"How could you believe I'd work over a poor little fellow like that?" Dwight asked Meg with a smile.

"I've got such a soft heart I couldn't have stood his screaming and begging, even when it came through the rag I stuffed in his mouth.

"I'd never have pulled his shoulder loose when I snapped one wrist behind him. I couldn't have picked him up when he passed out and hung him on a hook by his coat and waited for him to come to before I cracked his ribs against the garage wall."

He turned toward her with that same slow smile. "You know I couldn't have done anything like that . . . don't you?"

one monday
we killed them all

JOHN D.
MacDONALD

A FAWCETT GOLD MEDAL BOOK

Fawcett Publications, Inc., Greenwich, Conn.

prologue

AN excerpt from a statement in the Brook City Police file on the death of Mildred Hanaman, dictated and signed by Hans Dettermann, also known as Kraut Dettermann:

"You could say what she wanted was for McAran to notice her, and she was halfway drunk when she found us in a back room at the Holiday Lounge in the four-hand stud game for small money, just killing time. She called him all kinds of dirty names, then he topped her with some worse ones, and she cried and went out, but she came back in from the bar a little while later with a drink in her hand. She stood behind him, watching the way the cards were falling, and sudden-like she poured the drink on his head. He swung backhand at her and she dodged it, but fell down, sitting, because she wasn't so steady, and laughed at him. McAran went and got a towel and came back, drying his head and face, and she was standing up then, trying to make a joke out of it. There was music from the bar, and she did little dance steps in front of him saying something like, 'Remember me? I'm your girl. Dance with your girl. Be nice to your girl, please, please, darling.' But he pushed right past her not even looking at her and sat down to bet the pair of eights he had showing. She got real white in the face and she was breathing hard, and suddenly she jumped at him from behind, yelling and digging at his face. That was when he jumped up and she tried to run, but he grabbed her and backed her against the wall next to the door, and held her there and started hitting her. Pretty soon we knew somebody better stop him, so we stopped him. She slid down the wall and sat in a bent-over way. He came back to the table, and I remember it was his deal. After maybe three or four hands, she got up real slow. She held onto the doorframe. She didn't look at us, but I could see her face was messed up. She walked out. I'd say it was about quarter to one in the morning. I never saw her again. She was a real pretty girl, but I guess McAran got tired of her, the way she kept chasing him after he'd called the whole thing off."

i

WHEN you can count the time you have left in big numbers, count it in years; whole weeks can go by when you never think of it. But it dwindles down, and as the time gets shorter it seems to go faster. It came down to months, and then weeks, and suddenly it was time for me to go up to Harpersburg, up to the big maximum security prison and get my wife's half-brother and bring him home.

As the time got shorter I could see Meg tightening up. She'd look beyond me when I was talking to her, and I'd have to repeat what I'd said. She was short with the kids, impatient and abrupt.

"Five years out of the prettiest part of his life," she would say. "From twenty-five to thirty, all that good time lost and gone."

"It could have been more," I told her.

"What's he going to be like, honey? What's he going to act like?"

"You've seen him once a month for five years, Meg. You tell me."

She turned away. "We talk through the wire. I do most of the talking. He listens and sometimes he smiles. I don't know how he'll be. I'm—I'm scared of how he'll be."

I told her he would be fine, but I didn't believe it. I went with her to visit him the first time. He told me not to come back. He meant it. So I'd drive her up there when I could, and wait in the car across the road from the big wall and try to pretend to myself they were never going to let Dwight McAran out of the cage. She would always come out looking as if they'd whipped her, walking heavy, her face dull, and half the eighty miles home would go by before she'd begin to act like herself.

"I should go with you to bring him back," Meg told me.

"He made it plain in the letter. If we want to get him started right, we better do it the way he wants, honey. Maybe—maybe he just doesn't want to see you anywhere near those walls again."

7

"Maybe that's it." But her voice was dubious, her eyes uncertain.

And I wouldn't know why he made that request until he told me. With men like Dwight McAran it's little use trying to guess why they do things. We judge others by our own patterns. When a man doesn't fit anywhere into the pattern of most people, you might as well try guessing how high a bird will fly on Tuesday.

Down at the station they knew I was going to drive up and get him. There's more gossip in a place like that than any bridge club you ever saw. They'd even found out Meg wasn't going with me. It isn't very often a cop has a brother-in-law to bring on home from state prison. It would have been a rougher ride if I hadn't made Detective Lieutenant, but the rank kept most of the boys off my neck.

The bad situation, the one I knew was going to be bad, was with Alfie Peters. He marched through the squad room and into my office the afternoon of the day before I had to go get Dwight. We started rookie the same year and he'd thought of every reason in the world why he got a little bit left behind, except the right reason, he's too quick with his hands and his mouth. But he was the one who made the collar on Dwight all by himself, which is more than any one man should have tried or could have gotten away with, unhurt. All Alfie got was a dislocated thumb and a torn ear. Peters is a big man, quick and meaty.

He came in and stared at me and said, "The best thing you can do, Fenn, is drive him the other direction and leave him off some place."

"If you got to yell, Alfie, go down in the park and holler up at my window."

"You heard what McAran yelled at me in court."

"I was there."

"You give him a message from me. If I come across him any place at all in Brook City, and I don't like the look on his face, I'm going to hammer on it until I get a look I do like. He doesn't scare me a damn bit."

I stared at Alfie until he began to look uneasy. "If you have reason to arrest him, bring him in. If he resists arrest, you can take the necessary steps to subdue him. If it's a false arrest, I'll do everything I can to make the charge against you stick. He's not on parole, Peters. He served full time. There will be no arrests for loitering, for acting suspicious, for overtime parking. I've cleared that with the Chief. You're not putting the roust on McAran, and you're not working him over. And pickup order on him has to be cleared with the Chief."

"Nice," he said. "Real nice. Who gives him the keys to the city? The Chief or the mayor, or maybe we should invite the governor down?"

"Just handle yourself with a lot of care, Alfie."

"The picture is clear. That son of a bitch gets the special deal. The brother-in-law of Lieutenant Fenn Hillyer gets every break in the book. Is it on account he's a college man? He killed Mildred Hanaman and everybody knows it. You must be nuts to let him come back here."

I leaned back in the chair. I smiled at him, even. "I don't make the laws. He was arrested and charged and he stood trial and got five years for manslaughter. Now get out of here, Alfie."

He hesitated, turned on his heel and walked out. It certainly wasn't *my* idea Dwight should come back to Brook City. It was his, and Meg backed him up. She had some glamorized idea of Dwight becoming such a solid and dependable citizen everybody would realize they'd misjudged him. Personally, it had always astonished me he had gotten to the age of twenty-five without killing anybody. But what can you do when the woman you love is just using that natural warmth and heart which make you love her? She's two years older than Dwight. They had a miserable childhood. She did her best to protect him. She's never stopped trying. He's the only blood relation she has, and she has enough love left over for forty.

Chief of Police Larry Brint caught me in the corridor as I was leaving. He's sixty, a mild, worn man with a school teacher look, but with a deep and lasting toughness which makes Alfie's bluster look like a comedian's routine. He has made it known to me, without even putting it in so many words, that he wants me to have his job when he quits.

He fell in step beside me and we walked slowly toward the rear exit of our wing of City Hall. "Settle Peters down?" he asked.

"I hope so."

"This can be a rough thing. You've got to handle it just right, Fenn. McAran could make you look pretty bad."

"I realize that."

"If there's any slip, we can't afford an ounce of mercy. Does Meg understand that?"

"She claims she does. I don't know if she really does."

"How long is he going to stay with you?"

"Nobody knows. I don't know what his plans are."

We stopped in the shelter of the entrance roof. It had begun to rain again. Larry Brint studied me for a moment. "All prison ever does for most men like McAran is prime them and fuse them like a bomb. You won't know where or how that bomb is going to go off."

"Just watch and wait, I guess."

"Damn the rain." He started out into it and turned back. "Fenn, you try to get to him on that ride back. You try to tell him how it's going to be around here. He won't do Meg any favor trying to stay on here."

"Would that matter to him, Larry?"

"Guess not." He frowned and looked puzzled. It was a rare expression for him to wear. "Getting old, I guess. Thinking too much. Nearly every man I've ever known has been a mixture of good and evil, so it's mostly luck pushing them one way or another, and it's fair the law should give them equal rights and equal justice. But in my life there's been just seven I can remember that shouldn't come under the rules. There should be a special license for those, Fenn. A man should be able to lead them out back and kill them like a snake. Dwight McAran is the last one of those seven I've run into. God grant I never meet up with another. You be careful!"

He fixed me with a stern blue eye and walked off through the rain.

It was still raining when I left the house the next morning for the eighty-mile drive to Harpersburg, a cold pale dreary rain coming down through low gray clouds that nudged the tops of the hills. Brook City is in the middle of dying country. It's just dying a little slower than the hill country around it. They came a long time ago and pulled the guts up out of the earth and took what they wanted and went away, leaving the slag and the tipples and the sidings that are rusting away. There's nothing left in the hills but the scrabbly farms and the empty faces and the hard violent ways of living. Violence lifts the climate of despair and boredom for a little while. The government trucks come to the villages once a month, bringing food that's mostly starch, and when they collect it they try to make jokes about it, and the laughter is dutiful, and flat as the jokes. It's shine country, stomping country, old car country, a stale place left behind when the world moved on some place else, and the things most alive in the hills are the crows and the berry bushes, and, for a shorter time than seems fair to them, the young girls. Dwight and Meg came out of the hills, came from a village named Keepsafe, a small place now empty of people, with the road washed out and gone. I was born and raised in Brook City. With every year of my life it's gotten a little smaller, an old woman shrinking with the years, sighing at nothing at all, running out of time and size and money and hope.

Fifteen miles out of town I got stuck behind an ancient wildcat rig grinding in low-low up three miles of curves, overloaded with stolen coal, and when I finally passed it I caught a glimpse of the driver, a fat faded woman wearing a baseball cap. It didn't bother me to lose the time. I wished I could drive through the rain all the rest of my life and never get to Harpersburg. You can always tell when there's some part of your life that hasn't a chance of working out. It's like taking your cancer to the doctor a little too late. You wish you were somebody else entirely.

At the prison I went through gate security and was taken to the plywood office of Deputy Warden Boo Hudson.

"Fenn Hillyer, by God!" he said, pretending a vast, glad surprise. Way back, when I still wore a harness, he was Sheriff of Brook County and I knew him then, and it was always the same. If you had seen him twenty minutes before, the greeting was always the same. It had been over a year since I had seen him in the lobby of the Christopher Hotel at some time of political dealings, and he was unchanged, a sagging, flabby old man with a sourness of flesh and breath, hound-dog eyes the color of creek mud, seedcorn teeth, hair dyed anthracite black and oiled in flat strings across his baldness. He bulked heavy there in an oak chair, soiled and sweaty, the office thick with the scent of him, endlessly smiling, working hard at the effort of pumping the stale air in and out of his lungs.

Boo Hudson was Sheriff for twenty-two years until the signals got crossed somehow and he didn't get ample warning of a Federal raid on some of the back county stills in which he had some substantial interest. People talked and records were found, but over the years he had tied himself so closely to the men who run our state, and knew so much about so many existing arrangements, the worst they could do to him was force him not to run again after serving the last few months of the term of office. That was almost seven years ago, and two days after elections that year the State Prison Commission appointed him Deputy Warden at Harpersburg. We all knew it wasn't because he needed the money. During his years in office Boo Hudson had picked up bits and pieces of this and that, some leased warehouses and a beer franchise and that sort of thing, and we could assume there was some cash money here and there, where no court order could touch it, probably rolled tight in sealed fruit jars and tucked below the frost line as is the custom among our elected officials.

"Set and tell me how you been," Boo said.

I sat in a chair further from him than the one he indicated. "Nothing new," I said.

"Hear Larry Brint still ain't closed up Division Street and the women still yammering at him. Guess Brook City don't change, Fenn."

"It's the only way we can operate, Boo. We got a two-hundred-cop town and a hundred-and-twenty-cop budget, so we keep all the trouble in one place instead of getting it so spread out we lose track. They give Larry eighty more cops and twenty more cars, we'll close up Division Street right now."

He sighed, belched and said, "Sure, sure. I tell you, we're glad to see you around here. We're glad to be shut of Mc-Aran. Warden Waley, he says in twenty-eight years of penol —penology, he never see a con with absolutely no way to get to him. Nearly everybody, you can work them around with the food, or solitary or the work assignment or privileges, or some damn thing, and the ones left, those you can bust them up a little until they get the news. But a guy like McAran in a place like this, he turns into some kind of hero, and it gives a lot of punks the wrong ideas, and the whole setup gets harder to run."

Hudson chuckled in a phlegmy way. "The way you take him home, Fenn, you stop alongside the road where it's quiet, and blow the top of his head off, and then take what's left back to Brook City."

"When can I have him?"

"I gave orders that when you come in somebody should go get him straightened away for leaving, so he should be brought in here any minute now."

Hudson had just started to talk about Brook County when a guard brought Dwight McAran in.

He gave me one quick identifying glance and stood at ease, staring at the wall behind Boo Hudson, with all the massive patience of a work animal. I hadn't seen him since that first visit. Any last trace of boyishness had been gone for a long time. His face was a visible record of rebellion, the tissues brutally thickened, white scars shiny against the dull gray of prison flesh. His coppery hair was cropped close to his scalp. It was thinning on top and turning to gray at the temples.

He was dressed in the expensive clothing he had worn when they had admitted him. But such clothing no longer looked right on him. The jacket was too tight across the brute span of shoulders, and too slack at the waist. The huge stained hands, horny with callous, hung incongruously from tailored sleeves, curled into the shape of hard labor.

"He get everything back he brang in and sign the paper on it, Joey?" Hudson asked.

"Yes, and he got the cash money balance back from commissary, a little over fourteen dollars, Boo, and signed that paper too."

"He got any personal stuff out the cell?"

"He give what little he had to the guys on his row, Boo."

"Thanks, Joey. You get on back to work now."

Joey left. Boo Hudson put an envelope on the edge of the desk where Dwight could reach it. "In there, McAran, is your gate pass to go out, and the twenty dollars we got to give you by state law, and the three dollars and six cents which would be our cost on a bus ticket from Harpersburg to Brook City. Sign this here receipt saying you got it."

McAran hesitated, picked up the envelope and with an insulting thoroughness counted the money it contained. He put the bills into an alligator wallet with gold edges, flipped the nickel and the penny into Hudson's metal wastebasket. There was no trace of expression on his face.

Boo Hudson colored and said, "I hope that pleasured you, McAran. I hope it pleasured you the same way you bitched

13

yourself outa getting not one day of good time took off your sentence. If you'd come in here with the right attitude, you could have been walking free a year and a half ago, and you would have come off parole today."

Dwight turned toward me. He spoke with a minimum of lip movement. His voice was huskier than I remembered. "Is the sentence over now? Can I leave right now?"

"Yes."

"What would happen to me if I picked up this fat bag of ignorant garbage and ruptured it a little?"

"Now you hold on!" Boo Hudson said, his voice rising to a squeak.

"He'd probably have his people stomp you up a little and throw you out the gate, Dwight."

McAran turned and stared at Boo Hudson. "Not worth it," he said. "Too bad. Why don't you die a little faster, Hudson, instead of just rotting away and smelling up the world? Put your mind on it and you could be dead in a month."

"You'll be back in here!" Boo yelled. "You'll be back in here, by God, and I'll break you the next time, I swear. I'll have you begging and screaming like a girl. I'll tell them what to do to you, you—"

"Let's go," said Dwight McAran, and I followed him out of the office. We were escorted across an angle of the yard through the drizzle to the gate. The gate guards made a phone check on the exit pass, then gave the coded signal to the tower to lift the outer gate. We crossed the road to the parking lot. I suddenly realized he wasn't beside me. I stopped and looked back. He was standing under an elm tree with his fists on his hips, staring up at the rain-wet leaves. A small boy pedaled down the road on his bicycle. McAran followed the boy with a slow turning of his head. Then he gave a curious contortion of his body, a sort of massive shuddering shrug. Perhaps in that moment he threw off some of the hopeless weight of the prison years. At any rate, when he turned and walked toward me his stride was subtly changed, and his clothing seemed more suitable to him.

WHEN McAran got into the car with me, he was as casual as though I were giving him a lift from his home to the grocery store.

As we left the lot, he said, "Not much miles on this for a six-year-old car."

"It didn't have much on it when we bought it. Maybe it was turned back. We took one trip in it. Except for running up here once a month, it just gets used around town, and most of that by Meg."

"There was sixteen times she came up when she couldn't get to see me. Hudson could have let her know."

"At least she could bring you stuff those times and leave it off. That was something she felt good about doing, even when she couldn't see you."

"Stop where I can buy cigarettes, will you?"

I pulled into a gas station. When we were on the road again, I glanced over at him from time to time. Awkward silences can be created only between individuals who are aware of each other. Dwight McAran was so totally indifferent to any impression he might be making, he could have been sitting entirely alone. I glanced at him. In the line of the thickened brow, in the weight and placement of his pale green eyes, in the curve of the broken mouth, I could see a remote echo of the contours of the face of my beloved wife. It seemed a savage paradox that this could be true. It was as if someone had defiled a picture of her. His face was not a suitable place for this inference of warmth and sensitivity.

He is one of those men who do not seem particularly big until you notice some small detail, such as the great thickness of wrist. When you realize he is all in proportion to that dimension, he begins to look increasingly massive and indestructible. They comb our hills looking for these boys, knowing their merciless toughness, and, as in the case of Dwight, they give them football scholarships and keep them eligible to play as long as possible before losing them to the pro leagues. McAran was an All-State fullback. After a knee injury slowed him one step, the University converted him to offensive guard. He had time for one pro season as a rookie linebacker with the Bears before he killed Mildred Hanaman.

"You wanted me to come alone to pick you up," I said.

"So you can tell me what it'll be like before I get there. Maybe what you want to say, you couldn't say it in front of her."

"Why do you want to come back to Brook City?"

"To have a nice visit with my loving sister."

"Are you going to stay long?"

"I haven't decided."

I went into my speech. I hoped it didn't sound as carefully planned as it was. "Dwight, I can forget about Meg and look at it from the cop point of view. You killed Paul Hanaman's only daughter. You hadn't made yourself what anybody would call popular around town even before it happened. It wasn't like killing the daughter of—a mill worker."

"Wasn't it? Are you trying to tell me, Lieutenant Hillyer, everybody isn't equal in the eyes of the law?"

"Come off it, Dwight. Paul Hanaman is still publisher of the *Brook City Daily Press*. He's still a director of Merchant's Bank and Trust. He's still powerful in the party. None of that has changed. Neither he nor young Paul want you around town, reminding them of what happened to Mildred. With the kind of pressure they can put on people, how do you expect to get a job?"

"I won't need a job for a while, brother-in-law. I've got some money stashed."

I stifled the impulse to yell at him, and went back to my reasonable speech, delivered in a reasonable way. "I don't blame you for wanting to make—this kind of a gesture, Dwight."

"Gesture? Brook City took something away from me. I want it back."

"You can't get five years back."

"They took my freedom, and the way I earn a living, and eighteen hundred and twenty-six nights out of my life."

"Revenge isn't a very—"

"Revenge? On who, Lieutenant? I killed Mildred, didn't I? She was a sloppy pig with a bad temper, but you can't go around killing people because they have bad manners. It's antisocial."

"I guess I can't keep you out of town."

"Not legally. And you've got a lot of respect for the law."

"But I can tell you it isn't going to be smart to—to be conspicuous. There was an article yesterday in the *Press*. An editorial with a black border around it. It was called 'Rehabilitation, Modern Style.' It wasn't pretty."

"Should I sue?"

"Too many people don't want you to come back. If they get the idea they can't chase you away, they'll see if they can stick you back in Harpersburg."

"It's about like I thought it would be."

"It won't be smart to hang around too long."

"It's just the way I want it to be, Fenn. I wouldn't have it any other way. Hell, who can touch me? My sweet sister married the police force. She keeps telling me what a dedicated officer you are."

"But I won't be able to—help you very much."

"Are you trying to tell me there are nasty people in Brook City who would twist the law to suit their own purposes? Why, if they can do that, Lieutenant, what the hell are you dedicated to? Free apples and free coffee?"

"There are practical considerations you just can't—"

He slipped readily into the slurred nasality of hill country speech. "Law man can't protect his own kin? Ev'body watchin' you, make sure you don't protect me too much, maybe? What they sayin', boy? Pore 'Tenant Hillyer, got him a killer for a brother-in-law, but that Fenn, he smart enough to think him up some law duty over in the next county when we come around to stomp that ball-face killer face foremost into the mud." He chuckled and resumed in his acquired diction, "You're hung up right between Meg and your call of duty."

"I didn't ask for it."

"It's a handy thing Meg didn't marry a milk man. There'd be more money in the house, but it wouldn't have been so useful to me."

"It must be a nice simple way to live, Dwight, to think of people only in what way you can use them. You've used Meg all your life. You've used everybody who ever came within reach."

"You know, Fenn, that's my great trouble, and I'm grateful to you for lifting the veil from my eyes. Now I realize I should concentrate on what I can give instead of what I can take. True happiness lies in that direction. Service, unselfishness, devotion, humility. Yes sir, the meek will inherit the earth."

I glanced at him and saw that satanic smirk. "You haven't changed."

"How can you be sure? Maybe it's my heart's desire to be just like you. By God, it must be wonderful to be Fenn Hillyer, defender of the right! Why, if a man knows he's doing the *right* thing, it doesn't matter to him that any cheap member of the Common Council from the mayor on down can spit right smack in his face and walk away smiling. It doesn't matter he's never owned a new car and never will, and he can't afford a pair of shoelaces except on the years that end with an odd number. It doesn't matter at all that he's stuck forever in a dirty little city, because they let him carry a gun and a badge and they let him defend the rights of mankind. But, baby, now you are stuck with me, so keep your head down and let the sweat run free because you're never going to know from one minute to the next what I'm going to do, or how it's going to affect Meg or you or the kids."

I was coming down a winding grade, and in my anger I had pushed it up to seventy. I could have saved a lot of people a lot of agony if, at that moment, I'd snapped the wheel hard right and gone over the edge.

But what kind of an estate can a cop leave his wife and kids?

In a little while I broke a fifteen-mile silence to ask, "Was it really rough?"

"In the middle years. Not in the beginning. Not in the end. In the beginning it was easier because that Governor's Committee was still in session. But they were waiting, because they'd had the word. That's something every cop should know about prisons, Lieutenant. The word can be passed along, so that one man can do time so easy it's like a hotel—but without women. Or they can give you hard time, so hard you bitch your own record and serve the whole route. Hudson was giving out the old crap about how I could have been out a year and a half ago. They had the word on me, and they held off until that Committee was adjourned forever. And it got easier at the end, maybe because they plain got tired. Once you've convinced a man that even if he was to set you on fire you'd stand grinning at him until you fell over dead, once you've really convinced him, some of the heart goes out of him. But the middle years were bad. It isn't like the situation where they've got to worry about marking you. They can cuff you to the bars and work you over with half a baseball bat. When bats get cracked in a game they saw them off neat and save the handle half for Boo Hudson. He gets wheezing so bad from the exercise, you'd think he'd keel over. I was either in solitary, or stuck with the hardest, dirtiest, most dangerous jobs. I got the worst cell in the oldest block, unheated in winter and a furnace in summer. They beat me and sweat me and tried to burst my guts with castor oil. When I'd get in bad enough shape to start passing out, they'd put me in the hospital, but I never asked them one time to put me in. Yes, Lieutenant Hillyer, it would be a fair thing to say it was really rough. Maybe it wasn't supposed to be all that rough, even with the word to make it rough, but when a man won't beg, won't bitch, won't cry, won't change expression, won't even wipe the blood off his mouth, and keeps getting back up just as many times as his legs will hold him, it seems to get them all sort of carried away."

"Was that the smart way to play it?"

"I got exactly what I wanted out of it."

"Personal satisfaction?"

"Hell, no! I have a reason for everything, Fenn. You've never understood that. It made me some useful friends. Also, I got a bonus out of it."

"What do you mean?"

"I started something Waley and Hudson and all those underpaid screws can't stop. They lost control. They don't know how bad the situation is yet. But they will, Lieutenant. They will. They're in there with the lions, and those lions have got the idea they don't have to be scared of a whip and a kitchen chair and a whistle. That, I admit, gives me some personal satisfaction."

"The prison system in this state is—not up to national standards."

"No! Really!"

"There just isn't enough money to hire really qualified—"

"And Harpersburg was built to house eight hundred prisoners under maximum security conditions, and there are almost seventeen hundred cons crammed into there, Lieutenant, and they'd cancelled all prison tours before I ever got there, because there's things in there to see that would send a taxpayer running out into the street, yelping and throwing up."

"But don't public officials get a look at—"

"A fast tour of A Block, where everybody is always smiling, a look at one ward in the hospital, a little speech from the tame psychologist, and then plenty of bonded bourbon in the Warden's office. It's a great thing you do for law and order, brother-in-law, arresting the hard-nose cons like me and sending us up to Harpersburg for the rest cure."

"I don't decide what—"

"But you live with it, baby, and you're a part of the whole stinking thing, and you keep your mouth shut because if you open it, they'll lift your gold badge, and then good old Boo Hudson won't give you the big hello."

"So get hold of a reporter from the state capitol and fill him in on what it's like back there. Show him your scars."

McAran laughed with a good imitation of delight. "Lord God, I don't want to reform anything, Hillyer. I don't give a damn if they slice up the lifers and serve them for lunch meat. I'm just helping you be proud of the line of work you're in. I want Meg to be proud of you too, pal. And your kids should worship their clean, decent, dedicated old man, don't you think?"

"Say anything to Meg you want to say. Leave the kids alone."

"Or else? Settle down, Lieutenant. Ride it out."

The rain had stopped by the time I drove around the shoulder of West Hill where Dwight saw, for the first time in five years, the murky jumble of Brook City filling the valley flats six miles away. We came down the long slant and joined the heavy truck traffic on U.S. 60 and rode with it into town, past the junk yards, block plants and taverns.

"Take a swing through town," he said. "Go over Center Street and come back on Franklin Avenue."

I followed orders. Fifteen blocks over and fifteen blocks back. With his first show of alertness he sat forward on the seat, his big head turning from side to side. After the tour he leaned back and said, "A garden spot, isn't it? I didn't think it could happen, but it's gotten worse."

"Close to twenty per cent unemployed now. Most of them have run through the compensation. The furniture factory closed last year. Forty stores empty in the downtown area. Hasn't been a new house built in four years. Most of the big trucks don't even hesitate on the way through. Those who could afford to leave have left."

I drove to my house on Cedar Street. It's a small frame house about forty years old, but it's on a double lot and there are some good trees. A third of the houses on Cedar Street are empty, the weeds growing tall, windows boarded, paint peeling. It was almost one o'clock as I turned into the driveway. Though the street was empty, I was aware of the neighbor's eyes looking out at us. I guess it was enough of a drama to take them away from daytime television. The cop and the killer.

I parked short of the detached garage. Lulu came prancing, whining and grinning to offer greetings. She is a portly white dog, slightly speckled, and full of such emotional insecurity she convinces herself six times a day that everybody hates her, and goes around demanding affection with a sort of quiet hysteria. I dodged the frantic muddy front paws. She circled, frenzied with the responsibility of welcome, and lunged up at McAran. He punched her in the chest with a quick lift of his knee, so quickly and solidly she landed a-sprawl six feet away. She rolled onto her feet and stood for a moment, belly close to the ground, ears flat, tail tucked under, then give a shrill keen of spinster despair and scuttled across the lawn and around the corner of the garage.

It is perhaps somewhat sappy to read too much into such a small thing. I could have understood anger, or even a considered brutality. But McAran wasn't irritated, or even interested. It is difficult to describe the way it was done. If a fly buzzes around your face you flick your hand at it, and it is a matter of total indifference to you whether you cripple it, kill it or merely drive it away. The end result is the same—the fly stops bothering you. Were you to kill it and be chided by a Hindu, you would stare at him as if he had lost his mind. In order to have any understanding of his point of view you would have to go deeply into Hindu philosophy so as to understand why every life form is considered sacred.

The back of my neck felt cold. I was the Hindu facing the alien who could never comprehend my philosophy. He looked like a man and talked like a man, but we could not have been born on the same planet. I felt helplessly weakened by my own sentimentalities, by all the emotional baggage I had to tote around with me in a world where Dwight McAran was unencumbered. Up until that moment I had been apprehensive. With one casual jolt of his knee he had turned apprehension to a primitive unreasoning fear.

Meg came hurrying out onto the small back porch and down the steps and across the yard toward Dwight, making small sounds of gladness, and for one nightmarish moment I had a vision of the knee lifting again with a force suited to this larger object, to send her, too, tumbling onto the sodden ground.

I watched them embrace. And then they went toward the house together, with Meg asking questions he had no chance to answer. I followed along behind them into those kitchen aromas of the lunch which Meg hoped would erase the memories of five years of prison starch.

iii

AS far back as I can remember, I always wanted to be a policeman. Most small boys get over this. I didn't. I don't know why it should have been this way with me. Most men who become cops do so when other dreams become unattainable. They go onto the force as a compromise with reality.

Perhaps there is some order about it all which we do not yet understand. In every community of men there must be some who build, some who lead, some who heal, some who serve God. And every community must have laws, and men to enforce them. Just as every war has increased the percentage of male births in some pattern we do not yet understand, maybe there is some assignment of direction so that the communities of man will remain workable.

Without us, without the directed ones, you would not be safe in your homes at night, because it is too desperate a business to be handled entirely by the men who have drifted into it.

I am a good cop. It is a complex profession, laborious, drab and unromantic. I have a high school education. My army time, after basic, was spent in Military Police. I've had two tours at the FBI school. I study every issue of such technical publications as the *Journal of Criminal Law, Criminology* and *Police Science*. I do outside reading in these fields, as well as in sociology, psychology and public administration. I have learned the tricks and devices of command. I have a distinguished marksman rating. I have shot and killed two men, one in an alley and one in a bus station. I have wounded two others, and wish I had been able to just wound instead of kill the ones who died, and still dream about them sometimes, just as I dream about the time I picked up a woman's slender red high-heeled shoe at the scene of a violent collision just inside the city limits and found it heavy with the fragment of foot still in it. I have been shot in the meat of the thigh with a zip gun, and I have been slugged from behind with a tire iron. I have three citations on my record. I moved up from probation through two patrolman grades and three detective grades to gold badge rank in eleven years. I work an average seventy-hour week and receive no overtime for any hours worked beyond forty-four. Every two weeks I get a check which, after deductions, amounts to one hundred and eighty-six sixty. It is the most money I ever made in my life. If I stay in this same rank I can elect to retire after thirty years at one hundred and sixty-five dollars a month.

If I was not compelled to be a cop by some force I do not comprehend, I could not endure all the rest of it.

And the worst part, worse than the money, the hours, the idiotic inequities of the laws you have to enforce, is the constant need to rationalize. You can never do the job the way it should be done. So you strain to get the maximum out of tired men, obsolete equipment, an apathetic public. You wheedle and connive and bicker, knowing the best you can expect is a better degree of sub-standard performance. The roof leaks in five places and you have three wash tubs—

The way I met Margaret McAran, I was on regular patrol, but with an assignment to special traffic when the load got heavy, and on one afternoon of a light rain that froze as it came down, the body and fender shops were racking up a score that would keep them going for weeks. I was teamed with an older man named Lou Briss and we got a school zone injury case at quarter to three that afternoon at Hall Palmer Elementary School. It turned out to be a case of stupid rather than reckless driving. The crossing cop had made a blast with the whistle which startled an old guy into banging on the brakes, locking them so that even at fifteen miles he went into a long slow skid that swung the back end around so that it thumped a little girl, cracked her wrist and gave her a head laceration when she landed on the icy sidewalk.

The only adult witnesses were the crossing cop, the old driver and Miss Margaret McAran, first-grade teacher. She was there above and beyond the call of duty because it was such a crummy, dangerous, glassy day she wanted to help get the kids herded across the street before going back into the school and finishing up for the day.

The ambulance was loading the kid when we got there, and we found out from the crossing cop that the teacher who had seen it was inside calling the little girl's mother; so Briss and I split up what had to be done, but if he had seen the actual teacher instead of his mental image of the teacher, it would have been split a different way. I went into the school bracing myself to try to get some coherent information out of some semi-hysterical old spinster. She was in the administration office talking to some other teachers. They pointed her out to me. There was a dull gray pearly light in that room and some weak desk lights, but she seemed to have her own light—as if she had some trick of collecting and focusing all the light around her and reflecting it back. Maybe it was mostly that mane of dark copper hair, which looked metallic yet made you want to touch the softness of it. You would get the idea it was tousled, uncombed, but when you looked close you'd see it was as orderly as she could make it. Her skin was pale, but it had that glowing texture of superb health. Her eyes were a green that startles you because it seems too bright and clear to be possible. She was a big girl, moving with that protective dignity of big girls, but looking capable of explosive grace. I guess her features were a little heavy, denying her any classic beauty, but I can say that when she looked toward me in inquiry, there was an impact which dried my mouth and made me feel, in uniform, like a silly kid dressed up for a costume party. I learned later she was one day beyond her twenty-second birthday.

We went into a small room where I sat at a desk with my note book in front of me, and she sat in a straight chair beside the desk. Her voice was low and slightly harsh, and it had the intonations and elisions of the hill country hidden behind the grammar of her education.

Yes, she had seen all of it. She felt the traffic officer on duty had made a mistake in judgment. Under those icy conditions he should have let that car go by and stopped the ones coming which were further away. She saw the skid beginning, and so she had started herding and hauling the children back, and perhaps could have gotten little Shirley out of the way, too, had she not slipped and skinned her knee. Had she not been there, it was possible the rear of the car would have hit a half dozen of them. The driver had handled his car badly, had frozen on the wheel, the brakes locked, after the skid started.

Finally I had nothing left to write. I had her name and

25

her address and her telephone number, and my notes on all the information she could give me. So I had to look at her. She was so close. I had the hesitancy you get when you are tempted to look directly at the flame of a welding torch. If I thanked her, it was over.

I looked at her. There was a great calmness about this woman.

"This address, Miss McAran. Do you—live with your folks?"

"What has that got to do with the accident, Officer?"

I considered inventing some nonsense about how the phone was listed and so on. I discarded it. I looked into those bottle-green eyes.

"Absolutely nothing."

It was a challenge, and I saw it weighed and accepted. There was an aspect to this that you will not understand unless you grew up in an area where there are hills and flats, and people have lived there for a long, long time. Nowadays the differences are not as great, but they still exist and will probably always exist. Hill people think themselves tougher, shrewder, more realistic and more rebellious than the soft, conformist flatlanders. They compare their hard core of verbal honesty against the tricky legalistic antics of the flatlanders. They have a rooted distaste for all the symbols of authority. I am told it is this way all over the world, wherever there are mountains and old cultures.

We stared at each other across the fence our upbringing had erected between us. "Twenty-six Crown Street," she said, "is a private home. Mrs. Duke rents rooms to schoolteachers. There are three of us there. She operates it as a small boardinghouse. I've lived there since school started in September. This is my first year of teaching. What else do you have to know?"

She wore a dark gray skirt, a matching jacket over a green sweater, galoshes with buckles. She carried a gray cloth coat now placed across her lap. It looked cheap, threadbare and not nearly warm enough. She wore no rings, no watch, no jewelry at all. Her quiet hands rested on the cloth coat. The knuckles were chapped. Much later I learned she was self-conscious about the size of her hands and feet.

It must be just this way when the officer of an army of occupation must question a civilian girl. There is challenge, awareness, and the kind of contempt you cannot put your finger on.

I said, "A boy named Dwight McAran from this area plays for—"

"He's my half-brother."

"Do you have a car?"

"No."

"My partner went off with the traffic officer and left me the patrol car. I'm going down to the hospital to check on the child. Do you want to come along?"

"No thank you. She isn't badly hurt."

"Can I give you a lift home?"

"No thank you. I have work to do here."

"Maybe some evening we could—"

She stood up. "I seldom go out, thank you."

I could not get her out of my mind. The image of her grew stronger rather than fading. I began calling her up. She was coldly gracious, politely declining every invitation. I tracked down people who could tell me something about her. It was not easy. I put a lot of pieces together. She had been born forty miles back in the hills in the tiny settlement of Keepsafe, the only daughter of Red McAran, a vast, wild raging man who had not lived long enough to have other daughters. Meg's mother had died of meningitis when Meg was three months old. The tragedy had made her father more violent and unpredictable than ever. He had remarried, had come down to Brook City for his drunken week-end courtship of a Division Street slut, married the young dull-minded girl and taken her back into the hard hill country life. When Meg was two years old, the second wife gave birth to Dwight. Six months later Red McAran caught his new wife in a corn crib with a tough middle-aged neighbor, and took exception so carelessly he was knifed to death. Three days after the man who had used the knife—he was the father of nine—was sentenced to twenty years, the second Mrs. McAran left the two small children at the farm home of Red's uncle and disappeared forever, in the company of the eldest son of the man who had killed her husband. The uncle was a morose, arthritic, impoverished, childless man with a deaf-mute wife.

Had Meg not been such a bright handsome industrious child that the teachers in the Central School took a special interest in her, her history could have been quite different.

27

When she was ten and Dwight was eight, an ancient borrowed tractor rolled on her great-uncle and killed him. Her great-aunt was institutionalized. The farm was sold for taxes. Meg and Dwight would have become wards of the county had not one of her teachers taken them in.

After Meg began to win every award and scholarship in sight, Dwight began to come into his own as an athlete. She selected an all-expense scholarship for two years of State Normal School that would lead to her teaching certificate so that she could quickly begin earning a living and be able to help Dwight with his college education.

The most vivid picture I got during my off-duty investigation was from an old man who remembered how it had been for them. "I seen 'em go by lots of times, them two raggedy kids with that same bright-color hair, her the bigger one, holding his hand fierce and proud and strong. They was two against the world and she was the one knew it best, making sure his belly got filled before her'n, staring holes right through any sorry person tried to trouble them. When he pulled loose of her, and was playing rough games, and jawing at her, it was like a hen hatched a duck egg and can't stand for to see the little thing paddling out acrosst the pond. Later on, in the high school, when he was night roamin' with a hard crowd, with people older than she was, roamin' and fast drivin', turnin' theyselves ugly on 'shine, it was her fought to keep him out of worse trouble than he got in, and trouble is easy back there in the hills, with any old country dance turning quick into a stomping or a knifing or a shooting. He was thrice before the circuit judge up there, once warned and two times probation, and even with her fighting for him I'd say they'd chained him to work the roads a spell if it wasn't he was giving them the best football years back up there ever seen before or since. But what I remember is her hauling him along, those two heads shining in the sun, her chin up like a queen, coming barefooted down the dusty road with a nickel for stale bread."

She wanted no part of a flatland cop. Several times I humiliated myself by waiting for her at the school and walking the six blocks to Crown Street with her. She would answer a direct question, but that was all. By then I knew more about her, and I did too much talking, trying to tell her how the world had treated us a little bit alike. My own family had gone, but in quieter ways and when I was older than she had been. At headquarters they gave me a hard ride about it. Except for Alfie Peters, I kept my head down. But he said filthy things about her, so I had to wait until we were both off, and took him out behind the maintenance shed where such things were settled. They told me later he spent the first ten minutes of it laughing, clowning, dancing and knocking me down, and some of them were getting ready to stop it. I'm lanky and rawboned and clumsier than I would like to be, and I don't look half as powerful and durable as I've always been. Then they say there was a time when he stopped clowning and took his work seriously, trying to knock me down in such a way I'd stay down. But little by little he got arm-weary and he slowed down to the point where he couldn't duck enough of my slow, heavy, roundhouse punches, floating at him like sacks of stones on the ends of two ropes. After he started to go down I had longer and longer times in which to catch my breath, and finally he went down and stayed down. They told me I was kneeling beside him and shaking him and telling him to promise not to say anything more about Margaret McAran while his eyes were still rolled up out of sight. But after they treated us at the emergency room of City Hospital, he apologized in a way that satisfied me, and looked as if it hurt his mouth more than I had.

"Another time, pal, I'll know enough not to horse around at the beginning," he said.

"Name the time." I stared at him until his eyes shifted.

"I'll name it when I'm ready," he said. But he's never been ready, I guess.

On a May evening I stopped to check a badly parked car. As I straightened up after looking inside to see if anyone was in there asleep, sick or drunk, I heard a slight movement behind me, started to turn—and woke up sixty hours later with twenty-one stitches in my head. Severe concussion and coma. It had been a stolen car. The drunk who had stolen it had parked it fast to go into a vacant lot and throw up. He had taken the tire iron with him because he was scared of cats, he said. He could not remember hitting me. The paper gave it a big play, because had I died, which one of the doctors thought entirely possible, it would have been murder first committed during the commission of a felony. He made five fast miles before nipping a power pole off at the base. The lab matched my blood and hair to the tire iron.

I woke up on Thursday and was permitted visitors on Saturday. I opened my eyes after a cat nap Saturday afternoon and saw Meg sitting beside my bed looking at me with all her sweet gravity.

"How do you feel, Fenn?" she asked solemnly, using my name for the first time.

"I guess I feel pretty good. I guess I feel real good, Margaret."

"It's Meg, usually."

"I'm glad you came to see me, Meg, but it's—a real surprise."

"To me too. I guess I should tell you why I had to come."

"I—I'd like to know."

We stared at each other for a little while. Meg can lie readily about small things, those lies that make the life of every day an easier thing. But in the importances of life she requires of herself a truly terrible honesty which does not count the cost.

"They have kidded me about you, Fenn. The other teachers. I said you would soon give up and stop bothering me. I hoped you would. The paper on Tuesday said you might die without regaining consciousness. A friend said to me my problem was solved, trying to make a joke I guess, but it had an ugly sound. When she went away I found myself crying and I didn't know why. I took a bus to the end of the line and walked in the country. I could have sworn with all my heart, Fenn, I thought you were a pest. I thought of you often, and I believed it was because you were annoying me. But suddenly I knew that if you died, it would be—changed."

"You're crying again. There's no reason."

"It's been happening this way. The tears just—start."

"I think we better get married, Meg."

Her broad and heated smile nearly stopped my heart, but did not stop her slow tears. "After you court me, Fenn. Court me and ask me."

"I've been courting you."

"But it will be different, much different, now."

She touched my hand lightly and was gone from the room, and did not answer my call. She left the memory of the coolness and softness of her touch on the back of my hand. I kissed the place she had touched. They had to release me on Sunday or I would have torn the walls down.

It was as different as she had promised it would be. She was a girl to stand tall and proud against you, filling your arms and your heart.

"You have to understand about me," I told her. "There's a lot about me I can change if it's needed, but not being a cop. You'll have better opportunities, and you should wait for them, maybe, and select a—a more important kind of life in a prettier place in the world."

"You have to understand about me, Fenn Hillyer," she told me. "I belong where love is, because that's what I'm for. That's the meaning of me. I am for the man who is now my whole life, and I am lucky we are to cherish each other because you have—a goodness. I'd love you anyway because that is the way these things are. But, because of that goodness, Fenn, there doesn't have to be any end or limit or reservation to my giving, and I will make you so happy, so happy. So there just isn't any more important kind of life, and wherever we have to be, we will be in the prettiest part of the world."

Court is an old-time word, and she gave it all the old-time meanings, so that I could only guess at her passionate intensities, at what her kissings promised, until our honeymoon when, as though to refute all the sniggering ideas we flatlanders have about hill country girls, there was confirmed her hinted virginity. We had two weeks in late August, a borrowed station wagon and very little money. We spent the first two nights in a hotel in a city fifty miles away, and then went up into the hills, her hills, with food and camping gear, some new and some borrowed. She knew remote places and how to get to them. We camped twelve days and nights by a pond after lugging the gear two miles beyond the place where the logging track ended. It was wild country, with a wide misty view and no trace of man. We talked a lot, walked a lot, divided the chores, ate like wolves, and —in the best sense of the word—made each other's acquaintance.

We had no way of knowing we had not yet cured ourselves of a honeymoon awkwardness because we had no basis for comparison. An idiotic modesty still inhibited both of us. Our lovemaking had that dead protocol and inhibition which is the result of two people attempting to perform in all the ways they have read. We were each so determinedly anxious to inflict pleasure, it was all slightly forced, but we had no knowledge of what it could become for us.

I had used the entrenching tool we brought to enlarge a spring hole, and we would take turns bathing there. It took great will to clamber down into that icy water. On our fourth afternoon, I was collecting firewood and I thought I heard her call me. I assumed she had finished her bath. I went to the spring. The noise of the spring kept her from hearing me. I stopped, half-screened by brush, and watched her like a thief. White body, leaf shadows, yellow coins of summer sunlight, shining hair, black water. She stood up. The water level came just above mid-thigh. She plucked at the crown of her head and the piled hair came spilling down. She clambered cautiously up the bank. She was wearing a secret, private smile.

Suddenly, magically, I had the stupendous realization that the woman I watched was my woman, not just a honeymoon object to be anxious about. I felt as if weights had been taken off my shoulders. I went grinning toward her and laughed at her startled look, and pulled her down into the woodsy grass and took her joyfully, without protocol or borrowed knowledge or any worry about style or pace. I turned off my worried mind and did whatever my heart and body told me to do, and right there, with a great rumbling of her pale strong limbs, delighted gaspings and terminal frenzy we became man and wife at last in the only way that lasts. We grinned at each other, and we made bad and bawdy jokes. She felt that whatever it was which had so suddenly happened to us, there should be quite a different name for it.

In the days and nights left to us we learned of that curious paradox which seems to distort the lives of most couples. When two bodies are well-used in love, in forthright, honest, inter-selfish pleasure, sex becomes a familiar joy which can be approached in any mood, and thus becomes not only more important—in that it is an affirmation—but also less important because it becomes such a part of life it is not any more or any less serious than any other part. When bodies are not used in this honest way, there is an accumulated pressure of anxiety which elevates sex to a position of false importance, like a starving man obsessed with visions of food. Such trivia as the careful timing of mutual orgasm becomes a ponderously serious thing, whereas all true lovers know that the times of love are like an endless shelf of books. Some endings are happier than others, but all the pleasure is mostly in the reading, in how each story starts, and how it moves, and how the chapters fit together, and what little adventures the people have before the book finally ends. Each is a journey, and each is a story, and if one ending is a little less apt than usual, the next one will very probably be better, and every so often you will find a masterpiece. The anxious ones seem to feel they have in their hands the very last book on the shelf. They chant the words in a dead monotone, lose the thread of the story, plow joylessly through all the pages thinking only of how it will end.

I could put my hand on my schoolteacher and have her say, "Why sure!" or, "More beans or more franks?" or, "Go get your own can of beer." She could bend down and kiss the nape of my neck and I would either get up and go with her on a walk, or go get more wood for the fire, or turn and pull her down. The anxious never understand what is wanted. The lovers always do.

By the time we packed and started driving back down through the hills, I knew I had a prize more rare than I could have ever guessed, and marveled at my luck. The last bachelor suspicion had been leached out of my mind. I knew I had a woman who would last me all my life. We sang as we went down the winding roads. Neither of us can carry a tune. There is no sadness in the ending of a good honeymoon, but I understand there aren't too many good ones. We knew ours had been good. There should be two classifications of couples. Married and really married.

The only cloud on my horizon was so small I had to look close to see it. Her half-brother had taken time off from his summer job with a road builder in a neighboring state to come and give the bride away. It was the first time I had met him. I hadn't liked the look of him, or his manner.

But for Meg's sake, I had to say I thought he was fine.

Any professional lawman will tell you there is no such thing as a criminal countenance. There are murderers who look like earnest, dedicated young priests. There are simian professors, rodent-like bankers and Neanderthal ministers.

But if you keep pressing the professional police officer he will often admit being conscious of a kind of almost imperceptible strangeness about a man with the innate capacity

33

for lawless violence. It is idiotic to use a word like psychopath. That is a wastebasket word, a receptacle for all those people in whom we detect a kind of strangeness with which we can make no valid contact.

The police officer sees no specific clue. He suddenly has a hunch. The hunch is the result of an amalgam of many small impressions, any one of which would be meaningless taken by itself. For example, when a man is husky and has a lot of vitality, and dresses with great care and expense, and seems to have no strong opinions about any abstract thing, such as politics, and avoids anything that will require persistent effort, and is always enthusiastic about the next moment, but ignores next week, and hates to be alone, and has considerable surface charm and attractiveness, and is impulsive and unreliable, and likes to lead an active, eventful life, likes to exaggerate and dramatize, and lie about money, and make promises he forgets to keep, and has no specific goal in life, and tends to overindulge in anything he tries, and uses the people who love him and charms them into forgiveness, and forms no lasting emotional relationships, then small bells start to ring.

They are overly plausible. Their eyes seem to have a curious opacity. They laugh too quickly at your first joke, and wander away in the middle of your second one. Their smiles are practiced in front of mirrors. Any concern seems faked. There is never any evidence of anxiety. To them the great sin is not in sinning but in being caught at it. Add a constant need for and carelessness with money, plus a ruthless use of women, and the proficient cop begins to tighten up a little, because it is a pattern he has seen before, and when he has seen it before, it has caused him some work a little dirtier than usual. The cop will not say, "This one is going to commit violence." He merely says, "This one can be triggered. This one can blow. Let's hope it doesn't happen."

I met Dwight at the wedding, and I wanted to accept him because he was my bride's brother. But it did not take him long to give me the impression I was as close to him as I was ever going to get. His sister was throwing herself away on a flatlander cop, and it couldn't be stopped, but if she had any sense she would have gone where the money is.

I watched him operate, with her, and with the guests at the wedding, and with one of Meg's closest friends from

Normal School, and I liked no part of it. He leaned on the football hero bit with all the weight it would stand. Before we finally drove off he was recklessly drunk.

After we got back from the honeymoon we found out he had stayed away from his job so long he had been fired. He had talked his way into her room at Mrs. Duke's place, apparently, because her radio and her portable typewriter were gone. I traced them to Brook City's only hock shop and got them back, by using some pressure, for just what he sold them for—twenty dollars. He left Meg a note saying he was going to bum around for a while and he'd be back at school early in September. It wasn't until much later that Meg found out her pretty little Normal School friend, Ginny Potter, had gone right along with him. They used the car she had bought on the strength of her first teaching job. She wrote her parents she was taking a sightseeing trip with another girl. The last postcard from her was mailed in Baton Rouge. Two weeks later, several days after she was supposed to report back for the new school year, she phoned her people collect from a third-rate hotel in New Orleans, broke, sick, emaciated and desperate. Her brother flew down and brought her back. They never found any trace of the car. Dwight had walked out on her a long time ago. She couldn't remember when, exactly, and she didn't know what had become of all the clothes aside from the dress she was wearing. She came home and made a pretty good try at killing herself, and spent over a year in a rest home, then a few months later married one of her father's close friends who had lost his wife in a swimming accident.

I can remember what Meg said when she heard about Ginny. "Really, Fenn, Dwight didn't exactly *abduct* her, you know. She's over twenty-one. I think it was a stupid thing for both of them to do."

"So he didn't abduct her, but maybe he could have taken a little care of her."

"We shouldn't judge him, darling. We don't know what happened in New Orleans. And he's only a twenty-year-old boy, after all. Maybe he felt he was doing the right thing in walking out. Probably he thought she'd head for home where she belonged. How could he know she'd stay down there all alone until she got into such dreadful condition?"

"I think the money was gone."

"He knew she could *always* wire for some. I think he

35

began to feel—guilty about the whole thing, so he walked out."

"Maybe," I said, and changed the subject. What else can you do? You can't explain to your new wife that she is one kind of victim, and Ginny Potter was another kind, and there'll be many many more before he comes to the end of his life. And I was beginning to realize I was a victim too, second grade.

iv

SO I brought McAran back from Harpersburg and re-united him with his loving sister, and watched him kick our dog.

Meg took him to the room she'd fixed up for him. It was a two-bedroom house when we bought it. On nights and days off I'd turned a side porch into another bedroom, so Bobby and Judy could each have a room of their own. It had been Bobby's room for three years, and he hadn't been completely gracious about giving it up to move back in with his sister, even on a temporary basis. He had improved the decor of the room in the ways eight-year-old boys think essential, and it was degrading to have to move back in with a six-year-old sister, into a revolting tenderness of dolls and little dishes.

I stood in the doorway and watched her show McAran all she had done to prepare for him. She had packed his things five years ago, and recently she had put everything in order: pressed suits, slacks, jackets hanging in the closet above the row of burnished shoes, and the bureau drawers orderly with shirts, socks, underwear, sweaters. She even had his trophies on the shelf where Bobby had kept his kit models of racing cars, and all the cups and plaques were newly polished.

He looked at everything too quickly, too indifferently, and sat on the bed and said, "Nice, Sis."

Looking slightly crestfallen, she said, "I tried to make it nice."

He reached and turned on Bobby's radio, found some rickytick-imitation Dixieland and put the volume a little too high. "Rampart Street Parade."

She went to the bureau and picked up the savings account book and went to the bed and sat beside him. She explained the figures, speaking loudly to be heard over the music. "This was what was in the checking account after the lawyer, dear. And this is what I got for the car. I had them

37

figure the interest on it last week, so this is what you've got right now."

"How do I get it out?"

"What? Oh, we go to the Savings and Loan and make out a card for you so you can take it out any time, as much as you need of it."

"Can you take it out?"

"Of course."

"Then I won't need a card. Just take it out."

"But you don't want to carry that much cash——"

He snapped the radio off. "You just take it out, Meg. That's all. Just take it out and give it to me. That makes it real simple."

I didn't wait to hear her answer. I went out back looking for Lulu. I knew where she would be. I squatted at the right place and looked under the garage. She was wedged as far back in there as she could get, muzzle on her paws, rejected eyes staring out at me. I told her all the reasons why she was the world's most satisfactory dog, but she would have none of it. A horrid, frightening thing had happened to her in my presence, so I was a part of it, and soft talk would not cure a heart so broken.

I went back into the kitchen. Meg was alone there, staring at something in the oven. "What I liked most," I said, "was the way he kept jumping up and down and saying whee."

She stood up and gave me the slow turn, eyes like chips of green ice. "He's spent five years being a playboy in all the fun places of the world. That's why it's so easy for him to jump up and down and say whee at every little thing."

"But he could have——"

"Neither of us expect this to be easy. So let's make it harder for each other with a lot of smart cracks, Fenn. If we try hard, maybe we can make it impossible."

I went to her and held her close. I felt and heard her sigh. I could hear the sound of the shower running, and guessed our Dwight was scrubbing away the stench of prison. "We won't fight about him," I told her and released her.

She looked at me with eyes of woe, full of tears ready to spill. "Why did they have to do—so much to him? Why did they have to change him so much? What good does that do? What's the—purpose of a prison?"

"Punishment. A deterrent to others. Rehabilitation. Mostly, I think, it's formal, organized revenge. The ones the screws can't break, the inmates can. They exist because the shrinkers are still fumbling around. Some day when a man is found guilty, they'll strap a gadget to his head and it will buzz and clean his brain right back to the day of birth. They'll turn another dial and it will buzz some more and establish a whole brand-new set of abilities, habits, memory and desires, perhaps a pattern lifted intact from some sterling, productive citizen. But not for a long time, a very long time. Between now and then we'll lock them up and toughen them, coarsen them, twist them a little further away from the norm, and turn them loose. But that isn't my end of the business, and I don't like to think about it very much because it takes the edge off some of the good I think I'm doing—hope I'm doing."

"Did he—tell you anything about his plans?"

"Nothing specific. He thinks Brook City gave him a raw deal."

"He's right, isn't he?"

"Yes—and no. Yes, in that he didn't get impartial justice; no, in that that commodity is so rare he hasn't any rational reason to expect it. If he tries to tip the scales the other way, to get back some of the meat and juice he thinks was taken away from him, he'll just be trying to cut a loaded deck."

The shower sound stopped. She began to put things on the table. I went out and sat on the back steps. If he got a raw deal it was the same kind of raw deal I have tried to get used to, and which happens in every city in the country. It is one of the facts of life, and it is a flaw built right into the structure of our judicial system. Better minds than mine despair of ever correcting it.

This is the rub. The average public prosecutor is a youngish lawyer. Maybe he has political ambitions. Maybe he merely wants to make an impression that will help him when he is back in private practice. In either case his future success is going to depend on the good will of those men who call themselves the backbone of the community, the men who own and operate the stores, factories, banks, dealerships and so on.

The police force makes the arrest, files charges, completes the investigation and turns the file over to the prosecutor. The prosecutor runs a busy shop, usually on low pay and a limited budget. And so, in each case, he has to decide just how much time and effort to put into the prosecution. Suppose the crime has been committed by a good friend, relative or valued employee of one of the local businessmen. The prosecutor knows he will run up against a good defense attorney. Why should he use a lot of zeal, time, energy, expense in preparing the prosecution's case? Why should he make a careful investigation of the whole jury panel in order to be better able to empanel a jury which will convict? Why should he try to get it before one of the more severe judges? He can salve his own conscience by making a routine preparation of the case and then going after a conviction with every outward evidence of zeal. He can hammer hardest at the strongest parts of the defense case. If, on cross-examination of a defense witness, he suspects the existence of an area where he might be able to trap the witness, who can say that he steered his cross-examination in another direction? If it appears that a conviction is inevitable, cannot he inadvertently introduce some element which, upon appeal, will be adjudged reversible error?

But in a crime against the men able to directly and indirectly fatten his future, the spectators may think they are seeing exactly the same performance as before, but they are actually seeing a case put together as carefully as any ballistic missile. They are seeing an uncertain defense up against great zeal, in front of a tough judge and a jury as merciless as the prosecutor could make it. You see him slamming away at the weak spots, yet ever cautious to avoid any procedural error.

It is not this way in every city. It works this way in most of them. Suppose you were the prosecutor. Suppose you were not given, out of public funds, enough money to make a painstaking preparation of every case. Where would you save money and where would you expend it? It's a pretty problem, and it extends into the police investigatory work also. If you haven't the time or the men to make all files airtight, which ones do you concentrate on? Where there are professional public prosecutors appointed for long terms and paid well, the problem is lessened. And when you have that rare animal, the violent champion of the downtrodden, the outright foe of power and privilege, you still have the same problem—reversed.

In this sense justice is conditioned by who you are rather than by what you have done.

And Dwight McAran killed the only daughter of one of the most influential men in Brook City. The request for the change of venue was made too late, and denied.

Yet had he killed in the same way and for the same reason the same sort of girl his father found on Division Street, it might not even have gone to trial.

After his first full season of pro ball, McAran arrived in Brook City in the middle of January with the idea of setting up some sort of business connection which would support him during the off season, and one which might support him full time when and if he ever got out of the NFL. He rented a small layout in an apartment hotel, talked entertainingly at some service club luncheons, gave interviews and predictions to the local sports reporters, and started selling insurance for the Atlas Agency, for old Rob Brown who was getting too feeble to go out and dig for it. After two weeks and one sale he decided he didn't like it. Rob said later that the little venture cost him about three hundred dollars net.

He sold sporting goods for a little while. He spent one week behind the desk at the Christopher Hotel, and was fired for getting drunk. Traffic got tired of warning him about the way he yanked his blue convertible back and forth around town and started giving him heavy tickets. By then he was moving with a fast rough crowd.

I knew he had taken to hanging around the Division Street joints but I didn't know what it meant until Larry Brint called me in and shut the door and said, "Peters was working an informant for something else entirely and came up with something on your brother-in-law Dwight. He's on Jeff Kermer's payroll at maybe two bills a week."

I must have looked shocked. "Doing what?"

"Alfie's pigeon says Jeff is using him for muscle. People have moved a little bit out of line this winter because Jeff has been a little shorthanded. McAran is helping bring them back into the fold."

I remembered a brand-new hospital patient, the owner-manager of the Brass Ring on the corner of Division and Third. He'd walked in with two snapped wrists, a dislocated shoulder, some minor internal bleeding and a story about having fallen down his own cellar stairs. We had interrogated him at the hospital, almost positive we were wasting our time.

"Davie Morissa?" I asked.

"The word is that McAran did it, and Kermer liked the job."

"I don't like any part of it."

"So I'll talk to Jeff and you talk to the hero."

I got nowhere with Dwight. He was full of injured indignation. Jeff Kermer was a friend. He hung around Jeff's place, the Holiday Lounge, because Jeff had the idea he attracted trade and gave him a discount on his bar bill. He wasn't on anybody's payroll, honest to God. He had something real good lined up that might work out and might not. A couple of friends were loaning him money to keep him going. Hell, I should know that a guy in the pro league couldn't get tied up to anybody who'd been arrested a few times for gambling. They'd throw him the hell right out of the league. Getting a discount on drinks wasn't exactly working for a guy.

I had caught him at his studio apartment at the Brookway, at eleven in the morning. Just as it was apparent our little talk was going nowhere at all, Mildred Hanaman came strolling out of the bathroom wearing a big yellow towel in sarong fashion, and gave a great faked imitation of surprise. She was a lean dark girl, random as the March wind, spuriously elegant, her considerable handsomeness marred by a mouth too slack, too mobile, too given to framing every word with such labial exaggeration, she seemed to be speaking forever to a world of lip readers.

I was standing near the door. Dwight was sitting with paper, coffee, robe, beard-stubble. "May I present Detective Sergeant Hillyer. Sergeant, Miss Hanaman," Dwight said with sarcastic precision.

"Well, we've met," she said, with all the roving business with the mouth. "Haven't we just? Time and again, practically. You're a dear Sergeant, truly. Dwightie dear, you *must* make them do something about hot water up here. What did I do with my cigarettes? Oh, I see them."

Yes, we had met. People marveled at how completely unlike a brother a sister could be. Paul junior, four years her senior, had been fifty years old at birth and had always been totally solemn, totally reliable, completely proper. Their mother died when Paul junior was fifteen. Mildred had

42

been thrown out of every school they could get her into, including the Swiss. At eighteen she started receiving the income from a trust her spendthrift grandmother had left her. She lived like a sailor on shore leave, as if there would never be enough beds and bottles in the world, as if no cars could be driven quite fast enough, and no parties would last long enough. She went to far places on impulse, and her returns to Brook City were unpredictable. Whenever she was in town she became a problem to us. She was twenty-two. Her father's newspaper would, of course, kill any story about her. She was so used to having us pry her out of difficulties, she had come to believe we were on her father's payroll.

I had been in on one of the juiciest episodes, three years previous, when I was in the first detective grade. A well-to-do couple named Walker had taken a trip to Europe in the spring. Their son had brought two college friends back with him to the empty house for Easter vacation, a nice home in the Hillview section, not for from the Hanaman place. As we reconstructed it, the three boys had holed up in the house with Mildred and plenty of liquor, and the party had continued for five days and nights before the Walker boy's roommate died. We got there ten minutes after the mumbled phone call from the Walker boy. He was too drunk to be interrogated. We found the other boy in bed, snoring heavily. They had turned the house into a pig sty. We found Mildred Hanaman naked and passed out in a pink bathtub. Apparently the faulty drain had let the water run out or she would have drowned. The pink glow of the porcelain made her body look gray and lifeless, as inviting as a stacked corpse in a concentration camp.

The dead boy had been a high-fidelity bug. He hadn't been satisfied with the television picture they were getting. He had taken the back off the big set and stuffed his drunken clumsy hands in among the wires and circuits without unplugging the set. The shock had hurled him eight feet away. His dead face was redder than any sunburn, but we had to go through the pointless routine of resuscitation.

I wanted to blow the whole stinking thing a mile into the air, bringing every charge we could find in the books. When they found I was going to be hard to control, they pulled me off it. The Hanaman house servants put the Walker home back into immaculate order. Mildred was hustled off to a rest home to dry out. Somebody did an excellent job of coaching the Walker boy and his surviving friend. By the time the dead boy's parents had arrived, it had become one of those innocent, tragic accidents: three friends sitting around having a beer, and Ronnie volunteering to adjust the set and pulling the floor lamp plug out of the wall socket instead of the television set plug. Coroner's verdict—accidental death.

Larry Brint lectured me. "You are paid to be a cop, Hillyer, not a moralist, not a reformer. You don't enforce the Christian ethic. You enforce the laws. It was an accidental death. What good is a morals charge going to do anybody? What good would it do if we could prove the Walker boy waited twenty minutes, God knows why, before putting the call in? How would it help that boy's people to know how he spent the last five days of his life? This kind of a deal should make you feel sick, like it does me. Okay. If it didn't, we'd be bad cops and worse human beings. But don't let it carry over into what you're being paid to do. We're not going to change the way the world is. All we're going to do is make Brook City a reasonably safe place to live, and give them a buck and a half of protection for every buck they budget us. You're not a judge or a jury or a prosecutor."

I remembered his words as I looked at Mildred in her yellow towel. She lit a cigarette. Dwight reached lazily and she gave it to him and lit another. They were both looking at me and I suddenly realized how very much alike they were. There was an inevitability about this association. It wouldn't last long. They didn't lead lives in which anything lasted very long. But they had to be together for a little while.

"He came to tell me to stop working for Jeff. He gets these weird ideas."

"Jeffie is a dear man," Mildred said. "He's a fun sort. Sergeant, dear, we sort of run with the pack, but we're not employees, really. I did try to be one last year. I teased him to put me on a little telephone list, just to see what it would be like, but he was horribly chicken about it, scared of Daddy, truly."

"We don't want to keep you from your work, Fenn," Dwight said.

As I walked toward the elevator I could hear them laughing.

I learned Larry had made no headway with Jeff Kermer. Jeff had admitted just the casual association described by Dwight. We suffer the existence of Division Street. We need and use Jeff Kermer, and he needs and uses us. It is a realistic relationship which would horrify the reform elements if they knew how it works. In nearly all categories of major and minor crime, we run well below the FBI statistics for the national average. Nearby cities with a fatter per capita police budget run higher.

It is a power relationship, not a conspiracy. In the unwritten arrangement, Kermer keeps his operations pretty well centralized in the Division Street area, and can operate the clip joints, the gambling, the call girl circuits, the unaffiliated local union rackets and small scale protection setups, as well as jukes, pinball machines and punchboards, without any serious interference. In return he puts the whole city off limits for the organized narcotics trade, pornography, professional armed robbery, safe-cracking and car theft rings. We try to keep two classes of informers inside his organization, those he knows about and those he doesn't. We can't expect him to stop amateur impulsive crimes of violence, but we expect him to keep professional talent out of town. If any tries to move in, and he can't readily break it up, he sees that we get tipped off. If one of the independent operators within his sphere of influence gets too greedy, we are tipped off that Jeff wouldn't mind a raid and some arrests. This always pleases the reform elements. Because it is a controlled town, it is a cooling off place for out of town hoodlums. In return for the arrangement that they not ply their trade in Brook City, we agree to forego the dragnet technique of picking up strangers on suspicion.

As far as the police department is concerned, there is no grease involved. Kermer has a political budget, necessary to protect the status quo, but no bag man ever visits Larry Brint. And Jeff is too smart to try to buy the police. In a controlled town, when the police are purchased, it upsets the power balance, the town gradually becomes so wide open that the ever-present reform element gains enough power to take over and break up the party. Whenever any cop is so stupid as to try to extract grease, Kermer tips Chief Brint off and that cop is suspended. So corruption helps keep the force clean and professional, and giving a good return on the tax dollar.

For Larry Brint it is a working arrangement, a rational compromise. But he knows that such a balance cannot be maintained because it is a highly personal solution. Men sicken and die, and the ones who replace them have other ideas. Also, Larry was in a static position, and Jeff Kermer was getting stronger. Jeff had been expanding into legitimate enterprise for a long time, slowly allying himself with the commercial pressure group, acquiring new power of a different sort. And it was this duality of interest which kept him from making any attempt to obscure the details of the killing of Mildred Hanaman. Just as his extra-legal activities were at the mercy of Chief Larry Brint, his legitimate businesses were vulnerable to the pressure the Paul Hanaman group could bring to bear.

The killing occurred six weeks after I talked to Dwight and the Hanaman girl in Dwight's apartment.

These are the facts brought out by the police investigation. McAran had broken off the relationship. The girl was furious with him. Her pride was hurt. She was drinking heavily. He was staying out of her way. She found him on a Saturday at midnight in one of the private rooms at the Holiday Lounge in a four-handed game of stud poker. He told her to leave him alone. They called each other obscene names. She wandered out to the bar and came back with a drink and kibitzed the game for a little while. Without warning she poured the drink over his head. He swung backhanded at her. She dodged the blow, but was so unsteady on her feet she fell down. She laughed at him. He went and got a towel, dried his face and head and went back to the table, ignoring her completely. She worked herself into a screaming rage and catapulted herself at him, clawing at him from behind. He stood up, tipping his chair over, and walked her back against the wall beside the door, held her there with his left hand and worked her over with his right, striking her heavily with his open hand, backhand and forehand, until there was no resistance in her. He kept striking her until the men he was gambling with came and pulled him away. She collapsed, semiconscious. They went back to the interrupted game. After five minutes she was able to get to her feet. She left without another word. As she went out through the bar several people noticed her face was badly swollen and beginning to discolor. She left the Holiday Lounge at approximately ten minutes to one. A maid heard

46

her car enter the driveway at her home at about one-thirty. The trip should have taken no longer than fifteen minutes. She remained in bed most of the next day, complaining of a headache, nausea and a vision defect. She was up for an hour, but complained of dizziness and went back to bed. When a maid discovered her dead in her bed at noon on Monday, the coroner, using a thermistor bridge thermometer and the temperature extrapolation method, gave the estimated time of death as three o'clock on Monday morning. In view of the facial contusions, autopsy permission was requested and granted, and the cause of death was shown to be a traumatic rupture of a minor blood vessel in the left hemisphere of the brain with an attendant slow build-up of pressure which in turn starved the supply of blood to those deeper areas of the brain controlling respiration and heart action. No abnormality or malformation was noted in the area of the hemorrhage. Two consulting specialists concurred with the coroner's opinion that the facial bruises indicated blows of a sufficient severity so that it was *possible* they had also ruptured the blood vessel. The three witnesses to the assault were questioned separately. They willingly gave statements which were not contradictory in any significant respect.

The principle of reasonable doubt is one of the basic ingredients of the law. Any zealous defense would make much of the fact that the girl had been visibly drunk. The autopsy could not pin down the approximate time of the brain injury. She could have fallen before McAran beat her. She could have gotten out of the car on the way home and fallen. She could have gotten up in the night and fallen in her own bathroom.

McAran was charged with murder in the second degree. With all the Hanaman weight behind him, the young prosecutor, John Finch, made massive preparation. Midway through the trial it was easy to guess how it was going to go. The defense wisely requested a recess, conferred with Finch, and, with his agreement, entered a plea of guilty to a reduced charge of manslaughter. McAran was sentenced to five years at Harpersburg State Prison.

Had Paul Hanaman, Junior, stepped sufficiently out of character to have roughed up a drunken B-girl in one of the Division Street saloons, and had she walked out under her own power and died over twenty-four hours later, it is al-

47

most beyond the realm of possibility to believe he would have spent even five days in a cell. In his case, the doubt would have been exceedingly reasonable.

I visited Dwight in his cell after he had been sentenced and was waiting to be transported to Harpersburg.,

He gave me a rocky smile more like the lip-lift snarl of an animal.

"Dirty cop bastard!"

I leaned against the bars. He sat on the bunk, cracking his knuckles. "Sure. I framed you."

"It could have been fixed. Five lousy years! Jesus!"

"Fixed?"

"One of your prowl cops up there testifying he saw her pull over halfway home and get out and trip and fall on her stinking head."

"Oh, sure. We always do that for our friends."

"Why did Kermer cross me? Two of those guys taking my money in that game work for him. I told Jeff how to do it. They go on the stand. On the stand they change the testimony, and they say Mildred fell on her head hard after dumping that drink on me, and she acted dazed and funny, and her face was banged up before she ever got into that room, and all I did was slap her a little trying to bring her out of it. Was that so hard?"

"Did he agree?"

"He winked and told me not to worry about a thing. After they gave it straight, I knew I was cooked."

"Maybe Kermer needs Hanaman more than he needs you, Dwight."

"I wish I had that sloppy, drunken, big-mouth broad right here, right now. I'd kill her in a way that would give me some kicks. *Five years!*"

"More like three and a half if you handle it right."

"I have the strangest feeling I'm not going to handle it right, brother-in-law." He looked at me with a curious steadiness which made me uneasy. "I owe you, cop. I owe you and Kermer and Hanaman and this bastard town and this bastard system that's put me in every newspaper in the country. I'll be in the news again, officer. Wait for the day. Have yourself a nice five years with my sister."

"Don't talk nonsense. Don't talk like a punk kid."

He looked down at his big meaty right hand and slowly flexed the fingers. "A little too hard," he said softly. "And a

48

little too long. Should have stopped when she went loose, but I was in the rhythm of it, popping her face back and forth, catching it just right." He stared up at me with a corrugation of boyish forehead, a puzzled look. "By then I wasn't sore, you know? It was like—a game with a ball, where you catch the rhythm, and do it just right. It's like playing some kind of a game." His voice rose to a pitch thin and plaintive. "And what was she worth? A bag like Mildred? She didn't care about herself, did she? It didn't matter to her what happened, what she said, the things she did. All she wanted was her kicks. What she liked best was somebody watching. Jesus Christ, what makes her worth five years!"

"Meg wants to know what she can do," I said.

He came back from a far place and focused on me. "What does she want to do? Pack a picnic lunch?"

"Do you want to see her?"

"No."

"Do you need cigarettes or anything?"

He didn't answer me. He was staring down at the floor. I waited a little while and then I left. He didn't look up. I wondered how he'd adjust to Harpersburg. So did a lot of other people. All of us guessed wrong. We thought that toughness was a muscle reflex, that they'd peel him right down to a whimper. In this good guy-bad guy world it is too easy for all of us to believe in the myth of the gutless villain. So we all guessed wrong.

MEG called me from the kitchen door and I went in for the late lunch with the prodigal brother. He was in a yellow sweater, gray slacks, his cropped hair still spikey with shower dampness. Meg served the foods he had always loved best, in great quantity. She tried to talk in a spritely way of small funny things, but there was an edge of anxiety in her voice.

I knew what was bothering her and I had no good way to help her. I knew he was somewhat sullen and indifferent, but not as much as she believed him to be. It is the prison mark on them. We learn to recognize it in our work. I can walk down a busy city street and pick out the ex-cons who have done long time with a good chance of being right, but oddly enough some of the ones I pick out will be career enlisted personnel in civilian dress. They have lost the normal mobility and elasticity of the muscles of the face, the expressive muscles. There is a restriction of normal eye movement, a greater dependence on peripheral vision. The range of the conversational voice is reduced. There is a restriction of gesture and a reluctance to move quickly. Somewhat the same effect can be achieved as a parlor game with the normal person by asking someone to balance a book on their head and then continue to walk, sit, talk, drink.

"Is everything all right?" she would ask, too often.

"Everything is fine, Sis," he would say in the deadened voice of the cell blocks and exercise yards.

Once he looked down and plucked at the front of the sweater and said, "So damn bright. I keep seeing it. I'm used to that gray."

And I could see him consciously slowing himself down as he ate. Most prison disorders begin in the dining halls, so that is where they try to achieve total control. At Harpersburg they file in and line up at the long tables. No talking. The food is already served. At the whistle signal they all sit and begin to eat. No talking. The stick screws rove the floor and the gun screws watch from the gallery. At the second whistle, five minutes later, they stand up, facing the aisle, and start the file out, farthest tables first, carrying plates and utensils. Just outside the main door they split the file out into four check lines to get the cutlery count. 'From entrance to exit is a nine-minute span, so they gobble the slop, choke it down, gasping with haste, or endure a constant hunger.

I could see him trying to slow himself to the leisurely pace of freedom. But there was too much food, and it was too rich. Near the end of the meal he suddenly turned sweaty gray and excused himself hastily. We heard the wrenching distant sounds of his illness.

Meg sat with the tears running down her face. "He doesn't like anything," she said in a hopeless voice. "He doesn't like anything at all."

"It will take a little time."

"It isn't the way I wanted it to be, Fenn."

"Be patient."

"I've been trying so hard."

"You're doing fine. You're doing all you can do."

"But what does he *want*?" she cried. The phone rang. I guess it was a partial answer to the question she had asked. I took the call.

It was a girl's voice, young, husky, hesitant. "Is Dwight McAran there?"

"Who is calling?"

"Just a friend."

"I'd better have him call you back. If you'll give me your num—"

McAran appeared beside me, saying, "For me? Let me have it."

He was tense when he spoke into the phone. "Who?" he said. "Oh, it's you." He seemed let down. "Well, it's nice to be out. Sure. What else can I say about it? What? No. Not so soon. Later on, kid. Give me a few days. Let me get used to being loose. Sure." He hung up and looked at me. "You want a transcript of the call, cop? You want me to ask permission to use the phone?"

"Who is she?"

"A girl I've never seen, Lieutenant. But she's written me letters. A lot of letters. And she sent me pictures of herself." I was aware of Meg standing nearby. "She's just a little girl

51

whose been cheering me in my darkest hours, Lieutenant. She was only seventeen when they tucked me away in Harpersburg, but she's a full grown girl now."

"Who is she, dear?" Meg asked. "Do we know her?"

He shrugged. "You might. You might not. Cathie Perkins, a blonde kid. Stacked."

"There's a history teacher at the high school named Ted Perkins," Meg said. "They have five daughters."

"This is the middle one of the five," Dwight said. He smiled like a cat in a fish market. "I'm her hero."

"She's not showing much judgment," I said.

Meg turned on me. "What kind of a remark is that? They're a nice family. I think one of the Perkins girls would be good for Dwight, better for him than that Hanaman girl was, certainly. Because he's been in jail, are decent people too good for him? What kind of an attitude is that, Fenn? Really!"

Later on, I drove down to the station. We're in a sandstone wing added to the original pseudo-Grecian City Hall in the early twenties. It backs up against the block containing the Brook County Courthouse, a gray, cheerless, Federalist structure. I parked in back of our wing. As I pushed the door open I heard warning shouts and saw a girl running toward me, as fast as she could run. Even though I had a moment to brace myself, she knocked me back against the doors. She yelled and squirmed. I trapped her wrists. She kicked me twice before I could immobilize her against the wall, and then she tried to bite. Detective Raglin and the jail matron we call Iron Kate hurried up and took her off my hands. I was glad to get a little farther away from the fetid, grainy smell of the girl. She wore black jeans, an ornate motorcycle belt, a soiled pale green sweater with nothing under it. Re-caught, she stood quietly enough, breathing hard, staring down at the floor. Her parched blonde hair had long black roots.

"Sorry, Fenn. She just took off like a rabbit," Raglin said. His bald head was pink with anger.

"What is she?" I asked.

"New girl in town, trying to work a drunk in the bus station. Chuck West made the collar. He followed them over to Alderman Street, back to one of those empty garages. When he went in to break it up, her boy friend who was waiting right there had already coldcocked the drunk and they were checking his pockets."

"Tryna fine idennafacation," the girl said in a raspy voice. "Some drunk follows me and falls on his head, see, and so Tommy and I, we're tryna be decent, see, but we get arrested on a crummy rap."

"Off we go to the fish tank, dearie ,where you'll make a lot of new friends," Iron Kate said and put a come-along hold on the girl's wrist. Before they got to the stairs the girl started to resist. She gave a thin squeak of pain and went along with a new docility.

"Drifting through," Raglin said. "Working their way. Working the drunks. So they get a bath, a meal and a bunk, and a free trip to the city line."

"Except she was too ready to run."

"Huh?"

"Put out an all-points inquiry, then team with Rossman and sell them the idea we're going to use them to get that John Doe killing off our books, the bum somebody slugged too hard three weeks ago. She looked too case hardened to try that fool trick of running unless the reason was real good."

I saw Raglin respond to the idea. He began to nod. "Okay, but I'm supposed to go check the gas stations for—"

"I'll change the duty roster, Rags."

I went on up to the squad room. Eleven of the fifteen desks were empty. Three of the four men there were on the phone. Detective Sergeant Johnny Hooper was in my office with his feet on my desk. He jumped up violently, blushing and trying to hide the book he had been reading. It was my copy of *Leadership for the Police Supervisor* by Scott and Garrett.

"A quiet day, Fenn," he said anxiously. "One real quiet day."

Johnny Hooper is one of the good ones. He's twenty-eight and looks twenty, a big tow-headed country boy, newly married, newly promoted, slightly unsure of himself except when things start to get warm, and then you wouldn't want anybody else backing you up. He started to tell me about the small collar West had made, and I told him the orders I had given Rags, and he looked as if he was going to break into tears because he hadn't thought of it himself. I altered the duty roster and he went out into the bull pen to run the phone check on the gas stations himself. We'd recently had a loading dock theft of several cartons of assorted sizes of windshield wipers, about seven hundred dollars' worth, and it had the flavor of local amateur talent, the kind stupid enough to start peddling them locally, in the logical places. In fifteen minutes he came in and told me he had a lead and he would run out and check it out. I remarked that he'd come up with something pretty quickly, and he said he had ignored the alphabetical listings in the yellow pages and started with those on the west side. They seemed more likely outlets. So he got his lead in fifteen minutes instead of an hour, and that is the kind of thinking you can't go out and buy.

Larry Brint heard I was in and asked me to come up to his office. Chuck West had just come back, so I asked him to mind the store and went on up. On the way I stopped at C&D and checked the all-points inquiry which had gone out on the couple who'd been caught indulging in the most primitive-known variation of the badger game. I sat on Larry's green leather couch. He leaned back in his chair with a mild and attentive expression on his schoolteacher face while I told him about the trip to Harpersburg and my appraisal of Dwight McAran.

On his wall was a speaker with a separate volume control, hooked into the prowl circuit, the volume turned down to the point where it was a faint raspy buzzing, seemingly impossible for anyone to hear. Yet I had been in that office several times when one of the several emergency code numbers had been given and had seen Brint stop in the middle of a word and immediately reach over to the speaker and turn the volume up.

He didn't ask me what I thought McAran might do. He slowly bent a paper clip into new shapes. "One man in ten thousand, Fenn, you hammer on him long enough, you create a new creature in the world. Sometimes a saint. Sometimes a monster. Sometimes a harmless idiot."

The paper clip broke. He got up restlessly and went to the window and rocked back and forth on his heels, looking out at the city.

"Poor sad son of a bitch of a town," he said. "Seems as if could they forgive a man income tax, some smart greedy man could come in here and put together an empty factory and skilled men and make something people would buy.

54

Skip Johnson was in to see me this morning. Bought me a four-dollar lunch at the Downtown Club. Funny how out of an old family like that a man can come along you could stake out in the city dump and he'd get rich making coats out of rat hides."

"About McAran?" I asked.

"When he finally got around to it. He never came right out with it. A man like that never does. Old Paul Hanaman doesn't want McAran around town." He came back to his desk chair, sat down and sighed. "That's no secret. Jeff Kermer doesn't want McAran in town. That hasn't been as obvious. Skip Johnson is the link between those two because he's tied up to both of them in business ways. It seems to them that any reliable, efficient Chief of Police ought to be able to hustle any undesirable citizen on his way, and if said Chief can't do a little thing like that, the Common Council might request the Commissioner of Public Safety—if they can keep old Ed sober enough—to suspend the Chief and his most trusted assistants while they make a full-scale investigation of the operations of the department."

"What—what did you tell him?"

"He didn't come right out with it. But I guess I did. He kept smiling. That man never stops smiling. I said it would suit me. I can elect to be pensioned off right now instead of waiting the five years more. I'm an old widower, all alone in the world, with a son in El Paso ready any time to give me house room, and his wife is willing, and that sun will feel good. I said I'd go to the extra trouble of getting you and Johnny Hooper and a couple of other boys relocated in cities where the police don't work for a newspaper or a toad like Kermer. Then he and the Hanamans could sit back and watch the town go the rest of the way to hell. Then I thanked him for the lunch."

"Can you get away with that, Larry?"

He gave me a weary smile. "I don't much care. If I did care, he'd have me whipped, wouldn't he? By God, they've been walking around me for years, looking for the handle to grab and the button to push."

"It would be easier on me if we—eased him out of town. But it would have to be done in such a way Meg wouldn't know."

"Hell, while Skip was talking I figured how we could

do it, Fenn. Take a gun can't be traced out of our supply here and you plant it in his room where he won't run across it. Then I have you get Meg out of the way and we go in with a warrant and give him his choice of moving on or spending some more time with Boo Hudson."

"He'd tell Meg."

"She wouldn't know you were in on it. Neither would he."

"She has all that—unthinking loyalty. She survived the five years, Larry. If he had to go back, that way, it would tear her in half. I guess the marriage would survive, but there wouldn't be much in it any more, for either of us."

"You don't have to say all that. You know I'm just talking. I can't let myself be pushed around, especially when it would be damn poor judgment. McAran is after something, or he wouldn't have come back here. Until I know what it is, I want him handy. I don't want him chased back into the hills."

"But what am I going to do, Larry, if—they do go ahead and suspend you?"

"We'll go right to that good woman of yours and I'll tell her just why it's being done, and then we go to Ralph Kowalski who's the only lawyer in town the Hanamans can't scare, and we bring the Attorney General of this great state into the picture in such a way he can't wiggle out of it, and there'll be so many injunctions and so much stink they won't dare try anything."

"You didn't hint anything like that to Skip Johnson?"

"Hell, no!"

"Larry, did he say anything about—the spot I'm in? I mean, do they understand how a family thing like this can—"

"You ever been inside the Brook Valley Club, Fenn?"

"What? Yes. Once. When a dishwasher put a knife into a French chef."

"Your old man ran a steam hammer at the old A. Z. Forge and Foundry. You're a cop. A city has to have cops, mailmen, meter readers, trash men, street cleaners, ambulance drivers and telephone operators. About an hour from now Skip Johnson will belly up to the men's bar out there at the Brook Valley Club, and Skip will tell old Paul what a stubborn, arrogant old son of a bitch I am. If Jeff Kermer suddenly got hold of seven billion dollars in cash, all his own and tax free, he couldn't get into Brook Valley if he lived to be four hundred years old. They let him into the Downtown Club and that's about as far as he goes. Old Paul and Skip know one of my officers is brother-in-law to Mc-Aran. To them it is a strange little fact they don't have to try to understand. You're not important enough to mean as much to them as the bartender fixing their drinks, and they're not going to think of your problems on any personal basis of understanding. The best way we'll be home free is if Jeff Kermer is more nervous than I think he is."

"What do you mean?"

"If he happened to be very nervous, he could ask for a little help in return for what he skims off the top and sends out of town. He hasn't had to ask for that kind of help for over ten years."

"Oh. A specialist."

"In and out, like a fumigation job, with perfect timing and the ever-popular twelve gauge, and a pleasant trip home."

"But he isn't that nervous."

"No. But I have the hunch he should be. The years have softened him. He's had it his own way a long time. He's got too many kinds of letterhead stationery these days, and too much tax accounting and too many Rotarians calling him Jeff. What harm can come to a man who *always* gets a box for the World Series and comes up with a four-figure check for the United Fund?"

"We both know McAran thinks Kermer crossed him up, but—"

"But what"

"I can't see Dwight doing anything where—he didn't stand to make out pretty well."

"In five years a man might be able to think up a nice way to kill two birds, using a few things he could have learned while he was working for Kermer. I guess all we can do is wait it out and keep an eye on your—"

He lunged over to the speaker and twisted the volume up. It was a fire in a paint store on the north end of Franklin Avenue, and the first car there recommended four more be hustled along for traffic and crowd control. We went across the hallway to look out the windows on the north side. We heard sirens, saw the distant upward billowing of dirty saffron smoke into the gray afternoon sky, and saw a twinkling of flame inside the smoke, like lightning in a thunderhead. I followed Larry back into his office. He went over to the photo-map of the city which covered one complete wall—souvenir of the days when Brook City could afford such embellishments.

"In this block," he said. "Right about here. It's blown the roof, so it should take the ones on either side, but there's nothing directly behind it. Let's go take a look, Fenn."

He has always been like a kid about fires. We went out there. It burned hot and stubborn, with fumes which dropped a few firemen when they moved in on it, in spite of the masks. I went back to work. Johnny Hooper brought in one of the three men who had stolen the wipers. The man was eager to make a detailed statement implicating the other two, in return for a little special consideration. The moist chill night closed down across the flat expanse of the valley. I worked right on through the change of shift, checking the new duty sheet, reviewing the backlog that is always with us, comforting myself with the familiar pattern of the work. It is always the same. In the quiet times you assign your people to the legwork necessary to cut down the backlog, and you keep some of them loose to go to work on the new stuff coming in, and you ride hard on the clerks to keep your files and records as current as possible.

But you can't get so tangled in the routine you forget to be braced for something big. Say you have forty men. Seventeen hundred and sixty hours of specialist effort a week. But you operate every single hour of the week, and you have to adjust to vacations, sick leave, court appearances, training courses, compulsory time on the range, retirement, selection, promotion. You take what's left and try to fit manpower to the demands of each duty shift, and use the men on the things they do best.

With the coming of night the tempo always picks up a little. The patrolmen can handle all the trash arrests, but when it gets up to a certain category, they are required to call on the Detective Section. I kept telling myself I was too busy to go home, but I knew it was just another routine evening. The *Daily Press* called to complain about a half-dozen of their racks disappearing. A transient in a flophouse hotel on Division Street hung himself from the transom of his room with a child's jump rope after printing misspelled obscenities on his naked body with iodine. A salesman staying at the Christopher Hotel reported his room rifled, his clothes and samples gone. A teenage lover and his fifteen-year-old girl friend had taken off in her father's car. The pretty wife of a young doctor reported she had been receiving obscene phone calls and letters for over a month. At City Hospital a woman brought her eighteen-month-old child to the emergency room, so badly beaten by her alcoholic husband, his condition was classified as critical. A fast-draw clown, age fifty-one, blew half his right foot off with an unlicensed forty-five. A stolen car. Aggravated assault. An elderly woman in a dazed condition, unable to state her name or address. An indecent exposure over at Torrance Memorial Park. Vandalism at a church. A sad-eyed old man who came in to complain he couldn't locate the young girl to whom he had loaned his life savings.

These were the tensions and torments of the urban night. Stu Dockerty was there to report them. Brook City used to have four newspapers, if you count both the morning and evening paper Hanaman used to publish. When the only surviving competition died in 1952, Hanaman put out the evening paper for just one more year and then folded it. The *Brook City Daily Press* is put to bed at midnight. Stu Dockerty is the police reporter, covering us, the Sheriff's department a block away, and the criminal courts.

He is a dapper, elegant man in his forties, with all the devices of vanity—elevated shoes, military mustache, careful wave in the thick gray hair, tweeds, flannels, cashmere, solid gold accessories, languid courtesy, a faint hint of a British accent. New men on the force invariably make the wrong estimate of Dockerty. In time they learn of his three marriages, his merciless talent for any form of gambling, his astonishing capacity for liquor and that special kind of nerveless courage which turns any kind of danger into a game planned for his amusement. He reports accurately, spells names correctly, gives credit where it is earned, and defends the department against all improper attacks, even by his own publisher. He usually wanders in after lunch, picks up all he needs to know about the previous twelve hours, without getting in anybody's way, writes his own copy on the machine he keeps in one corner of my squad room, typing with a speed which intimidates my clerks. When he stops by in the early evening he catches up on any afternoon events. Only when things break late in the evening does he phone his stuff in to the copy desk rather than knocking it out himself.

He is also a wire service stringer, sells articles to the true crime magazines, ghosts local political speeches, and does some copywriting for a local ad agency.

I had told Meg I wouldn't be home for dinner, and had made my invented reasons sound plausible. As I was on my way out to get something to eat at about eight o'clock, I saw Dockerty stuffing copy into an envelope.

I stopped beside him and said, "No special events tonight, Stu."

He shrugged. "Man dangling on a jump rope. One-a-larry, two-a-larry, three-a-larry, four. Pathos and bad spelling, old boy. And a beaten baby. And the have-gun-can't-walk type. But I'll jerk the tears with the old moneylender."

"Nothing we can go on, you know. It wasn't a con game."

"I know. It was love."

"Want to come watch me eat, Stu?"

"Give me time to drop this stuff off."

I had franks and beans in one of the old mahogany booths at Shilligan's Courthouse Cafe, while Stu drank draught beer.

"I hear a killer is now living at your house, Officer Hillyer."

"You never know what kind of a brother-in-law you're going to marry."

"All of mine were splendid chaps. Got along splendidly with them. Found I couldn't stand their sisters, though. But I never lucked into a jewel like your Miss Meg, Fenn."

"She's not exactly dancing with delight. He's pretty sour."

"Just sour? Nothing more?"

"Bitter, incorrigible, smart, tough and dangerous."

"Trouble coming?"

"Probably."

"What kind?"

"I don't know, but I think it would be some kind that would make him a profit."

"Using your place as a base, eh? Can't help you much, you know. It won't improve your future."

"What the hell can I do! Little brother needs his big sister—she thinks."

"You can all do just what Chief Brint said you'd do, Fenn. You can wait for one legitimate violation of some ordinance commonly enforced, a violation plain enough so Meg won't blame you when he's pulled in. What does Meg really feel about him?"

I shrugged helplessly. "If she's doing any thinking, she's doing it with her heart. The trouble he used to get into, she thinks of it as mischief. Boyish pranks. When he was working for Kermer as an enforcer, I tried to let her know. She refused to believe it. Hell, she wouldn't even believe he'd worked the Hanaman girl over until she heard the eye-witness testimony, and then she said he wouldn't have really hit her very hard because he wasn't that kind of a boy. She was a zombi for six months after he was sent up, and she never has gotten all the way back to the way she used to be. Little brother! My God, you should see them together. It's like a kid with a loveable little kitten that grew up to be a tiger, and the little kid insists it's only a house cat. I can't reach her, Stu. The moment I start, all her defenses come up. Darling brother has had bad luck. As soon as he stops feeling sorry for himself, he'll get a nice job and meet a nice girl and settle down and go bowling with the fellows on Saturday night. When she looks at him she doesn't really see him. If she could really see him, she'd know she's been wrong about him all her life."

"What good is a woman who doesn't follow what her heart tells her? Who would want a woman who sees things the way they really are?"

"But—it's going to come out in some bad way for her, and for me, and there's no way to stop it. It's like a long hill and no brakes."

He looked at me with an unexpected compassion. "If you're lucky, Fenn, if you get the luck I think you deserve, maybe whatever happens will happen in such a way she'll get that one good look at him. And when she does, if she does, the spell will be over. She's strong. She started in a trap and broke out of it and brought him along with her. People not as strong as Meg have survived more horrible things. What was the name of that family five years ago? Brumbeck, wasn't it? Their only kid, a good-looking boy, an A student, confessing to two rape murders and dying in the chair."

"I know what you're trying to say, and thanks. They survived, yes. They kept on living. But how much joy have they got left? Meg was meant to be a joyful woman. Hum-

ming and singing and whistling around the house, making
fool jokes and playing tricks on her man and her kids, and
laughing at nothing when she feels particularly happy. When
they first put him away, it was like there wasn't a sound left
in the house. Nothing. I'd go home and feel like whispering.
I'd wake up in the night and know she was awake there in
the darkness, completely still, completely alone, and there
wasn't anything I could say to her."

Raglin suddenly appeared beside the booth, grinning, and
I asked him to sit down. "Jackpot on the pair," he said.
"Toledo got interested. Felony murder by auto ten days ago.
Knocked off a gas station and clobbered an old lady when
they went up over the sidewalk, they were in such a hurry.
Blew a tire on the curb and escaped on foot. Me and Rossman worked the guy for it first and he didn't know a thing.
So we got the girl out of the tank and said her boy friend
had fingered her for driving the car, and she figured we
knew so many details, the boy friend had talked. I guess she
never realized we could have been in touch with Toledo, so
she broke and when she got through screaming, she let us
have all of it. She'll sign the statement. Rossman advised
Toledo."

Dockerty had his copy paper out, and I left them there,
with Rags giving Stu the story. I walked back to the headquarters wing, remembering the wiry panic of the grubby girl,
the feel of her slender wrists in my hand. By the time they
would finally release her, she would be a cowed dark-
haired woman, heavy with prison starch, boiled rough-red
by the laundry years, perhaps unable to remember the face
of Tommy.

I arrived home a few minutes after ten. The kids were in
bed. Meg was on the couch, patching a pair of Bobby's
khaki pants. Dwight was sprawled in my chair, watching
a television serial. He looked up and gave a grunt of greeting. He made no move to give up the chair. Meg looked anxiously at me and then at him. She relaxed when I sat down
on the couch. We made some small talk during the commer-
cials. Dwight didn't join in. When the show ended at ten-
thirty he stood up, stretched, yawned and said, "See ya," and
went off to bed.

I turned the television volume down and went back and sat
beside her.

"How has he acted?"

"All right. He had a nap after lunch. He went out in the back yard for a little while. Except for when we ate, he's been watching television ever since."

"You act kind of low."

"There were four phone calls, dear. People called up and said—filthy things and hung up."

"Goddam them!"

"Don't be upset. They're just—sort of sick."

"But one of the kids might answer the—"

"I made a new rule. I take all calls. And some cars kept driving by, real slow, staring at the house."

"That won't last long."

"I told him this afternoon that if—he wanted to tell me how it was—it might help him. He said the best way I could help him was keep off his back."

"Nice guy."

"He used to get this way when we were kids, when something went wrong, or he was planning something he knew he shouldn't do. I don't think I could stand it if he got into trouble again, honey. I just couldn't bear it."

"We'll just have to keep an eye on him."

"Honey, he didn't realize you always sit in that chair."

"I don't have to sit in any particular place."

"It's your home. You ought to have the right to—"

"How did it go with the kids?"

"Dwight isn't used to children. I think they could get on his nerves."

"Now isn't that a damned shame!"

"He really didn't pay hardly any attention to them at all. Bobby seemed very reserved around him. But Judy jabbered at him a mile a minute. You know how she is. She's so convinced everybody loves her. That reminds me. That girl called again on the phone. That Cathie Perkins. He talked to her quite a long time. I was trying not to listen, but I got the idea she wanted to come over and see him, and he was discouraging her. I talked to Betty Robling on the phone about something else and I asked her about Cathie Perkins. Betty says she's a sweet girl, but sort of strange and hard to control. She didn't go back to college last year. She works in the business office at the phone company. It would be so good for Dwight if he could—find a really nice girl."

Again I remembered the stony starveling face of the girl

who had tried to escape. She seemed more suitable for Dwight McAran.

Lulu came cautiously into the living room, whined softly at us, and grinned in a rather abashed way.

"Darn you, Lulu," Meg said. "Every time she sees Dwight, she screams and runs under something."

"That's because he kicked her," I said.

She looked at me uncertainly. "Is that some kind of a joke, Fenn?"

"No. When we arrived, just before you came out, she started to jump on him. You know how she is. He gave her one hell of a thump with his knee."

"And poor Lulu thinks he *meant* to do it?"

"Yes, and so do I. She landed on her back six feet away, and ran under the garage."

"But—if he did kick her on purpose it was only because he—because it just happened to—"

She stopped and looked away. I put my hand on her arm. But she pulled away from me and stood up and went slowly to our bedroom. I heard the door close quietly. Lulu bumped her head against my leg. I scratched her behind the ears. She whined again. She did not like what had happened to her home. Nor did I.

But there was no way I could comfort Lulu—or Meg.

Without Meg I would become a dull beast, indeed, an entirely cold and rational fellow. I can erect all the structures of logic. But she has a warm heart and the knack of making joyful use of her days. Often I feel as if I have no good way to reach her, or reach anybody else I know in any deep and meaningful way. I can never say to her all the things which should be said. All I can do is hope she has the instinctive knowledge of me which needs no explanation.

Lulu stared at me, her eyes softly brown and adoring. I wondered if Cathie Perkins had eyes of that same vulnerable tone.

Two days later I went to the high school and talked to Mr. Theodore Perkins in his office after the day's classes were over. He was a big, bald, gentle man, quite willing to talk when he learned who I was.

"I have good girls, Lieutenant Hillyer. The two eldest are married, and one is very happy and one is miserably unhappy. Their mother died seven years ago. Her people were opposed to our marriage. We eloped. It was a good and happy relationship. You see, we have no right to force our children into our patterns and beliefs. Each heart has its own direction. Cathie is twenty-two. She is a woman. When this started she was a child, a dreamy, imaginative child. I thought she'd get over it. It was the kind of fantasy any young girl might have, I suppose. But how could I have known it would last for five years?"

I did not tell him what a familiar phenomenon it is, whenever any reasonably presentable man is convicted of a crime of passion and receives much newspaper publicity. Women respond, write letters, try to arrange visits, convinced they must patch up this broken life.

"For the past six months, Lieutenant, Cathie has been getting more and more tense, waiting for McAran to be released. She thinks she loves him."

"They've never met."

"I know. But they have corresponded. Perhaps—it might be right for her. How can we be sure it isn't?"

"McAran isn't right for anybody, Mr. Perkins."

"He's living in your home."

"Because he's my wife's half-brother, and she is a very loyal woman, and he's getting some kind of charge out of making me as uncomfortable as he can, because I'm a cop. I think he's a cruel, vicious, dangerous man."

I saw the expression of pain on his face. "I've been trying to tell myself he isn't like that, Lieutenant Hillyer. I—I can't talk to Cathie about it. This is a compulsion with her. Can you—talk to her?"

"I suppose I could try."

I met her by prearrangement when she left the phone company office at five o'clock. She was a tall, brown-eyed blonde, with a round, pretty, somewhat immature face. She was remote, slightly defiant and ill at ease. We talked over coffee in a luncheonette booth a half-block from the phone company offices.

"I wouldn't talk to you if my father hadn't made me promise I would."

"I'm meddling in something that's probably none of my business, Cathie."

It disarmed her slightly. "Probably," she said.

"Why did you write to him in the first place?"

"Because everybody was against him!" she said hotly. "It wasn't fair. There wasn't anybody on his side. They wanted to pull him down, like a pack of dogs. Now more than ever, he needs somebody on his side."

"How have you managed to get so emotionally involved with a man you've never met?"

"Oh, I met him. My father doesn't know this. Dwight doesn't remember, but I do. Maybe he'll remember when he sees me. It was when he was working in the sporting goods store. I was just a kid. I went in to buy bowling shoes. He was very sweet and funny, and he made me laugh. He was nice to me. I didn't have enough money, so he found a lot of wild crazy things wrong with the shoes I wanted, and he marked them down. That was before he got mixed up with that terrible woman. She ruined his life, and I don't think he killed her. I think he's so big and strong that a lot of little men had to put him in prison because they were jealous of him. And they didn't want him to come back here, but he promised me he would in his letters. You have no idea the wonderful letters he wrote me. Nobody else in the world really understands him."

"He used to be able to be very charming, especially to pretty girls."

She flushed. "His letters weren't charming. They were sincere."

"So what's the next step?"

"I don't know. I want to help him any way he'll let me, any way at all. But I'll just have to wait until he's—willing to see me. How—how is he acting, really?"

"He eats and sleeps and watches television. Sometimes he goes out into the back yard. That's as far as he goes from the house."

"I'm aching to be with him and talk to him. But I can't do that until he feels—ready to see me."

"What if you find out he isn't the kind of a man you think he is, Cathie?"

"But I *know* what kind of a man he is. He's hurt now, and angry, but way underneath he's a gentle man, if the world will give him a chance to be gentle."

"Listen to me. That gentle fellow went on Jeff Kermer's payroll at two hundred a week, cash. And Jeff sent him out to reason gently with a man named David Morissa, five-foot-six, a hundred and forty pounds. Dwight gently snapped both Davie's wrists, dislocated his shoulder and cracked half his ribs, and Jeff was very pleased with the job, because that was just what he was paying for."

Her brown eyes looked wide and sick. "You're making that up!"

"Why would I?"

She shook her head slowly. "I don't know. You must have some reason." She was a slender, vulnerable girl, shapely, fragrant, pretty, with a soft mouth, gentle breasts, fragile hands. "You must have some reason. Maybe you didn't come to my father. Maybe he went to you and asked you to do this."

"No. Here is the reason. I just don't want you making a lot of blind excuses for anything McAran says or does. I don't want you to be sacrificial about this—long-range romance, Cathie. I want you to just leave your mind open to the possibility that everything he has written you is part of a complicated lie, that there's no gentleness in him, and he wants to use you."

"It isn't that way," she whispered.

"But just leave room for a tiny little bit of doubt. And then give him the chance to eliminate that doubt, or increase it. Be watchful, that's all. And if he lets you in on his plans, and you don't think those plans are—exactly gentle, you let me know. You see, he's always had the knack of using women, and making them believe in him."

"But this time he—"

"If you think there can be some kind of a valid relationship, a little concealed skepticism in the beginning isn't going to bankrupt it, Cathie."

"Just tell me why you're doing this?"

"Because I have so much at stake, I can't afford to overlook the smallest chance. It's a table stakes game, and everything I own is on the table. My wife, my marriage, my job, my reputation, and the reputation of my friends."

"I see. When do you think he'll want to see me?"

"I don't know."

"I talk to him on the phone every day. I think he wants time to—be more like himself for me. More like he used to be, before they put him in a cage. And we probably both feel a little shy and awkward. I mean, after you write very personal things to someone, you worry about—saying the same sort of things face to face."

"I'm sorry, but I can't imagine him being shy about anything."

"Because you don't really know him."

"And you do?"

She lifted her chin. "I know I do."

"I could tell you other things, but you wouldn't believe them, would you?"

"No."

"But leave room for a little doubt, so you won't—get in too deep too soon, Cathie."

"I'll try," she said. "I have to go now. You've—been nicer than I thought you'd be. You're not like he described you in one letter. He said you're a cold, selfish, righteous man who doesn't give a damn about people, that all you care about is enforcing the law to the letter. He said he didn't know how his sister could stand you."

"I wonder about that myself."

She flushed again and said, "I thought that when a man got out of prison he'd be anxious to—see a girl." She sighed. "He's very strange."

"That's where we agree, Cathie."

After we left the restaurant, I watched her walk to the bus stop at the corner. The wind touched her blonde hair and tugged at the hem of her narrow skirt. She walked like a lady. I knew she was another victim. McAran collected them like beads on a string.

The days went by and I felt a restless impatience, an irritability. I did not enjoy going home, yet felt guilty when I stayed away needlessly. Even when he was in what had been Bobby's room and the door was closed, I could feel his presence. To me it was like a faintly acrid stench, unidentifiable, untraceable, the kind which makes you uneasy because it can mean something might break into flame.

I had to talk to Bobby again. I had a long talk with him before I brought McAran back from Harpersburg, at the time when the other kids first started to tease him. Meg told me he was acting very strangely. So on the next really pleasant Saturday morning, I walked with him to the playground and we sat on the bench. He was very reserved. I had hoped our kids would look like her, but both of them have my sallowness, and the dank black hair, and the sorrowful shape to their faces—though Judy is such a cheery child it is not apparent.

"I suppose the kids are giving you a hard time," I said.

"Not so much."

"Remember, I told you what to keep telling yourself, so it wouldn't bother you."

"Sure."

"Did it work?"

"I guess so," he said with elaborate indifference.

"Bobby, this is a very hard time for your mother. She loves us, but she loves her brother too. And she's known him a lot longer than she's known us. What we have to do is make it easier for her by—by acting as if everything is just fine, even though it isn't."

"I don't see how she can love him the way she does us."

"Love doesn't go by reasons, Bobby."

He sat still for quite a long time and then he turned toward me, his face pinched and white, and his eyes slitted and he said, "I *hate* that dirty killer son of a bitch!"

"Hey now! Steady!"

"I hate him! If he was shot dead right now I'd laugh and laugh."

"You're working yourself right into a paddling, fellow."

"Go ahead. I don't care what you do. It won't change anything."

"Now just what in the world has he done to you?"

I saw his face change, smooth out, become secretive. "He hasn't done anything to me." I've done too much interrogation work to have failed to notice the subtle emphasis on "me."

"To Lulu then?"

"No."

"Judy?"

"No."

"Your mother?"

"I promised I wouldn't tell."

It didn't take long to get all of it, because it was a promise he didn't want to keep. It was too much for him. She shouldn't have asked it of him. He had come home from school. Meg and Dwight had been arguing in the kitchen, talking so loudly they didn't hear him come in. He had seen Dwight strike Meg in the stomach with his fist and knock her down, then walk to his room and slam the door. Bobby had begun to cry. She had gotten up slowly and painfully and vomited into the sink and then taken him with her to our bedroom. She had lain on the bed and held him in her arms until they were both cried out, then made him promise he would say nothing. In the telling he cried again, but tried to conceal it. I would have held him, but he was eight years old, and there were friends of his on the playground.

He looked at me with wet eyes and said, "I guess she knew if she told you, you'd put him in jail right away. I think you better put him in jail. He hurt her. He hurt her terrible, Daddy. It—it's so different from a kid getting knocked down. It's scary. Will you go take him to jail right now?"

"Your mother wouldn't want him to go back to jail, Bobby. That would just be hurting her again, in a different way."

"But he—he's spoiling our *house*!"

I knew what he meant. Some of his friends had started to call him. He ignored them. "Everything is going to be fixed in a little while. Be patient, boy. Try to act like yourself so your mother won't worry about you. Now you go play with your friends."

"Are you going to tell her I told you?"

"That's up to you."

He frowned for long thoughtful seconds. "I think she better know you know it, Daddy. Will you hit him like he hit her, will you?"

I had to get out of that one in a way that would salvage some pride. "If she'll let me," I said. "He's her brother."

I sat and watched him racing around with his friends for a little while. I walked home. Meg was marketing. Dwight was in his room. When Meg came back I helped her carry in the groceries. I could hear the radio in Dwight's room. I sat on the counter top and watched her putting things away. I like to watch the way she moves. She has a balance, a deftness, a certainty about things.

"Stomach still sore?" I asked.

She stood motionless, her hand on the refrigerator door, then turned slowly to face me. "Bobby promised."

"You knew why he was acting so funny."

"I—I guess I did."

"So did you want me to pry it out of him? It wasn't easy, if that's any help."

"I don't *know,* darling! I don't *know!*"

"You've got an emotional stake in your brother. We've both got an emotional stake in these kids. So this is where I come in, with both feet. I don't want our kids over-protected, guarded from every unpleasantness in life. But Bobby saw something that didn't fit anything he's ever learned. He'll carry it a long time. It's a—dirty kind of thing, Meg."

"Dwight didn't know he was anywhere near—"

"What difference does that make? It's the whole setup that's wrong. For you, for the kids. You can't housebreak him. We can't live like this."

She moved close, and looked at me in a wary way. I had kept my voice calm and reasonable, with an effort she could only suspect. She forced a smile. "I guess a lot of husbands have trouble with their in-laws."

"It isn't that and you know it, Meg. You can't make this sound like such—an ordinary thing. We'll go tell him right now he has to get out. You got his money for him. Almost three thousand dollars. If you owed him anything, he cancelled it."

"Fenn, listen to me. Please. He didn't mean to do that. He told me how sorry he was."

"Nice of him."

"Listen, please. I know how angry you are. But listen. Don't blame him so much. An animal, Fenn, even an animal, if you chained it and beat it and then let it go free, it might snap at people trying to feed it. It wouldn't really mean anything. You have to be patient with—"

I caught her wrists and puller her close. "Tell me something, Meg. How about long ago? Tell me about this animal. Was this the first time he ever hit you?"

"Well—yes."

"Meg!"

"It was the first time—this way. I mean since we were practically kids. Kids quarrel, darling. You know that. He'd —get impatient. Sometimes the whole world seemed to be down on us. And—I was handy to take it out on. It never meant anything." She tried to pull away but I would not release her.

"For Bobby's sake, for Judy's sake, for your sake, honey, he goes."

71

She looked beyond me, thoughtfully, and I thought for a moment I had won, by using her need to protect our children against her loyalty to McAran, but I saw her mouth grow firm, reflecting her strength.

"Have I asked for very much, really? Have I made demands, Fenn?"

"No."

"He's waiting for something. I don't know what it is. He's just waiting here, the way people wait in bus stations. Since you brought him here, he hasn't been any farther away than the back yard. He won't even admit he's waiting for anything. That's what the quarrel was about, when I tried to find out. When I answer the phone, I'll look up and he'll be there, watching me. When he finds out it's just a friend of mine, he goes away. When the mail comes, he is standing in the hall when I bring it in. When a car or truck stops, he's at the window. Fenn, what does a man do, usually, after five years in prison?"

"He—does all the little things he hasn't been able to do. Walk down a street. Drive a car. Buy a meal. Go to the movies. Have a date. A lot of them just walk, day after day, for miles and miles, getting used to being able to walk where they want. The city boys walk the streets, and the country boys like to go walk in the fields and the woods."

"He isn't afraid to leave the house, is he?"

"No. You know I told him Larry Brint's promise. No persecution."

"So he stays here because he's waiting for something. And he's more restless all the time, Fenn. Whatever it is, it's going to happen soon. So I'm asking this of you. Let him wait here until it happens, whatever it is. I promise you I won't—do anything to annoy him. I'll know when it happens because he'll stop acting the way he's acting now. And if he doesn't leave then, I guess we can—we can ask him to leave." She yanked her hands free. "But I'll help him find a place to stay, and I'll visit him, and if he gets sick, I'll bring him back here, and if he gets in trouble, I'll be with him to help him."

"I wouldn't ask you not to see him, honey."

"Can he stay?"

"Until he stops this mysterious waiting, or until he cuffs somebody, or until ten days is up, whichever comes first."

"Two weeks? Could it be two weeks?"

As it was more of a victory than I had expected, I agreed. She kissed me and began putting away the rest of the groceries.

"Bobby wanted to tell me," I said. "But you made him promise. Promises are important to that kid, as they should be. He's going to feel funny about it."

She looked across the kitchen at me. "But, darling, as soon as you came in the door I told you about it, didn't I?"

When I realized all the implications of it, all I could do was sit and grin at her and admire her. A promise kept. The impression of trust between parents undisturbed. Women have that wonderful trickery based on the true wisdom of the heart.

She sat on her heels and began to rearrange things in the freezer compartment in the bottom of the refrigerator to make more room.

"If he knows there are people who love him, Fenn, he'll be all right."

"People? How many does he need?"

"Two might be enough. Me—and Cathie Perkins. She was here yesterday."

"You didn't say anything about it!"

She stood up and swung the door shut and looked at me quite solemnly. "She's a nice girl, dear. She has a loving heart. She's as worried about him as I am. I wasn't going to tell you she was here. I didn't want to give you another chance to meddle. You went and saw her. You didn't tell me anything about that, did you?"

"Did she tell you I'd talked to her?"

"No. Dwight told me, after she left. She told him."

"She shouldn't have done that."

McAran appeared in the doorway and grinned at me in a lazy way. "You can't expect my cute little girl friend to keep secrets from me. You tried to turn her into a cop stooge. That wasn't half smart, Hillyer. She's so full of love for me, I just couldn't keep her away any longer. She tells me everything she knows. She pours her heart out."

I looked at him for five long seconds. His glance didn't waver. I said, "I wasn't trying to turn her into an informer, McAran. I guess I'm just curious about everything that concerns you. If she was a tough little slut, I guess I wouldn't have bothered. But she seemed very nice. If I saw a child trying to make a pet of a rattlesnake, I'd warn the child."

"Fenn!" Meg said with shock and anger.

"Let him be the big saviour," Dwight said. "He's all cop through and through, Sis."

"Maybe all you'd do is swing on her and knock her down," I said. "Just smack her in the belly with your fist to prove you're all hard-nose."

Dwight looked inquisitively at Meg. "I—I told him," she said.

"None of his business, was it, Sis? Does he know that as soon as I did it, I felt like cutting my hand off?"

"He wouldn't believe that. I guess—it wasn't any of his business."

"He makes everybody's business his business, Sis. Like he told Cathie some crazy story about me, how I was supposed to be the muscle that brought Davie Morissa back in line. Now how could you expect such a sweet loving little girl to believe I'd work over a poor little fellow like that, right in his own garage where I was waiting for him to come home in his big pink Cad? I've got such a soft heart, I couldn't have stood his screaming and begging, even when it came through the rag I stuffed in his mouth. I'd never have pulled his shoulder loose when I snapped one wrist behind him, and then snapped the other wrist and picked him up when he passed out and hung him on a hook by the collar of his coat on the garage wall and waited for him to come to before I cracked his ribs and told him it was a little message from Jeff about not holding out any special private percentage of the take any more. Cathie knows I couldn't have done anything like that, just like Sis here, from now on, isn't going to tell you any family business because she knows it isn't good for me to have the feeling some in-law cop is hounding me. Go talk to Cathie some more, Hillyer, if that's the way you look for your kicks. I told her how eager you are to frame me back into Harpersburg. She thinks you're a monster."

He grinned, winked and walked away. In a few minutes I heard the sound of a ball game on television. I watched Meg. Her color was bad. "He was making some kind of a joke, wasn't he? A joke about that man."

"How did it sound to you?"

"It was a joke," she said, without conviction.

"I notice you didn't want to tell him it was Bobby who told me about him slugging you."

"Please don't talk about it any more, Fenn. Please."

"You got your first real look at something you've never wanted to see. And now you're trying to convince yourself you didn't see a thing."

"It's just—two more weeks. I promised."

"And I'll bet you didn't go off on any shopping trip so he could be alone with the Perkins girl, did you?"

"No, but—"

"How did they act together?"

"She was shy and nervous at first. He was very sweet with her. I could hear them in the living room, talking and laughing. I think she cried for a little while too. Before she left she had real stars in her eyes. She was glowing, Fenn. And he was wearing some of her lipstick, I noticed. Maybe darling, she can make him see that—"

I went to her and held her in my arms.

"I'm so scared," she whispered. "All of a sudden I'm scared. I'm scared for all of us, and Dwight too."

"Maybe it will work out all right," I told her. Maybe we even believed that, a little bit. Because, above all, you have to believe in your luck. You have to ride with it, even when you know the wheel is fixed, because once you are in the game, there's no way you can stop playing. No way at all.

vi

ON the following Tuesday morning I had to spend an hour in court, over in the Brook County Courthouse, watching one of my people handle himself on the stand in an assault-in-the-first-degree case which had gone before a jury. The prosecutor had told Larry that our man was a little less than adequate, so Larry asked me to go check it out. He was a bright kid named Harold Brayger, who had done so well on plain-clothes duty as a patrolman, we had hustled him a promotion to Detective Second. The defense attorney was T. C. Hubbard, a very shrewd man.

Brayger had been through my compulsory Testimony Clinic, and had signed the library sheet as having read the two assigned texts.

I sat and watched him blow the prosecution case, merely because he was unusually bright and articulate. But he wasn't as bright as Hubbard. A big vocabulary can hurt an officer called to give testimony. If he describes the defendant, in answer to one question, as being "adamant," and a little later as being "inflexible," the shrewd defense attorney will focus on the different nuances of those two words, and, in front of a wondering jury, lead the witness off into a semantic jungle he could have avoided by merely saying "stubborn" and sticking to it. Also, Brayger was, in the tension of giving testimony, forgetting one of the most basic rules, that of depriving the defense attorney, in cross-examination, of any chance to set the pace of the questioning. I teach my people to wait until the question has been asked, and, in the case of every question, no matter how simple the answer, take a slow five count before giving the answer. The easiest reminder is to sit in the jury box with your thumb on your own pulse. This spacing gives the impression of responsiveness, thoughtfulness, sincerity and reliability. And, as the questions get more complex, it gives you a chance to detect a trap, gives the state a chance to object, and gives the judge a chance to request a clarification of the question. When a trap is obvious, you can

76

wait out the five count and request that it be repeated. Brayger was being so quick and so responsive that he was entangling himself, confusing the jury, and giving too many personal impressions mixed with the actual facts of the assault.

It hurts to turn over a solid file and then lose because of some legal technicality. It hurts worse to lose because the investigating officer gets trapped into too much deviation from the file.

Thus, at a few minutes after noon, I had a flushed, sullen, indignant Detective Brayger in my office when Meg phoned me.

"It happened," she said, "what he was waiting for. And he went out. He called a taxi. Can you talk now, dear?"

"Hold it a minute," I said. I covered the mouthpiece. "Run along, Harry, and for God's sake stop feeling abused. Hubbard was doing what he's paid to do. If you can't be used on the stand, your usefulness around here is pretty damn limited. It's part of your job, and you're expected to do it well. Read the texts again. You'll go through the Clinic again the next time it's set up. Now go tell John Finch I want you to have a transcript of your testimony for study. After you've studied it, write me a special report on exactly what you think you did wrong."

As he walked out I asked Meg to tell me what happened.

"A special delivery registered letter came for him about forty minutes ago, dear. Addressed to him, care of me. He signed for it and took it into his room. Sort of a fat white envelope. He came back out in about ten minutes and called the taxi. He seemed kind of nervous and excited, but trying to hide it. After he left I looked in his room. There's black ashes in the big ashtray I put in there for him."

"What kind of cab did he call?"

"Blue Line."

"Did you ask him where he was going?"

"He said he was going to do some shopping."

"Thanks, honey. I'll see what I can come up with."

"He hasn't been gone ten minutes yet."

I checked Blue Line first. They're the biggest taxi outfit in town and operate on radio dispatch. The driver had made the pickup and then called in his destination as the corner of West Boulevard and Andrews. West Boulevard was Route 60, and Andrews was quite a way out, just beyond the city line. The driver, she said, would report the drop and probably request his lunch break in that area. I told her to find out from the driver when he called back if McAran gave him any clue as to where he was going.

I sat in considerable indecision after I hung up, wondering if I should send anybody to that area. She called back and said the driver said the fare was looking for a car to buy. It made sense. The big lots were out that way. He had enough money to buy a used car, certainly. I called Vehicle Registration in the basement of the courthouse and told them to be on the lookout for a new registration in the name of Dwight McAran and tell me as soon as any dealer brought the transfer in. The next step was a little more complicated. Post offices operate on the principal of making everything as obscure as possible. Going through official channels would have required a court order, so I had to use a friend I've used before. I phoned him and then, after lunch, drove over and talked to him. The letter had been mailed in Pittsburgh the day before, return receipt requested. The receipt was headed back to a Thomas Roberts, General Delivery, Pittsburgh. The envelope had been bulky, weighing an estimated six ounces. It had been printed in blue ink, probably with a post office ball point, and the flap had been reinforced with cellophane tape.

By the time I got back to the squad room I found one of my calls had been from Vehicle Registration. They had registered a transfer from Top Grade Autos to Dwight McAran of a two-year-old Pontiac wagon, and had issued new plates numbered BC18-822. One of the salesmen had brought the application in.

As I didn't want to bump into McAran if he was still out there, I phoned Top Grade and asked for him and was told he'd left twenty minutes ago in the car he had bought. I left Johnny Hooper in charge and drove out to Top Grade.

It's one of the bigger lots, perhaps a little more larcenous than most. It was a cool afternoon with bright sunshine and a high wind which flapped the signs and banners and awnings, and picked up towering dust devils. The aluminum sales office was in the middle of the lot. The special deals were lined up across the front of the lot, under a bright protective canopy, facing the busy divided highway. Two men were listlessly wiping the dust off the cars on special sale. One salesman was working on a young couple who were dubiously examining a pickup truck. The salesman was beaming and gesturing. I parked near the sales office, and as I got out of my car, a fat man came sauntering toward me saying, "We won't make much on you, friend. Any man who knows exactly how long to hold onto a car before he—"

"Police business," I said. "Who's in charge?"

His smile slid off. "Lombardo. He's inside."

Lombardo was a stocky man, younger than most of his salesmen, with a wide, white meaningless smile. He had been sitting in the office, chatting with two of his salesmen. He knew my name.

"Honest to God, Lieutenant, I was just saying to these boys, it puts a guy in a funny spot, this McAran coming up with cash like he did, and so do I tell him I can't take his money on account he served time? Do I ask him where he gets cash? Maybe I get a hit in the mouth, hey? When I send Charlie for the plates I have him hit the bank first and check out the cash. So it's good, so what else? The way the law reads, I sell something in good faith, then—"

"I'm sure you know how the law reads, Lombardo. I'm sure you have a lot of reason to look things up. Rest easy. It was his money."

He relaxed. "It's a good car, but I don't want it back. The way things are going, Lieutenant, it was the only clean deal in two months. You know what I got to do, the way things are going? I got to wholesale some good clean iron to pay the rent. Right now, believe me, I could make you one hell of a deal on your car, if that's yours you came in."

"It's mine. I use my own car on personal business."

"What can we do for you, friend?"

"I want to talk to the salesman."

"What for?"

"Because I can turn personal business into police business, Lombardo, faster than you can turn a speedometer backward. Your knowing he's my brother-in-law gives you no handle. By tomorrow I can have state inspectors in here freezing the title on everything on the lot which doesn't pass a complete safety inspection. That front canopy out there is in violation of county zoning on setbacks. The state might want to run a special audit on your sales tax records."

The white smile finally disappeared. "The salesman was

Jack. Jack Abel, out there, talking to those kids about the truck. Maybe—you could wait just a minute. I mean I could call him, but there's the chance maybe he's nailing it down and—"

"I'll wait."

"Thanks! Thanks a lot! You know, I got the idea, somehow, you—were sort of an easygoing guy, Lieutenant. I don't want any trouble. Believe me, I don't want any kind of trouble more than I got already."

"Everybody within fifty miles seems to know McAran, and knows he's my brother-in-law."

His smile had returned. "Anybody new here maybe doesn't. But anybody here five years ago isn't about to forget it."

I looked out the window and saw the couple start to leave the lot. The salesman turned and began to walk spiritlessly back toward the sales office. I went out and intercepted him twenty feet from the building.

"Abel? Lieutenant Hillyer. City police. Lombardo says you can tell me about selling the Pontiac station wagon to McAran."

He had a pink moon face, a soft paunch and a green tweed jacket. "Sure. He got a good deal on it. A real good deal. A nice clean wagon. Dark blue. No dings. Heavy duty shocks and springs, load levelers, radio and heater, power steering. Wagons always go pretty good. We wouldn't have had it around ten days, but things are slow. We had it priced twenty-five ninety-five, but account of no trade and not too much left in the rubber, it worked around to twenty-three even, tags thrown in. He got a good deal. What else you want to know. I figure you come from the office, you already know he put the cash money right down."

"Did he get what he was looking for?"

"I guess he did. He walked right in wanting a wagon, a good sized one, heavy, with a lot of muscle under the hood. That one's got the biggest engine they made that year. See that green and white Buick over there? He didn't like that one on account of the bright colors. Up there in the front, that dark green Chrysler, he didn't like that on account it has air conditioning, power windows, power brakes, power seats, all that stuff that pulls your horsepower way down. We took the Pontiac down the road. He worked it over pretty good. He left some rubber on the road starting up and stopping it too, and he took that corner onto Andrews like I was glad no cop saw it."

"Any other thing he was looking for in the car?"

"Not a thing I can think of. He isn't a man to talk. Lord God, he's a big hunk of man. And I stopped trying to make friends real fast. I just talked about the car. He wanted a car. He didn't want a friend."

"Did he hang around while you were waiting for the plates?"

"He walked over to that diner, and when he came back we were putting the plates on it."

I thanked him and went to my car and got in. I started the motor, then thought of something else, a semi-hunch, and went back inside and asked Lombardo about the money. "Twenty-three one-hundred-dollar bills," he said. "New, but not real brand new. Not off a roll or out of a wallet. By the time he came in here, and I'd okayed the price, he had the exact right amount in his hand. He didn't count it out. He just dropped it right there on the desk. I counted it. Twice."

As soon as I got back to my desk, I phoned Meg. She said he wasn't home yet. I told her he had bought a car.

"Does he know you know that?"

"No, honey. I checked it out. Be surprised when he drives in with it. I don't want him to know I'm checking on him."

"I wish I hadn't told you about the letter coming."

"Why not?"

"He shouldn't be hounded, Fenn. He's got a right to buy a car, hasn't he?"

"Of course."

"Is there anything wrong about buying a car?"

"No."

"Can't you just leave him alone?"

"Honey, we can talk about this later. When you drew his money out, how did you give it to him?"

"I just handed it to him, with the cancelled book showing the interest and so on."

"I mean what demoninations was it in? It was over twenty-eight hundred dollars, wasn't it?"

"Twenty-eight hundred and sixty-six forty-one. What do you care what denominations it was in anyway?"

"Please, honey."

"Well—he didn't say how he wanted it. So I wanted it in

a sort of handy size without being too bulky. So I had them give me ten hundred-dollar bills, and thirty fifty-dollar bills. There were six tens, and a five and a one so that makes three hundred in twenties. Why do you want to know?"

Hooper came in and I motioned to him to sit down. "He paid cash for the car. Twenty-three one-hundred-dollar bills."

There was a silence. I could hear her breathing. "Maybe he stopped at a bank and changed the fifties to hundreds."

"The taxi took him directly out to West Boulevard where the used car lots are."

"Maybe he went into town some other day, when I was shopping. I can't be certain he hasn't left the house, dear. I couldn't *prove* he never went to the bank. Cathie Perkins was here again, you know, yesterday, after she got out of work. Maybe she brought him some money."

"Meg, honey, why are you fighting the very simple and obvious answer that the money came through the mail?"

"So *all right!* So it *did* come in the mail. Maybe he borrowed it, or somebody owed it to him. Is it any of our business, really?"

"Then he burned the envelope."

"I shouldn't have even told you about it, Fenn," she said in a weary monotone and hung up on me.

When I hung up, Johnny Hooper was looking at me inquisitively. I hesitated, then realized this was no time to hide anything which might become a police matter. I gave it to him fast, cold and complete.

He whistled softly. "The man has friends. And orders maybe? Like stay put until you hear from me? Like burn this letter and buy a fast car. And he makes new friends, doesn't he? Why are such nice girls attracted to such dangerous animals? Because they *are* nice girls? I'll have somebody check out her bank book, just in case. Okay? And how about Pittsburgh covering the return receipt?"

"Not enough to go on. No evidence of any crime committed or being planned. Besides, it's a trick that's been used before. The man who sent the money doesn't want the actual signed receipt. He wants to know it was delivered. So he'll phone the General Delivery clerk and say he's Thomas Roberts, and is there anything for him, and they'll say yes, so he'll say he'll come down and pick it up. But he doesn't have to. It was the only time he used the name. So he'll know McAran got it."

"Tap the line and ask them to stall?"

"Nobody can stall long enough for a dial call to be traced. You know better than that, Johnny. It only works on television. Soon as he hangs up the connection is broken and can't be traced. And it's a half-day job to trace an open connection. The only chance is that routine of leave your number and we'll call back, and I somehow have the feeling that wouldn't work at all."

"He was looking for a station wagon? What does that mean?"

"Damned if I know. More room. When you're after bulky stuff, furs, clothing, liquor, a panel delivery makes more sense."

He looked at me with an odd expression. "Do you have the same funny feeling I have, Fenn? Do you have the feeling we're going to be outsmarted?"

"We better not be."

"And we both know where he must have made his Pittsburgh friend."

"I was thinking of how we could check that over. I can't see trying to do it over the phone. I think you're going on a little trip to Harpersburg. I'll clear it with the Chief."

Larry Brint listened quietly as I gave him the whole story.

"Under normal conditions," he said, "I wouldn't let loose of any man on something this hazy. He'd have to do it on his own time, and even then I might not want to clear it with Hudson. But the pressure is on me to roust him on his way. I've bucked it and I'll keep bucking it, but I just don't like to think of the mess there'd be if something gets pulled here, and he's in on it, and somebody gets hurt. Hooper can go up there tomorrow. I'll talk to Boo Hudson on the phone. Tell him to look hard at recent releases, going back not more than three or four months, as a guess. And I have the hunch he should look for a loner, not anybody out of organized crime, because everybody knows this is a hands-off town."

I set it up with Johnny, and I arrived home a little after six. The dark blue station wagon was parked on the grass beside my garage, doing the grass no good. I got out of my car and looked at it. The tread marks on the soft grass were sharply defined. I squatted and looked at the tires. He had new tires all around, heavy duty nylons with one of those all weather treads which are slightly noisy on smooth roads, but are good in mud and snow.

I looked in at the mileage. Fourteen thousand. I opened the door and checked the pedal wear, and guessed they'd turned it back about ten thousand.

"Like it?" McAran said, startling me. I hadn't heard him come up behind me.

"Yours?"

"Bought it today."

"Nice-looking car, Dwight."

There had been a sudden change in him. He looked amused, slightly wary, completely alert.

"Needs tuning. Runs a little rough."

"New tires."

"All around. Had them put on today."

"Doesn't leave you much money, does it?"

"Enough for a little while. I broke a law today, Fenn. After I bought the tires I was riding along and I suddenly realized my license ran out a long, long time ago. And that's the first time I gave it a thought. So I went over and took a test and got a nice new one, all in order. We law-abiding citizens have to do just what the law calls for. We don't like to take chances."

"I'm glad you remembered it. How about insurance?"

"Do I need any?"

"Next year it will be compulsory."

"But this is this year. I'll be careful."

"You've been very careful, ever since they let you out."

"I'm a changed man. I thought you'd noticed."

"Changed? I notice everything. Like the act with the Perkins girl. I'm astonished you haven't hustled her into bed. It would be so easy. She'd have to be convinced it was therapy. Maybe you just don't want any complications right now. Maybe somebody gave you orders to stay away from silly little broads."

"Nobody gives me orders, brother-in-law. You've got a cop walk and a cop mouth and a long, pointed cop nose."

"We can identify each other a quarter-mile away, Mc-Aran. You know what I am and I know what you are."

"Right now maybe you want to try your luck," he said. I watched the small changes in the way he stood, the planting of feet, lift of shoulders, lowering of chin. I should have been alarmed, but he suddenly looked ridiculous. I laughed at him. His face turned a dull red which made the notched scars in his brows look whiter. "We in a school yard?" I asked him. "A hillbilly picnic, maybe? You can whip lots of people, McAran. Mildred, Meg, Davie Morissa, Cathie Perkins. You could probably whip me, but I'll give you no chance. None. Come at me, boy, and I'll backpedal fast, and I'll be lifting out the Special, and I'll blow your knee into a sack of pebbles and kick your mouth sideways as you go down."

"Small-time cop," he said in a soft, sighing, dangerous voice.

"With nothing to prove about myself, one way or the other." I smiled at him and walked by him into the house. Meg wanted to know why I was grinning like a fool. I told her I'd been comparing muscles with her brother, and learned I had some he'd never heard of. I said I had admired the twenty-three-hundred-dollar automobile, and we'd talk about it later on. I went into the living room, inhabited by Lulu, Judy, Bobby and the Three Stooges. After a few minutes of flying pies, Meg called the kids to dinner. It was a new pattern for us, to feed them earlier and separately. It was easier than having the five of us at the table at once. That made too much tension for everyone.

Dwight came in and stretched out on the couch without glancing at me. We watched the evening news and weather. When it was over, an underwater adventure thing came on. He seemed to be watching it, so I didn't turn it off. I tried reading a weekly news magazine. It didn't mean very much to me. I don't think they mean very much to anybody any more. I suppose we should be interested. We're in these towns and cities, all of us, and an impacted wisdom tooth or an increase in the water rates, or three days of steady rain means more than the Congo. Maybe it was always that way. But now there's so much communication, so many people trying to tell you about the things that are shaking the earth, and behind it all is the chance of somebody suddenly turning you into nothing at all, by accident or on purpose. If you are in a room where eight or ten people are talking at you, all at once, telling you eight or ten terrible things, you stop listening to all of them and start thinking about when you'll get the haircut you've been needing for a week. It used to bother me, looking at Huntley and Brinkley and just watching their mouths moving and not hearing anything, as if I had the sound off, and then I found out it was that way with a lot of people. Everybody is telling us so much, you just hear the funny stuff.

I was trying to read about aid to education, because I thought I should know about it. But my eye was moving across the words, and I could have been holding the magazine upside down. In the top layer of my mind I was wondering what McAran was planning. I could hear his tone of voice in the car on the way back from Harpersburg. "Brook City took something away from me. I want it back."

And on the next layer of consciousness was the problem of how best to beef up the midnight shift with three men out with a virus. And what to do about three current files that were bogged down because the legwork wasn't producing anything new.

Meg called us to dinner. The kids took over the television for their final half-hour before bed. Meg continued her forlorn effort to make mealtime festive. I tried to help her. The unyielding presence of McAran made it like trying to play a banjo in a crypt. That was the biggest single change in him, that almost total withdrawal.

Near the end of the meal, as Meg was telling me about one of our neighbors deciding to move to Arizona to try his luck there, McAran dropped his fork onto his plate and said, "The kid can have his room back Thursday. I'll be pulling out about then. Let me see you cry real tears, Hillyer."

"Where are you going?" I asked.

"People on probation, people on parole, they have to say please can I go, sir. I don't. I went the route. You keep forgetting that."

"I haven't forgotten it for a minute. It was a polite question. Brotherly interest. Somebody says they're leaving. You say where are you going. Everybody does it."

"Please! Both of you!" Meg said. "Where *are* you going, dear?"

"No secret. I'm going back into the hill country for a while. The weather's getting mild enough now. Once I get the wagon running right, I'll pick up some gear and grub and go get lost back there for a while. It's been a long time since I've been by myself. I want to see what it feels like."

He smiled at her. Both the smile and the little speech had all the plausibility of Confederate money, but Meg looked delighted. She clapped her hands. "Dwight, I just think that's a *wonderful* idea."

"Better than sitting around your house, honey. I won't eat as good, or sleep so soft, but it's something I've been thinking of doing."

"You never cared to be alone, the way I always did."

"You appreciate it, Sis, when you can't get any of it. Like anything else I guess. I get too lonesome, I'll find a Saturday night dance and some little girl that might like camping out for a while."

"Now you be careful, boy, or you'll get yourself stomped some, or cut up." The hill cadences had grown stronger as they talked, and it was a kind of talk which closed me out.

"I'll find me one has nobody close about to fuss. Or maybe I should take the Perkins kid along."

Meg abruptly ceased smiling. "Don't do that to her, Dwight. You could talk her into it, probably. But that isn't what she wants."

"You so sure what she wants, Sis?"

"She wants to help you find yourself, if you'll give her the chance."

"In an all-electric kitchen?" he said, with a nasty grin. "After all those showers for the pretty bride? The whole routine, Sis? Little budget envelopes, take-home pay, diaper service?"

"What's so horrible about all that?"

"It would be heaven, Sis. The only way they can tell you're dead is when you stop smiling. I could be as deliriously happy as you are with this hound-face cop."

"If that's the way you feel," Meg said, "don't see that girl again."

"Have I been chasing after her? I'm going away, aren't I? What the hell more do you want?"

After a long silence Meg said, "What will you do after your—vacation, Dwight? How long will you stay up there?"

"I don't know. I can't make any good plans until I can unwind. I don't know how long it will take. I've got a few hundred left. I could make it last through the summer if I have to. Then I don't know. Maybe I'll come back here. Maybe I'll move on some other place. I'll let you know."

She gave him a fond, warm smile. "I'm happy about it, Dwight. I was afraid you were—too bitter about everything, and you'd keep on brooding until you—got into trouble."

He stood up. "They gave me the dirty end of the stick. But that's over. If I stick around here, they might jump me again. And I know it's been hard on you too, Fenn. If it'll take some pressure off you downtown, why don't you just tell them you threw me the hell out."

He went to his room. I stared down into my coffee cup and slowly shook my head. "How stupid does he think we are?" I looked over at Meg and saw the luminous joy fading.

"What is that supposed to mean?"

"I guess it means he'll never make it as an actor, honey."

She looked at me with an expression too close to hate. "You won't give him any kind of a chance. You won't give him any benefit of the doubt, will you? You don't want him to have a chance! You have to be so hard and cold about everything, don't you?"

"You aren't being very fair about—"

"He's trying to do the best thing—"

"What best thing, with whose money? Can't you see he hasn't had a single normal reaction to anything since he got out? Can't you see he's been playing a part since he got out? Can't you see how careful he's been? He doesn't act like a man just released after five years in prison. He acts like a man holed up."

"But now he's—"

"He's got word from somebody, so now he's through waiting. He's on the move."

She looked pleadingly at me. "Can't we trust him a little? Can you do that much for me?"

"I'd like to know just what he—"

"But if he's trying to straighten himself out, it isn't fair to have you—doing things like talking to that girl."

"When I think of her, I think of her as poor Cathie. There's a sort of inevitability about it, Meg. Poor Cathie."

"Fenn, you have to promise me you won't keep checking up on everything my brother does. There's something so changed about him it—scares me a little. But I have to believe he wants to stay out of trouble."

I crossed my fingers, a childish hedge against deceit. "Okay."

"Your work has made you too suspicious of people, darling."

"Probably it has."

She looked content again. "He knows those hills. I miss them sometimes. Could we go camping this summer? Bobby and Judy have never really had a chance to get to love it the way I do. I spent the most miserable years of my life back in the hills, darling, but it wasn't the fault of the hills."

"We can try to do that."

"Golly, I wish we could afford to buy just a little bit of no-good land and put up a shack, and a little garden patch." She stood up, smiling in a wistful way. "And a yacht and a villa and a peck of diamonds, huh? I've got to shoo the animals off to bed. You going back?"

"A little later. Got to straighten out the late shift, steal a few patrolmen, maybe."

She poured me more coffee, and marched in to break up the gunslinger group.

On Wednesday the memory of my crossed fingers did not make me feel any less guilty when I traced the garage which was working on McAran's new car. I hit it on the fifth phone call, and they said they would have the work finished by three that afternoon. I sent Rossman out to the Quality Garage at four o'clock and he was back forty minutes later to report. He is a quiet and thorough young man who looks more like a bank clerk or insurance adjuster than a detective. But, unlike Hooper, he has no liking or talent for administration.

"Like you remembered, Fenn, that's the place that makes a specialty of hopping up the stock cars and the carts. It cost him eighty-eight cash for the motor job they did for him. Racing plugs and points. Changed the jets. Gave him a manual control on the dash for air intake. The guy that worked on it, he told me it will do a legitimate one-thirty, and take off like a bomb."

"Did you cover, in case he comes back for more work?"

"I couldn't cover your phone call, but from what you said, there's no reason they'd mention it. I just asked what they could do to give my car more steam, and when they got to telling me about the Pontiac that was just in, I kept them talking about it, what was done, what it would cost me and so on. Do you want me to write this one up?"

I didn't like the question. It made a personal inference. I have learned that in the management and manipulation of human beings, control can best be exercised by responding to a question with a question.

"Can you think of any reason why you shouldn't?"

Ben Rossman looked uneasy. "There's no file, is there?"

"If you turn in a report, there'll have to be one."

"What's the classification?"

"How would you classify it, Ben?"

"Well—we've got him classified as a Known Criminal, and there'd be a registration number. So I guess we'd just set up a sort of open file, an activities file, and cross reference it to that registration number?"

"Exactly as we've done other times, Ben. With a verifax copy of the ID sheet, and, when Harpersburg ever gets around to it, the abstract of the prison record and the release photos."

"I guess I just thought that—"

"There's more reason to have a complete file on him, wouldn't you say?"

"I guess so. I'm sorry, Lieutenant. I hadn't thought it all the way through."

"The file is already established, Ben. I set it up the day after I brought him back here. Do you think it's going to be useful?"

He looked slightly startled. "When he uses that car, for whatever he wants it for, yes. We better have a file."

"Maybe he just likes to drive a bomb."

"Maybe we could all get lucky, Fenn. He could drive it into a tree."

90

vii

SERGEANT Johnny Hooper got back from Harpersburg at eight-thirty that evening, and phoned me at my home. He said he had something which sounded interesting. Mc-Aran was sprawled in my living room, and Johnny was about to sit down to the meal his new little wife had saved for him, so I arranged to go over to his place.

When I told Meg she gave me a rueful smile and told me she hoped it would be a boy. It is a family joke. Early in our marriage she read a magazine article about how occupations can interfere with togetherness. It told how the wives of obstetricians are the ones least likely to be able to plan anything in advance, and dedicated business executives run second. They made no mention of the wives of cops, so she accused me of operating an obstetric business on the side.

I remembered the joke when Mimi Hooper answered the door. I hadn't seen her in several months, and I estimated she was now about eight months along with their first child. She is a small vivacious girl, as dark as Johnny is blonde. They lived in a pleasant, spacious apartment in one of the old houses west of Torrance Memorial Park. Mimi was a Littlefield, and the house was built originally by her great grandfather who made his money in hardwood timber. She is distantly related to the Hanamans. There isn't much left of what was once a substantial fortune for this area. The Merchants Bank and Trust administers the estate, and divides the income between Mimi and her two brothers. The estate owns the old house and, in return for letting Mimi and her husband have the apartment, subtracts a very nominal amount from her share of the income. She gets a little over a hundred dollars a month. It makes a fine arrangement for a career cop. I think it would be a lot easier to put up with all the rest of the harassment if you didn't have to wage that constant losing battle with the household budget.

They were almost through dinner. I sat and had coffee with them. Johnny appeared tired and depressed. Mimi seemed to be using the most innocent remarks to take small stabs at him.

Finally he sighed and said, "Mimi stands on the side of the poor oppressed criminal being persecuted by the gestapo."

She frowned at him and turned to me. "When a man has served his sentence, why can't you leave him alone? Isn't society supposed to be able to—reabsorb people like Dwight McAran? He was just a—professional athlete who got mixed up with the wrong kind of people, and with a perfectly horrible girl."

"There's been a lot of pressure on us to push him around, Mimi."

"And you feel you have to?"

Johnny said, "I keep telling her we haven't done any such thing."

"Sometimes, Mimi, for reasons which seem good, we move people along, strangers in town, usually, who want to set up something we don't want. We have a special list of city ordinances, the ones we can't enforce under normal conditions. Littering, loitering, spitting, jaywalking. We assign men. The municipal judges co-operate with maximum fines, and if the man or men involved don't get our message, we start adding jail sentences on top of the fines. Running any city is the art of the possible, and in a controlled town like this one, it's a little bit easier to discourage people who want to upset—the local balance. Personal factors have to be considered. If I wasn't in the job I'm in, or if he wasn't my brother-in-law, maybe Larry would have put the machine to work, and McAran would be out of town by now. He hasn't any influence here. But we're not leaning on him."

"Then what was Johnny doing at Harpersburg?"

"Chief Brint, Johnny and I—and some others—think McAran is dangerous. We think we know the type. Meg can't believe he is."

"I know he *looks* sort of tough, but you can't judge a—"

"We don't like the way he acts or the things he's doing. We have to protect ourselves. If he does some violent thing, it's going to look like contributory negligence on our part. And the powers that be will break up our team. We think it's a good team. And it's a help to us if our wives—believe we know what we're doing."

She smiled. "I guess I consider myself spanked, huh?"

"I didn't mean it that way," I told her.

She tilted her pretty head and looked at me questioningly. "I guess I'm still adjusting, Fenn. I never expected to marry a law man. I think I've adjusted to the idea that some horrid little spook could—hurt him. But he's happy doing what he wants to do. God knows he isn't doing it for the sake of the money, and neither are you. But what bothers me is —how you can keep up this sort of dedication you both have, when the whole situation is so sort of grubby. I mean the working arrangement with Jeff Kermer, and the way you make the law work one way for some people, and another way for others, and the way you have to do things in a sort of—political way."

"Social institutions are imperfect. Meg can tell you about politics in the school system. Everybody gets the same choice. You can try to operate in spite of the crud, or you can live with it until you enjoy it, or you can get out. I don't know about Johnny, but I take a kind of upside down pride in it. Cynical pride. I do the cop job, and feel like an idiot for trying. Cop movies and cop television make me feel like laughing or crying, and I'm never sure which. With a citation and a dime you can ride a city bus, and if you get killed, the city chips in on the burial expenses. If I arrest the wrong lawbreaker, I get chewed, and if I can't find the one I should arrest, I get chewed. When I testify in court, I'm fair game for the defense lawyer. The public thinks I'm a cop because I'm making it on the side, or I'm somebody's relative, or I'm a sadist, or I'm too stupid to make out doing anything else. The best respect we get is from professional criminals, who know a good cop when they see one in action."

"I'd like to know why I don't quit," Johnny said. "The only thing I can figure out is that it's like the boy who ran away from a wealthy home and when they located him forty years later he was with the circus, working every day with a big shovel, cleaning up after the elephants. They told him all was forgiven and he could come back to the bosom of his family, and he said, 'What! And leave show biz!' "

She gave him a fond little punch and said, "Okay. I'm learning. Go on in the other room and practice your trade while I clean up."

We went into the front room of the apartment. He sat

and scowled at the empty fireplace and said, "Right now this business makes less sense than usual."

"Harpersburg?"

"I never spent a day there before."

"Of the fifty states, Johnny, our prison system is rated forty-fifth. Keep that in mind. Prison systems need money. So, having very little money, and a legislature which can't come up with any good ways of getting more, we have a bad prison system, a bad school system, bad programs for the aged and indigent, bad state and county highways. We're a poor relation, Johnny, like West Virginia and Mississippi."

"Jesus, the way they're jammed in there, Fenn! All it does is keep them out of the way for a while, then turn them loose like sick animals. I've put some people in there. What good does it do?"

"According to Boo Hudson, it makes them damn anxious not to come back."

"Anyhow, maybe I found out what I went after. It took a long time. They had a rat they were keeping in solitary because the kangaroo court gave him a death sentence. He was knifed but he lived through it, and they're trying to get him transferred, but Hudson says that even if they do, it'll probably catch up with him in the next place. He was on the fringe of the group McAran was a part of; before they found out, one of the guards had turned him into an informant. McAran was a loner for two years before he was accepted into that little group. It made a hard-nose quintet, with McAran serving the shortest time of any of them. The leader was Morgan Miller. Here's a photostat of the prison ID card on him."

I studied the sheet. The corner photo hadn't reproduced well in the positive photostat. A balding head, a lean, closed face. Two previous convictions in Ohio. A pattern of professional theft. Several arrests without convictions. One rap for breaking and entering. One for armed robbery. And he had been given fifteen years in our state for a bank robbery in Kinderville, up in the northern part of the state.

"That bank job was a very smooth operation," Johnny said. "There were three of them, and nobody could get a line on it for seven months. Then a woman talked, and from that tip, the Bureau put a tail on one of them. The take was a little over ninety thousand. The one they were tailing led them to Miller, eventually, and when they moved in, the one they had been tailing got killed. They made recovery on over fifty-five thousand. Miller wouldn't talk, but by backtracking his movements, they decided the third man had been somebody they already wanted. Miller said they had cut the take and split up the same night they'd taken the bank. The man eluded them for three years. They found him in California. He died of some kind of sickness while they were getting set to extradite him."

"Miller led the bank job?"

"The witnesses testified he was the one giving the orders."

"And it was professional?"

"Fast, rough, nasty and well-planned. They went in a few minutes before closing, slugged the guard, herded everybody into a rear office, pulled the main switch, cutting off power to the alarm system, locked the doors, cleaned out the cages. A three-minute job."

"His group of five, where did they fit into the prison set-up?"

"No known affiliations. Off by themselves. Nobody wanted to mess with them, prisoners or officials. All older than McAran. None of them getting any kind of special deal, except the kind McAran was getting. Two of them, Deitwaller and Kostinak, are lifers. Kelly has thirty to go."

I looked at the ID record again. "Morgan Miller got out two months ago."

"After the full fifteen. Down there in the corner is the psychologist's estimate of likelihood of continuance of criminal activity. Ninety per cent. It would be a hundred, except they never mark anybody a hundred. Ninety is tops."

"Was he turned down for parole?"

"He never applied."

"And he went back to his home town?"

"Youngstown, Ohio."

"Which is how far from Pittsburgh? Sixty miles?"

"Not much more than that, maybe less."

"We'll check it out with them tomorrow."

"Fenn, if it was Miller who sent McAran the money, where would he have gotten it?"

"Hell, look at the arrests and convictions. This is an old pro, Johnny. How old is he now? Forty-seven. And he's spent twenty-one years of his life in prison. Two years, four years, fifteen years. He's sort of a loner, and he likes to run things. He'll swear his luck has been bad. He considers robbery his line of work. He knows it takes financing to set up a job. It probably took a month to set up that bank in Kinderville. So he would never let himself go broke, because if he did, he'd have to take a chance on some small stuff in order to bankroll himself. So as standard procedure, he'd stash funds to finance the next job. A few thousand sealed up in a jar and buried. Some of them get compulsive about it. I've read of cases where men have been burying half their take for years. They're frugal men, temperate, quiet. They don't seem to want the money for what it will buy. They seem to want the charge they get out of planning to take it and taking it. But they have to get into bigger and bigger operations, to keep the kick from diminishing, and they need more people helping them, and the more people you have in on something, the sooner somebody is going to talk. They tell themselves they'll make that final big one and live in Mexico forever, but it's a dream that never happens because it isn't what they're really after."

"Would a man like Miller hook up with an amateur like McAran?"

"They couldn't break Dwight at Harpersburg. That would count heavily with a man like Miller. He's big, quick and tough. That makes him useful. He's bright enough, and educated, and he's full of hate. I'd say Miller might wish he had three Dwight McArans."

"Will they—try one of the banks here?"

"Hanaman is a director at the Merchants. But we better not get carried away. If we add two and two and keep getting seven, we may not pay enough attention to four."

"Something simpler?"

"Miller may have something in mind a long way from here. McAran could leave a little gift of arson on his way out of town."

"He's leaving tomorrow?"

"I've gutted all three shifts to keep him under hundred per cent surveillance. Unmarked cars, good men and an emergency communications link. They picked him up this afternoon when he left a repair garage, and they're standing by right now a half-block from my house. So let's hope the town stays so quiet I don't have to pull them off."

"But tomorrow he heads for the hills."

"Maybe. But we lose him after he crosses the city line. For two years I've had a poop sheet in my desk about a gadget I wanted Larry to buy. It's a short wave battery pack transmitter, about so big. It transmits a standard signal for about sixty hours, with about a two-hundred-mile range. It comes with two directional antennae you can substitute for the fish poles on two police cars, and you can triangulate the location down fine enough for all practical purposes. You can hide that transmitter on the average car in about thirty seconds."

"Nice!" he said. "Very nice! But it isn't the sort of thing you'd have a chance to use very often—"

"Larry said never. It took me four years to talk him into the wire tap gear, and five years before he'd let me get the smaller interrogation room bugged. There's no use wishing for something you don't have. Johnny, thanks for the job at Harpersburg."

"That place gets me. I think it's ready to blow. All day it made the back of my neck feel funny."

"Hudson seem nervous?"

"I think they're too close to it to sense it. You get the feeling that everybody in every cell knows just what you've said thirty seconds after you've said it. The men move on command, but they sure God take their time. In the exercise yards there doesn't seem to be much, and no laughing or horsing around. They all seem to be standing and watching and waiting for something important."

"Maybe it's always like that," I said, and stood up.

"You have to go? How about a brew?"

Mimi appeared in the doorway. "Don't leave so soon, Fenn. I haven't had enough chance to be sociable."

"I thought I'd just take a run down and—check on the shift."

"Mind if I come along?" Johnny asked earnestly.

"If you want to. You don't have to."

Mimi laughed hopelessly. "He will, Fenn. He'll come along. And you'll both find something that needs doing right away. And I'll say my good nights to Jack Paar."

Three minutes after it was reported to me that McAran had left the city at quarter-to-five on Thursday afternoon, heading south toward the hill country on Route 882, Meg phoned me and said, "Dwight left just a little while ago, dear."

Somehow I managed to keep myself from saying, "Yes, I know." I said, "Oh, did he?"

"He told me to tell you good by, and thank you for letting him stay with us. He was as excited as a little kid. His station wagon was really loaded."

I knew that too. I had a partial list of what was in it. "I guess you need a lot of gear if you're going to camp out."

"When are you going to be home, dear?"

"A little after six, the way it looks."

I hung up. I knew McAran had gone on another errand, earlier in the day. And I'd been wondering about it ever since I'd gotten the report. He'd parked near the phone company office and made a call from a drugstore booth. Then a girl matching Cathie Perkins' description had come to the car where he was waiting. They sat in the car and talked, and then he drove her to her home. He went in with her remained inside for twenty-five minutes, then came out quickly, slammed the car door and screeched the tires as he started up.

I finally succumbed to curiosity and tried the phone company. I was told she had been taken sick in the middle of the day and gone home. I tried the house. I asked if I could speak to Cathie and the girl's voice which answered said, "She can't talk. She's sick." I asked to speak to Mr. Perkins.

"Oh, Lieutenant Hillyer," he said. "I was wondering if I should call you. I can't get anything out of Cathie. She isn't—in very good shape. McAran was—alone here with her today. I'm worried about her. Maybe she might talk to you."

I told Rags to phone Meg and tell her I'd be a little later than I promised. Cathie was in her room. It was a two-story frame house. Mr. Perkins stayed downstairs with the two younger girls. Her bedroom door was open. She sat at a small desk, half-turned so that she faced the window, in a pallor of evening light. I coughed and said, "Can I talk to you, Cathie?"

She did not turn or move. It seemed a very long time before she said in a weak monotone, "Come in and close the door."

When I was standing six feet from her, she slowly turned her face toward me. One brown eye stared at me with childish gavity; the other was puffed fat and shut, blue as a plum. There was a scratch on her cheek, a lesser bruise on her chin. She wore a pale blue quilted robe.

With very little lip movement she said, "Oh, you were so right—you were so right."

I sat on a chest in front of the window. "What happened?"

"He phoned me at work and told me where he was parked, and I came out. He wanted to talk to me. He seemed very happy and excited, not at all like times I talked to him at your house. He said I should secretly pack some clothes so I could be ready to leave at a moment's notice. He said he was going away today. He said he'd get word to me in a couple of weeks or maybe less about where to meet him. He said to keep cash around so I could buy a ticket to wherever it would be. He said I had to be "cute" about it. He said I should take a bus or an airplane to some other city first, and make sure I hadn't been followed by going in and out of department stores by different exits, and then go somewhere and dye my hair a different color and pick a new name to use, and go to the city where I'd meet him. I was confused. I said there was no reason for anybody to follow me, and he said by the time I get the message, there'd be a reason, because the police would want to follow anybody who could lead them to Dwight McAran. He said we'd live rich and have a ball. I said I didn't want to live like that. We sat in the car and we argued, and I had to tell him about ten times before he began to believe me. He said he thought I was in love with him. I said I was. He said then I ought to come running when he called. I said I could love him but I had to respect him too, and respect myself, and that meant being married and having kids and not hiding from the police. He said we'd never be caught, so what difference did it make. He said I was a stuffy, conventional little prude. By then I was crying because he was a different person from the man I thought I was in love with. Then all of a sudden he changed back again and said he guessed he was wrong. His voice even trembled when he told me that. He said he was in a terrible jam and he was going to be forced to do some bad thing that would get the police after him unless I helped him. He said if there was somewhere where we could be alone, he could explain it all to me. So I came here with him, and the very second he was sure the house was empty, he started laughing and humming and pulling my clothes off, saying he was so glad to find out I was willing to give him a little farewell present, seeing as how I wouldn't join him later on. He said it was a really sincere gesture on my part, and a nice sentimental end to our five-year romance. By then I was sobbing and screaming and trying to keep away from him. It happened right down there in the living room. It was like the nightmares where you can't move fast and you can't make enough noise, and some animal thing is coming at you and nobody will come and help you. He twisted my arms and tore my clothes, and started raping me on the couch, and we fell off, and he finished raping me on the floor, and when I hurt him with my knee, he hit my face with his fist, but he didn't get mad. He kept laughing and chuckling and humming. I stopped fighting him as soon as he—was actually raping me, and I think I was in kind of a half-faint. Then I was alone and crying without a sound. I crawled up onto the couch and covered myself with the old green Afghan. I heard the refrigerator door shut and in a little while he came in, and he was eating a cold chicken leg. He threw the bone in the fireplace and licked the grease off his fingers and put his clothes on. He smirked at me and said he wished he could have spent more time, but he had a lot to do. I knew he was going away and I would never see him again, and suddenly I realized it meant I would never have a chance to kill him. I didn't even know I was thinking about killing him until all of a sudden I was able to make myself stop crying and make myself smile at him. It surprised him. I said that now he'd have to take me away with him. He came over and sat on his heels beside the couch and stared at me and told me he had been just about ready to point out how stupid it would be for me to go to the police about this, because I'd brought him here knowing the house would be empty, and he could prove I'd been visiting him at your house, and I should remember that the first thing I did when we walked in was phone the office and tell them a lie about being taken sick. I made myself laugh. I told him I loved him. When you feel the way I do and tell a stinking animal like that you love him, you feel as if the words would rot your mouth and make your teeth fall out. I said I'd join him whenever and wherever he wanted me, and on his terms. So help me God, I think I made him believe it. He said it was a funny way for it to work out, and I said maybe I was just that kind of a woman and couldn't help it. He was still a little cautious. He didn't say I definitely would hear from him, but he said maybe I would. I made myself kiss his filthy ugly mouth and say love words to him. You see, I couldn't let him walk out of my life and never give me any chance to—ever see him stretched out dead and know I helped do it to him. I said I'd be packed and waiting. I never knew I would want to kill anybody. I can't tell my father all this. I don't know what he would do. Dwight actually strutted when he walked out, as if he'd done some wonderful thing. I was going to come and see you and tell you all this. He walked out and then I could cry some more. I got up and picked up the clothes he ruined, and did what I could do to try to be sure I won't have his baby, and I threw up, and then I had a hot bath, and I took two of my father's tranquilizer pills, and I've been sitting here ever since, not really thinking of anything, but just hating him. I want him to send for me. And I'll go to him. For a little while I thought I wouldn't say anything to you. But suppose it goes wrong? Suppose he sends for me and it goes wrong and I can't hurt him? I'll have to make certain you'll get him. So if he sends for me, I'll tell you. If he comes for me, I'll find some way to leave you a message. Who did I used to think I was? A missionary? A princess? Why did he seem so romantic? I'm not stupid any more, Lieutenant. I'm a deadly weapon. I'm very smart and very strong. Some day he's going to know he made the most terrible mistake, the most terrible, terrible—"

The small controlled voice stopped. The mouth moved and crumpled, and she laid her head on the desk blotter, nested in her young arms, and I could not tell whether she was crying again. When I put my hand on her shoulder, she shuddered. I took it away. I looked at her room in the fading light. On a high shelf was a collection of small dolls in different varieties of peasant dress. My little girl has a Mexican doll she adores. A large tortoise-shell cat sat on her shadowy bed, staring directly at me.

"Cathie?"

"Yes."

"If you get a chance to, I think leading us to him will be enough. We won't let you endanger yourself. You're a very brave girl, a very fine girl. I'm going to send a doctor here to check you over. Dr. Sam Hessian. I'll brief him. He's a damn nice old guy. I'll tell your father it's because that eye should be looked at. I'll also tell him that you came here with McAran and quarreled with him, and he pushed you and you fell and he walked out, and you've been in this daze because you saw him for what he really is, and your heart is broken."

"My heart is broken. Yes indeed," she said, and straightened up. "I thought you had to be insane to really want to kill anybody."

"Your father better not come across your ruined clothes."

"He won't." I stood up and she stood also, her face twisting with the pain of that effort. "Everybody tried to tell me," she said ruefully. "I wouldn't listen to anybody. I knew it all. When I went on dates I felt bored and superior because my shining white knight, my poor persecuted hero was in a cell, yearning for the time when they would free him and I would soothe him and mend him with my glorious gift of love. He helped me make a fool of myself, the things he wrote to me. Why did he bother?" Suddenly she looked at me more intently, and said, "Why did you come here? Did my father phone you?"

"No. We've been tailing McAran, right to the moment he crossed the city line and went up into the hills at five o'clock. The report said he was here for twenty-five minutes with you. I wondered about it. I phoned."

I stopped at headquarters again before going home. I called Sam Hessian from there, and he said he wanted his nurse in attendance, so he'd take the Perkins girl down to his office and take her back home if he found no reason for hospitalization. He does a lot of police work aside from his duties as coroner. He's examined a lot of rape victims. He always says his attitude toward the rapist is unworthy of a doctor of medicine. He says they should all go free, after an orchiectomy he would be willing to perform without fee. After talking to him I sat at my desk and knew I was entirely too anxious to tell Meg what her beloved brother had done. But he was gone, and I had the feeling he would never return, that he was going to make it impossible for him to ever come back.

So all I would be doing would be to sadden Meg, and prove what a flawless fellow I was. Telling her would not change the course of events. And I did not imagine Cathie wanted any more people to know about it than had to know. So I made myself feel somewhat noble by deciding to keep it to myself.

I thought of McAran up there in the hills, in the night, equipped for some dirty adventure, and I wondered what it would be. He knew that after it had been done we would want him badly.

In retrospect I could see an increasing merit in the suggestion Boo Hudson had made the day I picked McAran up at Harpersburg. If I'd blown a hole in his head, Cathie Perkins would not be in despair. And I had the sickly feeling that by the time it was all over, Boo Hudson's idea would look even better.

But that is dangerous thinking for an officer of the law. And ludicrous thinking as far as I am concerned, because it is something I know I could not do. I could not be an executioner. McAran would have laughed if he knew what I was thinking about. I wondered what he was thinking about at that moment. But the quick dark shapes of his thoughts were beyond my capacity to imagine. Nor can we ever know what visions sweeten the dreams of the crocodile.

Before I left, all the reports were in, and I had a typed list of what he'd bought—for cash. He'd shopped at a supermarket, Sears, a hardware store, an Army-Navy store and a few other places. Camp stove, ax, hatchet, gasoline lantern, shelter halves, blankets, ground sheets, camp shovel, rope, Japanese binoculars, transistor radio, almost a hundred dollars' worth of canned food, pots, pans, paper plates and paper cups, a case of bourbon, a half-dozen packs of playing cards, outdoor clothing, saw, hammer, screwdriver, drill, nails and screws, fifteen ten-foot lengths of two-by-four, hinges, builder's glue, several sheets of quarter-inch plywood, one big flashlight and two small ones, two air mattresses, two sleeping bags, ten dollars' worth of magazines and paperbound books, a spinning rod and fresh water tackle, a large first-aid kit, two sheath knives, swim trunks, an extension tape rule, a big canvas water bag, a canvas camp bucket and water purification tablets.

I took the list to Larry Brint and sat and watched him study it, making small red checks opposite the items which most interested him.

"Doesn't expect to be alone," he said.

"It doesn't look that way."

"Can't figure out the tools and materials."

"I think there's some place he knows of, some shack he can patch up with that stuff."

"Probably right. Be nice to know where he's headed."

"Yes indeed."

"See what Bub Fischer can do for us. See him in the morning, Fenn."

"It won't be much."

"Fischer isn't much of a Sheriff."

We had the evening meal with our kids, and it seemed as if McAran had been with us for six months instead of a little less than two weeks. Afterward I found out from Meg that her brother had taken the rest of his stuff with him. I asked questions about the load until she told me about the lumber sticking out over the tailgate. She said she had asked him about it, and he had made some joke about it, something about building a garage for his new car.

After the kids were in bed it seemed particularly nice to have our house to ourselves again. I knew Meg felt that way too, but didn't want to admit it to herself because I guess it seemed like a kind of disloyalty to her brother. But she seemed in a smiling mood, and later, when it was time for bed, she gave me a look that turned my throat dry, and I knew that even though she would never admit it, we were going to celebrate being alone again. When I turned out the kitchen light the last thing I saw was Lulu's maniac grin. She had grinned at all of us, all evening long.

I went over to Sheriff Emery "Bub" Fischer's courthouse office on Friday morning at ten o'clock. He is a living example of the idiocy of making any law office on the operations level an elective office. He's been the Sheriff of Brook County for three years. He's nearly sixty years old, and he has been on the county payroll since he was eighteen, through the simple device of running in the primary for any office which happened to have several people on the ticket, then making a shrewd guess as to who would win the runoff, and throwing his few hundred votes to the right man. He filed for Sheriff on the same old basis, but three days before the primary the most likely winner dropped dead, and the number two man was slapped with a tax fraud suit, and Bub Fischer learned to his complete astonishment he was going to be the new Sheriff of Brook County.

He looks like a Sheriff is supposed to look, in a bad movie. Big, portly, white-headed, with a big homespun voice, faded whipcord outfits, semi-western hat, gunbelt and silver gleam of badge. Forty years of cheap whisky has broken enough veins in his face to give him an outdoor look, and forty years of cheap politics has convinced him of the basic error of ever offending anyone.

"*Glad* to see you, Fenn! *Real* glad! Take a load off your feet, boy. Don't see *near* enough of you. Everything going fine with you?"

As I told him what I wanted, I could see the conviviality draining out of him. His expression changed to that of a baby beginning to wish somebody would come and change it.

"Not as easy as it sounds, Fenn. Not easy at all."

"All that hill country is the biggest part of Brook County, Sheriff."

"Now you don't have to tell me that on account of all I have to do is look at that map over there."

"Doesn't anybody ever break the law up the hills?"

"They break it pretty complete, as I guess you'd be knowing. But I got a working agreement with those folks." He got up heavily and waddled over to his wall map. I followed him over. "You see right here there's only three towns up there big enough to have any kind of law. That's Laurel Valley, Stoney Ridge and Ironville, and they all got chiefs of police with a couple men helping, and a car to use and a place to lock up the drunks. There's four smaller places has a town constable system, like you can elect to have in this here state, and for those it's a part-time job. The way it works, they take care of their own unless it's a killing or a rape or something, or maybe a smaller thing they got reasons they don't want to handle through a justice of the peace setup, so then they invite me in on it, and we go up and bring back whoever it is and the statements and so on. This here 882 is the only road the State Police patrol, and they don't do it often, and never at night. These people up in there, they like to take care of things their own way. I got nice co-operation now, Fenn, and I worked for it, and the quickest way I can upset the whole thing is sending anybody up in there just looking around. They don't want me or you or game wardens or tax fellas or any Federal folk looking for stills."

"Boo Hudson used to be welcome."

"Not because he was Sheriff. And he made deputies of a couple of boys up there, to sort of look out for his interests. Those old boys quit the day Boo's term run out. That hilly piece of my county is about sixty miles by forty miles, which comes out to twenty-four hundred square miles, Fenn, with most of it tilted sideways, and maybe six or seven thousand people scattered all to hell and gone across it, with too many of them willing to shoot your hat off when you take the first step across where they think their property line is. And you know, Fenn, men have tried to hide out up in there, but sooner or later they mess with some of those people and get in trouble."

I remembered Larry Brint telling me about something which had happened way back in the early years of the depression. During the night a car with Kentucky plates had been parked and abandoned near the courthouse. It checked out as belonging to a Lexington businessman who, with two friends, had gone up into our hill country deer hunting. All their gear was stowed in the car, even to the rifles. It was over a year later that a rumor drifted down out of the hills to the effect that a fifteen-year-old girl had come upon their camp site by accident, had been given whisky, had spent the night and been misused. But the girl was never identified. It was believed to have happened in the Stoney Ridge area, but that was never established. There was never any mystery about what happened to the men. One was in the front seat, on the passenger side of the big LaSalle automobile, and the other two were lashed in place between hood and front fenders, the same way they would have brought the buck deer down out of the hills. All three men had been shot high in the spine, the same kind of expert shot which will bring a running deer down in a long boneless sprawling fall.

"But McAran is hill stock himself."

"Then likely he won't have trouble. I can ask you something, Fenn. How many people are there up there you'd be real glad to lay your hands on?"

I shrugged. "Thirty, forty, I don't know exactly."

"They ever come down to town and give you a chance?"

"Not that I know of."

"You ever try to get 'em brought down to you?"

"Before I knew any better. One spindly-looking old man

put two husky young cops in the hospital He knocked them down, stomped them, and dropped their guns in a corner mailbox. I traced him to Laurel Valley, and I learned his name. I couldn't get them to arrest him. I took a day off and went up to see if I could bluff him into coming back with me. He listened very politely, and then followed me down into Laurel Valley in his old car and introduced me to five good citizens who were willing to swear old Tom hadn't been down to Brook City in over a year. As I was ready to take off he leaned down to my car window and said, 'Thank you kindly for being so nice and polite. I kin prove I was never nowhere near the city that evening you had the trouble. Anyhow, I was standing in the nightime looking at some pretty rings in a store window, and two young squirts come up on me from behind, slappin' my pockets, pushing me rough like, and a-callin' me pappy. So I told them I would have no layin' on of hands, but they laughed and pulled on my beard, and I got a temper I've been tryin' to cure all my life. So I whipped 'em and come on back home earlier'n I planned. If I felt I done a wrong thing, I'd walk down there barefoot in the deep of winter. You tell those young men they'll do better having respect for grown men. You told me they reported me drunk. Had I been drunk they'd have been kilt too dead to report. On my twenty-third birthday I drank heavy and come to myself a month later, five hundred miles from home, with not a penny. I walked home in eleven days and eleven nights, and took the pledge and ain't tasted a drop since. Had you come up on me talking rough, you would be a long time getting back to talking and walking.' Then he nodded and walked away, big as a minute and tough as a berry patch."

"So when you came over here, you didn't have much hope of my doing anything for you, did you?" Bub Fischer asked the question hopefully.

"Not too much."

He looked relieved. "You know how it is."

"Maybe you can think of some way of finding out what I want to know. Some easy way, Sheriff. Something that won't cost you a vote."

"Now if a man spent all his time thinking about votes—"

"He'd keep getting elected forever."

"Now you know I wasn't going to say that." There was

107

a slight whine in his voice. "I'm trying to run this job right."

I stood up, wondering why I'd wasted my time. The few reasonably adequate deputies had quit in disgust. He'd filled the slots with his no-good buddies. Their budget was still substantial, because Boo Hudson had pushed it as high as he could, and government operating expenses never go down. But the money wasn't going into law enforcement in the unincorporated areas of Brook County. Their radio network was deteriorating, their vehicles were growing ever closer to the final breakdown, their central records setup was falling way behind. The "unsolved" rate was shooting up. The county prosecutor was turning cases back for more investigation, which wasn't getting done. Convictions were reaching a new low for the county. And Bub Fischer was attending every Sheriff's conference within seven hundred miles. I could have told Bub what would happen, but he wouldn't have believed me. He'd been riding a long streak of luck, because nothing really hairy had happened in the area under his control. But it would. And he wouldn't know how to handle it. Then the State's Attorney would send in some investigators, and Fischer would be suspended for incompetence, and a new Sheriff would be appointed. Ironically, if the appointee was a professional officer of the law, he wouldn't be able to keep the job by getting elected to it later on, not unless he was a combination so unusual he'd be too smart to waste his talents in Brook County.

"How are your boys coming with that hit and run?" I asked him.

"The way it looks to me, Fenn, we just plain don't have enough to go on. It's more'n a month now, and——"

"Not enough to go on? Good Lord, you know the make and color and the year from the spectroscopic analysis report on the paint ground into that boy's pants. You know the car is registered in this state, and you've got the first two numbers of the plate, even. I told you, you have to send a man upstate to pull all those numbers and make a list of the cars of the right make, then use plain old shoe leather to locate the ones painted that shade of red, or repainted since it happened."

He shook his head sadly. "I wish I could do just that, boy. But I swear to you, we got such a work load around here, I can't turn a soul loose to go do it your way."

108

I could hear his cronies laughing and talking in the outer office. "Is there another way?" I asked him.

He winked at me. "We got a lead on it. Don't you worry. We got a little lead we're tracking down right now."

I had seen the police pictures of the boy who'd been hit by the car. Estimated speed at moment of impact— seventy to eighty m.p.h. I wished I could not remember the pictures so vividly. I could not trust myself to speak to Sheriff Emery Fischer at the moment, so I walked out.

"Come round more often, you hear?" he called after me.

viii

THE days and nights went by. I settled gratefully back into the old routines. I was aware of tension, of anticipation of trouble, but I realized I had merely traded one variety for another. In the last months before McAran had been released I had been dreading it. Now it was a more formless worry, but no easier and no more difficult to bear.

Meg was very merry and happy during that period. She had found it easy to sell herself a brand-new dream about Dwight. He would summer in the hills, and return refreshed and make himself a new life. Also, she felt she had a better chance, this year, of getting back into the public school system in the fall.

A dwindling city creates unusual problems. All public utilities work at less than capacity. There is always plenty of room in the hospital. Young people are the ones who leave a shrinking city, and that means fewer kids, empty classrooms. They need teachers only to fill retirement vacancies. By the time Judy had entered kindergarten, we knew we couldn't have a family as big as we wanted. So Meg had applied that year. One house wasn't enough to use up all her awesome energies. She had applied again last year, and narrowly missed being taken on. Now she was very near the top of the list, and they told her she could practically count on it. Her hours would be so similar to the school hours the kid had, there was no special problem. It would take some of the financial pressure off us.

She wondered aloud when we were going to hear from Dwight. I made the casual, unheard answers, in the right tone of voice.

Larry Brint wondered when we were going to hear from Dwight, too. So did Johnny Hooper. So did I. Cop sense, you call it. We hear a lot of bluffs. They're part of the business. Nine hundred and ninety-nine out of a thousand aren't worth the breath it takes to shout them in open court.

110

The thousandth one makes you wonder.

Even when you're busy, you keep wondering. We kept busy. Crime in a depressed area has its own pattern. We were spared professional felonious ventures. Jeff Kermer saw to that. And the people with jobs were particularly careful not to get jammed up, because jobs can be lost that way. But for a long time we had been getting more than our share of those vicious, random violences which are born out of despair. Kitchen quarrels turn into an ugly business with a carving knife. They look for all the kinds of blackout which mean escape for a little while—driving a car at top speed, knocking off the cheap half-pint bottles in one long spasmodic gulping in the alley nearest the liquor store because it works faster and harder that way, losing money too fast in Kermer's rigged games and then trying to waylay a winner on his way home, messing with the neighbor's wife, or his daughters, swinging with a maniac frenzy at the man who accidentally jostles them, beating wives and children too long and too hard, committing impulse thefts of ridiculous clumsiness, writing bad paper that makes even the most stupid store clerk wary.

These are the crimes of a hard-times town, and they fill the cells with all that aching remorse of men and women who know, in their hearts, that nothing like this would ever have happened if—the furniture factory hadn't closed, or the lawnmower plant hadn't moved away, or the bake shop hadn't failed, or if Sam hadn't insisted on coming back to this lousy, dirty, crummy, stinking town way back when he got out of the army.

We worked at our trade, hating a lot of it, trying not to forget the uses of mercy. And while we worked, we tried forty ways of getting some crumb of information out of the hill country. But it was as though big McAran and the big car with the big load had melted into the mountain ground.

A week after McAran left town, Paul Hanaman, Junior, came to see Chief Brint, and Larry sent him down to see me. We walked over to Shilligan's Courthouse Cafe. It was the first genuinely hot afternoon of the year, and I was technically off duty, and I wanted some of the dark and bitter imported brew Shilligan keeps on draught. Also, I thought young Paul would be more off balance there than in my office. We sat in a booth and he ordered probably the only iced coffee served that afternoon in Shilligan's.

He was uneasy, and I was not going to make it any easier for him. He has a pudding face, a pudding wife, and two doughy children. He lives with his father in the old Hanaman place out in the Hillview section. He dresses twenty years older than he is. His eyes bulge slightly, and are vaguely blue. His mouth is puckered and prim. He has the idea the world has been established in order to provide him with an agreeable environment, and it is his obligation to pay the world back by living up to the responsibilities of wealth and social position. His public title is Assistant to the Publisher of the *Brook City Daily Press*. He serves on a dozen civic groups and committees. He gives a hollow imitation of his father's effortless, merciless authority, but he is the sort of man who would march righteously to quiet some foul-mouthed drunk and end up apologizing to him for bothering him. I have sensed from the very beginning of it all that his sister's death was a source of great relief to him. Despite her wildness, she was the old man's favorite. She constantly embarrassed young Paul. She shamed him.

"Chief Brint said you could answer my questions, Lieutenant." By a small emphasis on "you" he managed to convey his impression that it was a preposterous idea.

"I'll try to be real bright."

"What? Well—I'll appreciate it, certainly. My father is curious about—Dwight McAran."

"What does he want to know about him?"

"My father has felt it was a terrible miscarriage of justice when the court accepted a plea of guilty to the reduced charge of manslaughter. It made him—very bitter."

"McAran thought it was a miscarriage of justice too, but not exactly the same way."

"My father thought it practically obscene that he should be permitted to come back here to Brook City."

"You people made that clear in the paper. And you stirred up a lot of other people, too."

"He shouldn't have been allowed to come back here just as if nothing had ever happened."

"If you'd bought the city and put a fence around it, you could have kept him out."

"Is that some sort of a joke, Lieutenant?"

"It's the only legal way I can think of—to have kept him out."

"Things like that can be arranged."

"Sometimes."

"But he came back here and he actually—lived in your home."

"We've been scrubbing and fumigating it ever since."

"You have a strange attitude, Lieutenant."

I studied him for a few moments. The future I planned for myself might well depend on the good will of this pompous young man. The canny police administrator will maintain excellent relations with the influential members of the community.

I sighed and smiled at him and said, "I'm not exactly charmed and enchanted by your attitude, young Paul."

"I beg your pardon?"

"My wife, whom I dearly love, happens to love the Mc-Aran monster with all her heart. She made sixty sad pilgrimages to Harpersburg. She cannot believe evil of him. If the Brook City Police had bowed to Hanaman—and Kermer—pressure, and framed McAran back into prison, or chased him the hell out of town, I would have had to choose between my wife and my job, and properly so. I would have chosen Meg, not the job. Larry Brint knows I am the best he has, the best he is likely to get, and his logical eventual replacement. Even so, he might have played it your way, for the sake of expediency, but you all pushed a little too hard. And he is a stubborn man. So he backed me, backed my marriage, gave McAran safe haven. So if we want to have any kind of constructive thought on this hot afternoon, let's forget what might have been, or what you and your father think should have been, and stick with the facts."

He moistened his lips, tugged at his collar, and tried to drink out of his empty glass. "You certainly—speak right out, Lieutenant Hillyer."

"And I realize I'm talking to the only newspaper, the biggest bank, the biggest of the two radio stations, and miscellaneous holdings here and there."

He coughed and said, "You'll understand it's difficult for me to really comprehend an officer of the law giving house room to the person who—murdered my sister."

"We've covered that, haven't we?"

"Yes. Yes, of course. My father has been informed that McAran left this city of his own free will one week ago today."

JOHN D. MACDONALD

"Correct."

"He bought a fast car and a lot of—outdoor equipment, and just drove away."

"That's what he did."

"Where is he?"

"I haven't the faintest idea."

I think he tried to assume an intimidating scowl, but it looked as if he was suffering a temporary gastric disturbance. "Isn't it your business to know?"

"How do you mean?"

"Shouldn't the police always know the whereabouts of a person like that?"

"My God, Hanaman, you can't have it both ways, can you? If we'd chased him out of town, we wouldn't be able to keep a finger on him. We knew where he was when he was here. It's a good bet he did go up into the hills."

"Isn't there some law which says he has to tell the police where he is?"

"He is *not* on probation or parole. He doesn't have to report to anybody. He's lost some of his civil rights, like the right to vote or hold public office or obtain a passport. Presumably no bonding company would bond him. Aside from that there's no more restriction on him than there is on you. We'd *like* to know where he is, but we've got about as many informers in those hills as we have in the hills of Chinese Turkestan."

"My father and I want him found and arrested."

"What for?"

"For this," he said with a slightly girlish indignation, and took a postcard out of the inside pocket of his jacket and handed it to me.

It was a comic postcard, in color, showing a photo of a chimpanzee sitting in a little rocking chair, wearing a top hat and smoking a cigar and smirking at the camera. It had been mailed the previous day in Polksburg, a city half the size of Brook City and situated ninety miles to the south, beyond the far edge of the hills. The card was addressed to the elder Hanaman, fat backhand writing in purple ink with printed capital letters and little circles instead of dots over the i's. The message read, "See you soon, Popsie." It was unsigned.

"This isn't McAran's writing."

114

"I know. It's Mildred's."

The room seemed to shift out of focus. "It's *what!*"

"It's an imitation of Mildred's handwriting. She always used that purple ink, and a broad nib and slanted the letters backwards. It isn't really a very *good* imitation, but it's close enough to be—very disturbing. And she was the only one in the world who ever called him Popsie." He pronounced the term with a marked distaste.

It was such a clever viciousness, so loaded with implications, it made my skin crawl, and I could only guess at the effect it would have had on the old man.

"I think you used the wrong word," I said. "You said your father is curious about McAran. I'd think he'd be highly nervous."

"My father isn't a timid man. We want McAran arrested."

"On what charge?"

He looked at me in a dim questioning way. "For sending this card."

"Let's be just a little realistic. There's no charge that will stand up. No fraud. No obscenity. Even if anybody could prove he sent it. This is not, for God's sake, one of those feudal setups where we're your personal armed guard and you can send us off to whip one of the serfs because he gets impertinent."

"It isn't necessary to say that. My father's life has been threatened."

"But too indirectly to stand up in court."

"But not so indirectly, Lieutenant, we can't demand police protection."

"We can't spare the men, honestly."

He looked triumphant, as though I had left him a wonderful opening. "Then it would be a lot more efficient to just arrest him, wouldn't it?"

"If he's in the hills, that's Sheriff Fischer's territory."

"How about the State Police?"

"Once upon a time the State Police had a Criminal Investigation Division. But the legislature knocked it out and split the money between all the county Sheriffs and the investigation staff of the state attorney general. That staff helps the counties nail down major felony indictments."

"The—uh—F.B.I.?" he said faintly.

"And the National Guard and the Strategic Air Force and

115

Central Intelligence. We'll get them all excited about this post card."

"You don't have to be rude, Hillyer."

"Will you just understand that you've come to us with an impossible request?"

"Will we get protection or won't we?"

"Why don't you and your father go away on a trip for a while?"

"That's out of the question."

"Will your father maintain his normal routine?"

"Of course."

"We'll make your house out there a special check point on the night patrol for that area." I wrote a name and address, tore the sheet out of my notebook and handed it to him. "Joe Willsie hit compulsory retirement six months ago. He lives with his daughter. He's bored. He's a rugged old man, with good reflexes. A dead shot. He knows protection routines and emergency procedures. On his real talkative days, he'll sometimes say ten words. For sixty bucks a week you people can buy a lot of safety. Let him do the driving for your father. Fix him a place to sleep out there."

"Can't you—assign a regular officer to do the same thing?"

"I won't, and I won't recommend it. But Larry Brint could reverse that decision. Is it the sixty a week that stops you?"

He looked indignant. "Of course not! It's my father's —attitude about all this. It makes everything very difficult. He thinks you people were wrong in giving McAran such a short sentence and then letting him come back here. So he thinks it's your responsibility. And if he had to pay to be protected—it's almost like an admission of being wrong. And my father has never—never in his life admitted being wrong. It's very difficult to explain anything to him. It always was, but it's worse since Mildred—passed away. I'm afraid he's going to—demand protection."

"Does he have to know who's paying Joe Willsie?"

Young Paul looked blankly at me, and then with unexpected humble gratitude. "Would this Officer Willsie be able to—understand?"

"He's more than bright enough, believe me. And he'd like it because it would make the job easier. Your father will do what Joe tells him if he thinks Joe is still on our pay sheet. You talk to Joe. If you see any question in his mind at all, you have him phone me."

Unexpectedly, young Paul wanted to shake hands. "People don't talk to me the way you have, Lieutenant Hillyer."

"I had to explain our side of it, my side of it."

"I'm beginning to understand why Chief Brint thinks highly of you. Have you ever thought of—some line of work that might be a little more profitable?"

"No thanks." We were standing by the booth. "Let me know right away if you hear from McAran again." He said he would, and walked out into the hot bright afternoon. I stood in the tap room gloom, directly under one of these slow, old-fashioned ceiling fans with the wooden blades, wondering if my thirst for a second stein of dark was more important than the thirty-five cents it would cost me.

"Buy ya one," a raspy intimate voice said. I glanced down at the upturned face of Kid Gilbert. They say he used to walk straight in, hooking with both hands, and grinning because he enjoyed it. If he'd fought in a heavier class, he'd now be institutionalized or dead. But he was a bantamweight, fought at 118 pounds, fought over a hundred times and retired over twenty years ago. He now weighs at least a hundred and fifty. He looks as if he had been worked over with ball bats and tack hammers, stung by giant bees, then left out in the weather. Small bright blue eyes stare at you out of the ruins. He's Jeff Kermer's clown, a creature of idiot routines, half-punchy, half-shrewd, completely trusted. He tells us exactly what Kermer wants us to know, and he has to be handled with care or he will take back more information than he gives.

He's safe to be seen with. Even in a controlled town, caution is required. He has no record. He owns two parking lots and three laundromats, and visits them all twice a day to pick up the money. He will not admit ownership. He claims he is the front man for the one who really owns them. But we know they're his.

I looked around Shilligan's to see who might take any special interest in my talking to the Kid, and saw Stu Dockerty talking to a couple of men from the County Highway Department at the bar. I sat down in the booth again and let the Kid buy me the second stein..

"Jeffie gets greetings from an old buddy," the Kid said.

"Like a postcard?" I asked him.

It was the first time I was ever certain I'd caught Kid Gilbert off balance. He choked on the first sip of his drink, wiped his leathery mouth on the back of his hand and stared at me.

"Like a postcard from Polksburg?" I continued. "With a monkey in a high hat?"

"So you got the mailman, huh? So why let me know?"

"No mailman, Kid. It was a guess."

He stared at me for a few moments. "Other people got cards too."

"All over town," I said.

"So what I was saying, a couple of times Jeffie tries to get in touch, in Harpersburg, to explain how things had to be the way they had to be, maybe to say there can be some good breaks to make up for the bad break. But he can't make a contact, and he gives up. It bothers Jeffie when he can't give protection."

"It fills him with remorse."

"Huh? I guess so. Sure. So then he's in your house, and Jeffie waits and there's no contact. So he sends Lupo to make an offer, nothing great, but not a bad deal you understand. You know this?"

"No. He didn't say anything."

"Lupo, he waits around until there's nobody home but McAran, he phones from a couple of blocks away. McAran is nice, he says come to the back door, so okay. It's understood Lupo comes with a deal. Knocks on the back door. The door wings open and slams shut, and Lupo is on his back out in the yard, with a nose this wide, but thick as a piece of paper. Three hundred to rebuild the nose, but it won't be right, and you know Lupo, always making people tell him he looks like Gregory Peck. Now he hates himself. Anyhow, that's the answer he takes back. So Jeffie stops going through doors first, like old times. It eats him because he's mostly legit, and he shouldn't have to live that way, and he wonders if it's important enough to maybe have somebody help out. McAran, he thinks, can be some kind of a nut by now."

"But he felt better when he found out McAran left town."

"Until the card comes."

"What did it say?"

"It just said 'We got a date,' and it was signed Millie. That broad didn't like anybody calling her Millie and it was Jeffie and McAran used to get her steaming mad calling her that. Jeffie is real sore."

"So what does he want me to know?"

"You should know something more? When he was in town, just before he left, you were tailing him."

"Were we?"

"When he comes back, maybe you shouldn't. Not right away."

"*If* he comes back."

"Jeffie thinks he's coming back. After a couple of days you can tail him, if you can find him. I gotta run."

He left. The message from Kermer was clear. Kermer had told me, in effect, "McAran has now made me so nervous I'll feel better if he can be put permanently out of circulation. I'm importing some people to handle the problem. If the police follow McAran, it will complicate things. Let me do it my way, and you won't even have a body to worry about."

I could guess at the method. They'd have to transport it at least forty miles to unload it in the modern manner. You take it to where the bulldozers have been, out in front of where they're laying the foundation stone. It's easy to dig, and it doesn't have to be deep. A few months later fast traffic is rolling over the grave. Estimates of how many are under the New Jersey Turnpike vary from three to fifteen. Perhaps it isn't a particularly modern method. Maybe there are bones under the old Roman roads. At any rate it is more convenient than those problems of logistics involving wire, weights and a boat.

I could have sent Kermer a message through Kid Gilbert, preparing him for the possibility of McAran traveling with a small hard-nose pack.

I closed my eyes as I drained the last portion of cold dark brew, and when I opened them, Stu Dockerty was sitting across from me, looking like a British consular agent trying to get us to buy more tweed and Jaguars.

"Running a consultant service this afternoon?" he asked me.

"Bring your problems to Doctor Hillyer."

"Doctor, I want to ask your advice about a sick city."

119

"I've had time to examine the patient. It is in a run down condition, susceptible to infection."

"By a special virus?"

"A very special one, with a five-year incubation period."

"When I came in, Fenn, you and young Paul were making faces at each other. Something fell into the fan over at our print shop, and it hasn't filtered down to me. Should I know about it?"

"You won't be able to write it up."

"Can you imagine what this town would be like if I wrote up all I know?"

So I told him about the comedy postcards. I told him to go and fake Paul Junior into showing it to him.

Dockerty burlesqued astonishment. "Good Lord, my dear fellow! I do not speak to Hanamans. The old one tells the young one who tells the managing editor who tells the assistant managing editor who tells the city editor who then tells me."

"So you just admire the Hanamans from afar."

"The surviving ones, yes. I had a closer contact with poor Mildred, though. Long ago, when she thought it would be jolly to be a girl reporter, and they tucked her under my wing. It took two months for her to find out it's very dull work. Fenn, does the kiss-and-tell ethic cover the dead as well?"

"You wouldn't bring it up without a reason, would you?"

"No. I guess not. She was a forlorn beast, you know. She tended to exaggerate the importance of her bounty. I was supposed to be full of tremulous gratitude. But she wanted to use her favors as a club, and hammer all males into dreadful submission, a constant condition of begging. But her talent was without sufficient discipline or selectivity, and so, for this antique lecher, it just wasn't that good. And she deprived me of any lengthy pleasure of pursuit. I did not realize at the time that it could be called research. But our little pleasures did give me a chance to be realistically accurate when I sold her slaying to two different magazines under two different names, for a total gross of five hundred and fifty dollars, later on. And I made the bitch far more enchanting than she was. But now it occurs to me that of all who shared that slender fortune, perhaps McAran and I are the only two who quit before she was ready to quit—which was for her the most horrible insult possible. Our reasons might have been identical, a distaste for the female usurpation of our primitive right of aggression. I struck her too. Go ahead and look surprised, dear boy. You are right. It was out of character. She waylaid me at my place, drunk, abusive and hysterical. I took her in and tried to calm her down. After too much clawing and kicking, she decided to scream until my patient neighbors called the police. So, as she started the second scream, I popped her with great care, with a fist wrapped in a dish towel, a short right chop on the jaw, caught her as she fell, placed her on the bed. Ten minutes later she started snoring. It was half-past midnight. I phoned young Paul to come and get her, and bring somebody to drive her car back. I thought it would be too awkward to be there when he got there, so I told him I'd leave the door unlocked. She woke up before he got there, and she was very busy when he arrived, working her way through my wardrobe with a razor blade. We settled out of court, of course. I made a careful estimate of damage, bought the replacements and charged them to him."

"A lovely girl."

"A sick girl. Sicker than any of us realized, I think. And the damage continues. It isn't over yet. The face of Helen sank the thousand ships. McAran is Mildred's agent in this world, Fenn. And he has a few more errands in her name. Those postcards are not quite sane."

"I feel that too."

"But you can't tell Meg, can you?"

"No."

"But if you have to find him, Fenn, if it becomes imperative to find him, Meg is the one who can go up there and find him, because they'll talk to Meg. Have you thought of that?"

"I've been trying not to."

"You would have to trick her, wouldn't you?"

"That would depend on why we wanted him."

"You aren't really the one in the middle, Fenn. Meg is the one. Larry knows she could find him."

"He hasn't mentioned it."

"When there's a good reason, he'll have to."

"Think up a reason, Stu."

"Mmm. A gaudy one? He slips into town, kills jolly old

Jeffie Kermer and fades back into the hills. But there is an eyewitness."

"So he'd know he was wanted for murder? And you think I'd try to send Meg up there? She could probably find somebody who could tell her where to look for him. But she wouldn't get any information unless she was alone. Meg's positive her dear brother wouldn't harm her. By God, I'm not. I don't think he'd harm anyone he could use, and I think he'd kill anybody who might harm him. All I would ever do is try to talk her into finding out where he is, so we could go in and get him. I'd have to level with her, not try to trick her and follow her in. And I don't think she'd set him up that way. It would take a lot of hard solid proof to make her even consider it, and I just don't think we're going to get that kind of proof on anything McAran does."

"And if you can't convince her, it would look as if you're protecting McAran."

"Are you having a lot of fun with this, Dockerty? Heaps of glee?"

"I'm trying to be your friend. If McAran hits and runs back into the hills, there's going to be pressure on you like you never saw before. So just be braced for it, old boy. Decide in advance just which way you'll jump and how far. The *Daily Press* will be screaming for your scalp and Larry Brint's."

"Sorry. I didn't mean to get sore at you, Stu."

"I want you to survive, Lieutenant. If you and Larry get pushed out, I'll be working with dolts and savages. I think you might need help from any place you can get it. Even me."

ix

HARPERSBURG State Prison erupted into overdue violence on the following Tuesday. The timing was perfect. It happened at ten minutes before noon, the one moment in the day when the maximum number of prisoners were outside their cells. And it took advantage of a vast, intense, windy thunderstorm which had knocked the lights out, and was impeding the guard routines on turrets and catwalks. There were three gates in the prison walls, the main pedestrian gate, the truck gate for incoming supplies and outgoing products of prison labor, and the railroad gate which hadn't been used in over ten years. The truck gate had not only been reinforced to the extent that no vehicle could smash through it, but it was also protected by a low interior wall built to force outgoing vehicles to approach it at a curve which obviated any buildup of speed. The double pedestrian gate was too narrow to be broached by a vehicle. But somehow the vulnerability of the unused railroad gate had been overlooked. The weak point in prison security was the unthinkable prospect of somebody trying to take a vehicle through the railroad gate.

Subsequent investigations showed that the vast majority of the prison inmates were unacquainted with the escape plan, but had been incited to rebellion so as to provide a maximum diversion while the actual escape took place.

In the first vicious scufflings three guards and two prisoners lost their lives. Eleven hostages were herded into D block. The laundry, the metal stamping mill, and the paint storage shed burst into flames. Under cover of the storm, the confusion and the black choking smoke, a prisoner jumped the ignition wiring on a heavy truck parked at the loading dock, pulled out and picked up speed all the way to the railroad gate. It smashed the inner gate of riveted steel plates and plunged partway through the outer gate before becoming solidly wedged. Thirty-one men followed it to the railroad gate, running at top speed. They made their escape by dropping to the roadbed and crawling out between the front wheels of the truck. By the time more men had discovered the escape route, the ruined truck had burst into the flames and the heat drove them back. The man who wheeled the big truck had taken a calculated risk. It was discovered, when he was recaptured, that he had been a stock car driver, and knew that he could be injured only if the gates did not give way, thus stopping the truck in its tracks instead of the lesser impact which would result from smashing all the way through, or partially through. He told of crouching on the passenger side, working the gas pedal with his free hand and steering until the last moment, then flattening himself against the firewall. The truck doors were jammed in a closed position by the impact. He dropped out through a side window just in time to join the first group crawling under the front axle. By the time the flames blocked this only exit from the prison the escape siren was bellowing, competing with the thunderous spring storm, and all police installations in the area had been alerted to set up the roadblock plan designed to seal the area.

By one o'clock the demoralized guard force had been strengthened and all prisoners had been driven back into the cell block area, and the firefighting equipment could be brought in through the truck gate. During the armed search of the administration offices they found Deputy Warden Boo Hudson, semiconscious and incoherent, half under his desk, slashed once and deeply from gullet to groin, yelping and dying in the hot spill of viscera. By that time the camera crews were racing to the scene, radio programs were being interrupted for the news flash, the wire services were fattening their coverage, all roadblocks had been fully manned and in operation for at least forty minutes, a contingent of the National Guard was being assembled, and we were getting progress reports over the police teletype network.

By two-thirty all confinement areas except D Block, where the hostages were being held, had been subdued through the use of fire hoses and tear gas. One more prisoner had been killed and seven injured. Also, by that time, eleven of the thirty-one who had escaped had been recaptured by State and County Police. But because it was impossible to take a head count until D Block was subdued, the number still at large was not then known, nor could the identity of those who had escaped be established.

Early reports said a hundred desperate men were roaming through the countryside.

The spokesman for the prisoners holed up in D Block said he wanted to negotiate, but that he would not negotiate with Warden Waley. One hostage guard was released to relay his message. The guard said that one lifer in the prisoner group, a moronic lout, had agreed to personally slit the throats of all the other hostages if the prisoner demands were ignored. By then the State Superintendent of Prisons and Reformatories was on the scene and ready to begin the familiar charade of negotiation, that meaningless procedure whereby the authorities listen to complaints and demands and then, with mock reluctance, agree to honor the demands. Because these demands receive newspaper coverage, the prisoners have the quaint belief public opinion will keep the authorities from welching on their promises. Sometimes conditions do improve, even for as long as two or three weeks. More often they worsen. Once the hostages are released, the authorities state proudly that they managed to trick the prison scum.

Johnny Hooper came into my office at three in the afternoon. I had a table radio tuned to the Harpersburg station, to a disc jockey who kept giving information about ten minutes sooner than we were getting it on the teletype. Johnny had a troubled look on his boyish face. He sat on the corner of my desk and said, "I've been thinking, Fenn. When they do find out who's missing, I'll bet a buck I can give you three of the names."

"Deitwaller, Kostinak and Kelly," I said.

"You too, huh?"

"Yes. Because I don't believe in coincidences either."

We stared at each other for a few minutes.

"He bought that bomb, that wagon," Johnny said.

"So it could have been waiting for them in a pre-arranged place."

"Fenn, do you think it could have gotten through before the roadblocks were set up?"

"Doubt it. They put them far enough out so no car can cover that much distance in the time it takes to get them set up. It would be more likely for McAran to have clothes aboard, and identification, and figure on getting through the roadblock that way."

Johnny shook his head. "Four men traveling together? No

125

matter how you dressed those guys, they'd look wrong, boss. It would have to be some other way. Like McAran dressing like a farmer and stashing them under a load of carrots or some damn thing."

We suddenly discovered we were nodding solemnly at each other. We grinned. I sent him after a road map. Suddenly, as if he'd become telepathic, my disc jockey friend cut in and told about the traffic tieups at the five roadblocks and he named the locations of the roadblocks. I jotted them down. When Johnny spread the map out on my desk I marked in the roadblocks.

"Easy to seal that valley right off," Johnny said. "No secondary roads at all. Just those five roads leaving the valley. Nice."

"Now listen to all the 'ifs' I can string together. If those three are loose, and this whole thing was planned to spring them, and if McAran went over there after them, and if he parked in some hidden spot as close to the prison as he dared get, and if they made a bee line to the place where he was waiting, and if he wanted to bring them back to the hideout he's fixed up in his familiar hills, the fast logical way back would be through Polksburg, where those postcards were mailed. The other way would be a little longer and it would bring him practically into Brook City before he could turn onto 882. So he'd go through this roadblock, at Melton. And it's—let me see—about eighteen miles out of Harpersburg. Suppose they were in the car and rolling by a few minutes after noon. He'd roll it well within the speed limits. Make it twenty-to-one by the time he got to the roadblock. By then the roadblock would have been functioning for about fifteen minutes. That might be a help."

"Why?"

"The troopers are more likely to remember the cars they worked for the first hour. After that things begin to blur. Do you think it's too wild a chance, Johnny?"

He shrugged. "You told me a long time ago, Fenn, that in this business if you never take a chance on looking real stupid, you never had a chance to look real bright either. But right now those people aren't going to be thinking about how maybe somebody got through already. They're going to be trying to stop anybody else who tries to get through."

I could see the merit in that. So I held off. By seven-thirty that evening the truce had been arranged. Nine more escapees had been nailed. The lockup and sorting out had begun. The National Guard climbed onto their trucks and headed home. The inventory and damage report was begun. The railroad gate had been given emergency repairs, after a wrecker had yanked the blackened skeleton of the truck out of the way.

By nine o'clock the head count was complete, and three more prisoners were en route back to the prison. Eight were still at large. Names and descriptions of those eight were sent to all area installations, with photographs to follow.

At ten o'clock Johnny came into my office. The radio news from Harpersburg was just reporting that one of the eight, a William Fogg, age twenty-six, serving twenty to life for armed robbery had tried to cut around the Melton roadblock in a stolen car, had flipped at high speed when he tried to take the ditch, and was in critical condition.

Johnny put the list of the eight names in front of me. He didn't have to say a word. I drew a red line through Fogg's name. I made three check marks—beside Kelly, Kostinak and Deitwaller.

"So let's say we've made some good guesses, but we're one step behind them," I said heavily. "And let's say that if we had any sense and guts when we first started this game, we'd have got right on the wire and had them set up another roadblock near Polksburg, with a pickup order on that wagon, and it would have been in time to catch them before they made it into the hills."

"But it was a lot hazier then than it is now, Fenn. Maybe you better go on home. You look whipped."

I didn't sleep well that night. I was wide awake at dawn, wearied by half-forgotten dreams of violence, and I managed to sneak out of the bedroom without wakening Meg. I got the six o'clock news on the radio, at a volume where I could just barely hear it.

They'd picked up two more. Five were still at large, a man named Price, a man named Seckler, and the three hard-nose friends of Morgan Miller and Dwight McAran. By the time Meg and the kids got up, I'd had too much

127

coffee, but I had lost that sour feeling of having spent a restless night.

I went in and stooged around headquarters, unable to concentrate on lesser matters, waiting for Larry to come in. As soon as he came in I asked him if I could make a run over to Melton on official business.

"What for?"

"Fifty to one it's a waste of time. But if it isn't, it's worth the trip. It's all so vague and iffy, I'd rather wait and tell you about it if it works out."

He looked dubious, then shrugged and told me to take off.

It was about sixty-five miles and I made it in just under an hour. The State Police Barracks on the eastern outskirts of the village of Melton was the usual cinderblock structure with flagpole, radio tower, manicured lawn. The duty Sergeant was named Boscatt, a florid man with a cold blue eye. He relaxed, but only slightly, when I showed the gold badge. Our troopers have great morale. They are carefully selected and trained, and fairly well paid. He said he was the ranking man on the station at the moment, and what could he do for me. All of them are unimpressed by city police officers, apparently believing we are all pallid, grafting, untrained nephews of politicians.

"It's about your road block operated by this barracks, Sergeant."

"Kind of far from your city limits aren't you, Lieutenant?"

"About sixty-five miles, approximately."

We tried to outwit each other. I won. He said, reluctantly, "What would it be about our roadblock, Lieutenant. We took it off less than an hour ago."

"Aren't there five men still—"

"Four still loose. We take our roadblocks down when it's time to take them down."

"I guess that must be a sensible observation, to a roadblock expert, which I am not. Which one was picked up?"

"Kelly!"

And suddenly I lost ninety-nine per cent of my assurance. I felt like a fool. It knocked a fine theory in the head. "Kelly!" I said faintly.

"One of the reasons we took the block down. A farmer found him in a ditch thirty miles east of here, a ditch on

128

a side road, fifty yards off the main road to Polksburg. The farmer's dog kept barking. Kelly was dead. A slug had hit him from behind and smashed his shoulder all to hell, and he'd lost a lot of blood, but what killed him was being strangled by somebody with a lot of strength in his hand. Dead since some time yesterday afternoon they think. When all those fellows were running, and that tower guard finally came out of his daze and fired a long burst at a high angle, he claims he saw one of them fall and get up and keep running, so it must have been Kelly they think now. So he couldn't have been driving the shape he was in, and because he got by one of the blocks, they figure some of the others maybe went by the same way, so there's no point in stalling all the traffic in the area."

"How was he dressed?"

"Prison twill. Why?"

"I've got an idea how he got through your block, Sergeant. He and Kostinak and Deitwaller."

"Nobody got through it, Lieutenant. Not the way we run it. Around it, maybe, walking up and down hills and hiding from the search planes, but not through it."

"I'd like to talk to the troopers who were checking the cars yesterday, the ones who handled the first trick on the roadblock."

"There's no point in it. Sorry, Lieutenant. We know our business. I can't pull men in off the road because you maybe got some weird idea."

"I'm asking for your co-operation on an informal basis, Sergeant. If I can't get it this way I'll go after it some other way. And, believe me, I can get it. Now just suppose your people did slip up. Wouldn't this be a better way to run it down than by bringing a lot of other people in on it?"

"Okay, if you want to put it that way, suppose you tell me what your idea is, and I'll pull the two men in off the road if I like the sound of it."

"No dice, Sergeant. Pull them in, order them to co-operate, and listen to me ask the questions." As I saw him hesitating, I said gently, "After all, Kelly got through somehow. And he wasn't in any shape to walk, was he?"

That did it. The two men were each on single patrol, and their names were McKeen and Golden. He had the dispatcher call them in. McKeen arrived an minute or two ahead of Golden. They were huge, tanned, husky, moving with creak of leather and purr of whipcord, with deceptive indolence and watchful eyes. They were as skeptical of me as Boscatt had been. They bought Cokes out of the machine and we went into the small lounge off the day room and sat down.

"I want you men to think back and see what you can recall about a Pontiac station wagon, two years old, dark blue, local license BC18-822."

"We were on that block until ten last night, Lieutenant," McKeen said. "There were a *hell* of a lot of station wagons. We don't keep any license number record. Anyhow, Kelly couldn't have got through us in a damn station—"

"This particular wagon would have come along pretty soon after you got set up over there. Probably in the first half-hour, when you were still having to explain to people what it was all about."

"But if it was a station wagon, Lieutenant," Golden said, "there isn't any chance we'd—"

I put a lot of edge in my voice for the first time. "I'm not interested in hearing you people tell me how well you run a roadblock. I've asked you to remember a particular car, even if it was as obviously empty as a bass drum."

"Humor the Lieutenant," Boscatt said in a growling voice.

"Hmm. Right soon after we opened the store, huh?" McKeen said. "Hey, Goldy, there was the broad. Did you get your eyes off the front of her sweater long enough to check me out if it was a Pontiac. I know it was dark blue."

"Pontiac it was Mack, and a Brook County tag. Not too long after we opened the store. Twenty minutes? A little more, a little less, because the rain had quit by then. But she was alone."

"The wagon was empty?" Boscatt snapped.

"Well, not exactly," McKeen said, looking uneasily at Golden.

"Load of lumber," Golden said. "Two by fours. Right up to the roof and out onto the tailgate. Solid two by fours."

Boscatt's heavy face turned tomato-red. "*Solid* two by fours, Goldy?" he asked in a dangerously quiet voice.

Golden licked his lips and swallowed. McKeen said, "Well, I suppose you could fake that kind of a load so it would look like—"

"Give that broad back to me, piece by piece, boys," Boscatt ordered.

Golden licked his lips and swallowed. McKeen said, eyes and was silent for about five seconds. "In her thirties some place. Green sweater, jeans, some kind of a jacket she wore unbuttoned. Hefty but not fat. Hair dyed blonde. Some fresh sunburn on her forehead and nose. Husky voice. Talked with a cigarette in the corner of her mouth. A little on the hard side, maybe. Couple of storewrapped packages in the seat beside her. Let me see now. She wanted to know what the hell was the idea of stopping everybody. I told her. She said she was just another truck driver, making a joke sort of. Said her husband was a builder in Polksburg and sent her over to Harpersburg to pick up the lumber. McKeen had walked around the load by then. He nodded and I waved her on and told her not to pick up any hitchhikers. That was a joke too."

"Ho ho," Boscatt said.

Boscatt left us alone for fifteen minutes. When he came back he said, "There are three lumber outfits in Harpersburg, and not one of them sold any station wagon load of two by fours yesterday morning."

"So we goofed it up," Golden said. "But how would this—this Lieutenant figure that was the way—"

"I didn't know how it was done," I said. "I just had the idea that that car was used and they came out this way. I have no idea who that woman can be."

Boscatt slammed a red fist into his palm. "Kelly!" he said. "So they're in the middle of that fake load of lumber and Kelly maybe starts to moan or thrash around at the wrong time, so while my troopers are making punch lines with the blonde, somebody is strangling Kelly a couple of feet away." He looked at me. "How about a little more news from you, Lieutenant?"

"Two men were recently released from Harpersburg, Miller and McAran—" He listened intently as I told him my reasoning.

"I don't think we want to publicize this," I said. "They should believe the gimmick worked, so they'll feel okay about using it again. We know in a general way where they are. Miller likes banks. There are a lot of reasons why they'll want to hit my city. If we keep this quiet, they won't split up and run."

131

"I'm not going to buy any space in the paper for this," Boscatt said. "But I'll have to put in a confidential report that'll go all the way upstairs, right to Major Rice. That south half of Brook County is rugged country. And you say McAran was raised there. And I know you got practically no Sheriff at all over there. And as soon as they rest up, they'll be ready to make their move, eh? We better be in on it. Either going in after them, or being beefed up to seal the area. These aren't young punks. Take that Kostinak. A sentence of a hundred and ninety-eight years.."

I thanked him and told him that my Chief would undoubtedly make a special request for State Police assistance, probably directly to Major Rice, but I couldn't predict what that request would be. I said I'd tell my Chief that their co-operation had been of great help.

By then the three of them had become very cordial. I was not misled. Their contempt for city cops was intact, but they had classified me as an exception. I hurried back to Brook City. Larry Brint was anxious to hear how my fifty-to-one shot had come out. I brought Johnny Hooper in on it. I gave them the whole story, and they made a very alert audience indeed.

AFTER we had talked our way up one side of it and down the other, we adjourned the meeting. Larry called me back in his office later in the afternoon. He said he'd had a long phone conversation with Major Rice.

"One thing we agree on, Fenn, nothing is going to be gained by letting what we know leak out. But that's where we stop agreeing. Rice thinks we should mount a joint operation, and hit that hill country all of a sudden with everything we can collect, up to and including the National Guard. Seal all the roads, set up a continuous air search procedure, and narrow the perimeter until we grab them."

I shook my head slowly. "Twenty-four hundred square miles of rough broken country, Larry. A hundred ways to sneak out once they found out what was happening. And all that display of force would do would be to challenge those hill people to help McAran and his pals in every possible way."

"He couldn't sell me his idea, and I couldn't sell him yours, Fenn. He says we're making too many assumptions. He says we're assuming they're going to hit something here in Brook City, we're assuming they'll use the load of lumber gimmick for the getaway, that they'll come down out of the hills on Route 882, but, most importantly, that we can give them the initiative and still grab them without somebody getting hurt. He says there could be more than the four of them, and the woman, whoever the hell she is, and they could have other vehicles, and some more cute ideas, and an entirely different target in mind. And he's right. You know it and I know it, Fenn. And even if we did spot them coming into town, following your plan, it's no sign that when we move in they're going to come shuffling out with their hands up and saying shucks."

"But—"

"Now you listen here, and stop trying to tell me this long shot you want to play is a sure thing. Get this whole thing in focus for a minute. Yesterday we had one of the worst prison breaks and riots in the history of the state. A lot of men are dead. Three were guards. One was the deputy warden. Violent and dangerous men are still at large. There is a growing stink about this, and it's going to get worse. Warden Waley has been suspended. Now let's just suppose we tried to use your plan and it went sour. Inevitably, dammit, it's going to get out that we all *knew* those men were up in the hills and we sat around and waited for them to come to us. What do you think that would do to Rice's career, to say nothing of yours and mine, fella?"

"I—I see what you mean."

"Prince and Seckler gave themselves up. I got the call just before you came in here. They'd been hiding in a barn six miles from the prison. That leaves just two men loose— Kostinak and Deitwaller. While we're talking here, Fenn, some smart reporter may be digging around at the prison, and he will be wondering if those two had outside help, and he'll come up with the names Miller and McAran."

"I guess it could happen."

"And when they check Youngstown to find out about Miller, they'll find out just as we did that he dropped out of sight three days before McAran was released. And when they start checking here on McAran, what do we say? That he bought a fast car and loaded it with supplies and went up into the hills and nobody knows where he is? Does it take a genius to figure out Kelly's body was found near a road that leads from Harpersburg into our south county hills?"

"Larry, I can understand all that, but—"

"And so can Major Rice, believe me. And so all I could do was stall him for a very short time. I've got to go back at him with a third suggestion, one that he'll buy. And you know the key to the third suggestion without my telling you. The key is Meg. All that loyalty of hers is fine, but we've got to use her now, Fenn. There's two possible ways. Either you level with her and get her co-operation, or you sell her some yarn that will send her up there to find him, and we follow her in."

"I won't do that to her. You know I wouldn't do that."

"Then you have to make her co-operate."

"I don't know if I can."

"You'd have to make her see she'd be helping him, because it would give us a chance to grab him before he gets in so deep he'll be put away for life."

"If I could make her believe those people are up there with him, and his car was used in the break—yes, but she's going to think he's just up there camping out, and we're trying to frame him into this whole deal."

"Then she'd be doing him a favor by locating him for us so he can prove he had nothing to do with it."

"I can try, Larry."

"Then start trying. Start this thing rolling. And get the answer to me just as fast as you can."

We talked for a little while about what the operational plan would be, *if* she agreed. And then I went home. It was a little after five. She stared at me and pretended to feel faint, and asked me if headquarters had burned down. I tried to smile, but it was an effort. She realized something was wrong and became concerned about me.

"I have to talk to you, Meg. I have to explain a long complicated thing."

"Has something happened to Dwight!"

"No. At least not yet. But it's about Dwight."

"What are they trying to make you do to him now?"

"That's the attitude I don't want you to have, honey. I want you to please, please listen with an open mind, and ask all the questions you want to, but please try not to be —emotional about it."

"Whatever you have on your mind, that's a poor way to start, to ask me not to be emotional."

The kids were playing in the back yard. We went into the living room. I started at the beginning, making a full confession of the file I'd started on her brother, the close surveillance that neither she nor he had known anything about. She sat quietly, her face still and pale. I knew that this was the time to tell her about Cathie Perkins. I had the feeling I was throwing stones at my wife, that the words were stones and I was taking slow and careful aim. I brought the account up to date, explaining to her the attitude of Major Rice and Chief Brint.

There were evening shadows in the room when I had finished. She got up slowly and went to the mantel and moved a small blue vase to a new position. I heard her sigh. She stood there with her back to me.

"It satisfied *you*," she said. "You don't want me to be

135

emotional. You build the whole thing so it points right at Dwight."

"With all the facts, yes. The supplies he bought prove he expected guests. The plywood and two by fours and carpenter tools he bought were what he'd need to build a fake load of lumber, with the back end of it hinged.

"But you don't know it was his car, and you don't know who the woman was. All of you—all of you are so anxious to prove you're right about him, you twist everything to make it fit. I know he's wild and impulsive, and he's done bad things—but I can't seem to see him *planning* so carefully."

"Morgan Miller would be the planner."

She turned and faced me. "What makes me really sick is Cathie. Could she have been lying?"

"No."

"Then Dwight must have some kind of sickness. Those five years did something to him."

"Then help us find him, Meg."

"I don't want him beaten or hurt in any way."

"I swear we'll try to take him without any fuss. He'll be given every chance."

"What do I have to do, dear? How will it be arranged?"

"Do you think you can find out where he is?"

"Not right down to within a dozen feet, but certainly to within a mile or so. I'll ask around Laurel Valley first, and from there I might have to phone old friends in Stoney Ridge or Ironville. At first it will be sort of eliminating the areas where he's not, and then narrowing it down and finding somebody who's seen him coming or going, or seen lights at night."

"We can do it carefully now, Meg, and take the time we need to do it right, so there won't be any slips. We'll want to block every road out of the hills when you go in. And when you get it narrowed down to one small area, then you come on out and we'll move in on that area."

"I wouldn't see him?"

"Not until we've brought him out."

"It's a strange thing to—do to your brother, Fenn."

"I know."

"If you hadn't told me about Cathie I wouldn't do it. I think all this other stuff is nonsense, really. I think he'll be alone up there. But if he could do that to Cathie, and come right back here and act as if nothing had happened —then I think he needs help. I don't think he should be alone up there. Would I be able to—talk to Cathie about it?"

"I guess she'd expect me to tell you."

"Why didn't you?"

"What would it have accomplished?"

"You're a strange man, Fenn. It would have hurt me, yes. Not having you tell me hurts me too, in a different way."

"I have to call Larry."

"How many other things do you hide from me?"

"Larry will want to know right away so he can phone Rice."

On that Wednesday evening I phoned Larry. He said he knew Rice would agree that we should all plan it carefully and use maximum manpower. On Thursday we began to plan it. And it was on Thursday we made a positive identification of the woman who had been driving the station wagon. Larry had a hunch she might be Morgan Miller's woman. Trooper Golden was flown to Youngstown. He found her picture among the mug shots on file. Her name was Angela Frankel, also known as Angel France. At the time Morgan Miller had been picked up for the bank job, she was living with him. She was a young stripper. In the first few years after Miller was sent up, she got into several kinds of police trouble, extortion, badger game, drunk rolling, soliciting. Then she apparently learned how to keep her name off the blotter. For the past few years she was believed to have been operating a call-girl ring. She had left the last address they had for her, and they could get no line on her.

I went home that evening to my strangely subdued wife, who treated me as if I were a stranger she had been asked to be polite to. Just as she started to tell me she'd talked to Cathie Perkins, a phone call came for me.

"Fenn, this is Johnny. Kermer just died on the way to City Hospital."

"Who did it?"

"Relax. They say it was a heart thing. He collapsed at his own place, at the Holiday Lounge. Just keeled over."

"What a hell of a time for that to happen."

"I know. The king is dead. So who gets to be king?"

"What's the Chief's reaction?"

"I saw him for about two minutes. He's talking to himself. There's no number-two man. Kermer didn't trust anybody enough for that. Played everybody against everybody else. So somebody local is going to turn up in the saddle or we get a syndicate moving in. Either way, Larry seems to think things are going to be hard to control for a while. And it isn't going to take them long to start making their moves, and Larry says we're going to be busy people around here. Do you think McAran will be terribly disappointed?"

"I'll eat and come back down. Let me know if anything happens."

I hung up and turned toward Meg. She had her head tilted on the side and she was frowning at me. *"Every* night, darling? *Every* darn night?"

"Tonight, anyway." I told her what had happened. She couldn't understand why we expected trouble. I said, "Power keeps things in equilibrium, power exerted in several directions. Suddenly there's a vacuum, and things are going to have to rush in to fill it, and in a rush like that, things can get upset. If we just had the damn manpower, we could move in. Somebody will end up with all the marbles. If they want to be reasonable, we can eventually get back to something like the Kermer years. If they want to tough it out, we'll have a long term mess, one I might inherit from Larry."

"But you hope you can—make a deal."

"In a whipped town, honey, even vice is an essential industry. It meets its payroll and keeps the money moving and pays property taxes. Feed me, huh?"

The emergency call came just as Meg was pouring my second cup of coffee, and I had to leave it right there. I met Larry at the hospital. The coroner was already there. We went down to the morgue, and walked through to the autopsy room where Dr. Thomas Egree was standing beside Kermer's body, chatting with one of the interns. Egree is a heart specialist and one of the most well-known and important doctors in Brook City, a blond-gray man with stern gray eyes, a large lumpy nose, a face pitted with the acne scars of long ago.

He spoke to each of us in turn, "Sam, Chief Brint, Lieutenant."

Jeff Kermer was naked under the merciless glaring white of the big overhead operating light. He was blue-white, grotesquely dwindled, puddled as if the light was melting him down. The ruff of hair on his chest was white. His eyes and mouth were half-open. The left side of his chest looked mangled.

"Gentlemen, I was in the hospital when it became known they were bringing in what was presumed to be a massive coronary infarction, so I went down to emergency and made the necessary preparations. Dr. Walsh here was on duty. The patient was apparently D.O.A., with no respiration, no perceptible pulse. Dr. Walsh injected a stimulant directly into the heart muscle while I opened the rib cage to gain access so as to manually massage the heart itself. As soon as I touched the area I knew I was faced with a different problem. The pericardial sac was full of blood. I opened the sac, removed the blood and tried to find a wound in the heart wall. When the heart is not beating, this is most difficult when the perforation is small. I had ordered an immediate transfusion. I turned the heart slowly, squeezing it gently, and finally found the perforation on the underside of the left ventricle. By then there was no need to suture it because the patient was unquestionably dead. With the heart back in its normal position, I found a matching perforation in the rear of the pericardial sac."

He motioned Walsh around to the right side of the body, lifted the left arm of the corpse across the chest and said, "Dave, please pull a little, roll him just a little way over. Gentlemen, here is the primary entrance wound."

It was a very tiny, bloody mark about four inches below the bottom of the shoulder blade, and well toward the left side.

"What do you think, Sam?" Dr. Egree asked.

Our county coroner, Dr. Sam Hessian, bent and examined it at close range for what seemed a long time. When he straightened up, the intern let the body settle back into it's previous position, and put the left arm neatly back at the side.

"Clean puncture," Sam Hessian said. "Like a goddam knitting needle. Point of entry matches what you found?"

"An upward angle, assuming he was sitting or standing

erect at the time it happened. Call it about a thirty-degree angle from the horizontal."

"Lung?"

"Of course. But you've got a spongy tissue, and an extremely sharp object, so you'd almost get a self-sealing effect, much the same as you would in the pericardium. Not perfect, of course, but not enough hemorrhage or leakage to have much effect on him in the short time between when it happened and when he died. It skimmed past the aorta. It had to be sharp to slip through the gristle between the ribs. Flexible, to a certain extent. Eight to ten inches long. The same diameter for the whole length of it. I'd say the absolute maximum would be an eighth of an inch. Sam, I don't know what the autopsy ritual should be, in any legal sense. I have a perfectly straightforward cause of death here which I will certify, and I wouldn't have come across it except for the emergency measure I took."

"Nobody would have come across it," Sam Hessian said sourly. "But I better get a regular autopsy request and go through the routine."

There was a silence in the small room. I noticed that Jeff Kermer's body still wore dark silk socks and a gold wedding band. The disinfectant smell was acid-sharp in the still air. I looked at Larry Brint. He met my glance and looked away. But there had been an affirmation in that moment. This was what we were for. This was the ultimate felony.

"Just a couple questions," Larry said. His voice sounded almost bored. "Wouldn't he know he was stabbed? Wouldn't it hurt like hell? Wouldn't he yell?"

"We can assume he was drinking," Dr. Egree said. "A certain anaesthetic effect there, of course. He would appear to have been in his late fifties, overweight, with bad muscle tone. A man like that would be accustomed to pains and twinges, discomfort in the upper torso, gastric pains—some of them quite sharp. The most sensitive area would be the epidermis, but with a very sharp instrument used quickly, that would be so minor as to be barely noticeable. A good nurse can give an almost painless injection. We can assume further penetration, quickly done, would cause almost no pain at all until the heart wall itself was pierced. Then there would be growing pain and discomfort, and a feeling of breathlessness."

"How long between the time he was stabbed and when he'd pass out?" Larry asked.

Egree shrugged. "He'd start to feel extreme discomfort almost immediately. The pressure inside the heart would be pumping blood through the puncture wound in the heart wall. The pericardial sac would fill quite quickly, causing an external pressure that would severely tax the heart muscle, causing it to labor and slow down and founder. He'd feel faint, breathless, dizzy, much as if he had a small aortal rupture."

"And it would look like a heart attack, eh?" Larry said. "Doctor, would it take a lot of skill to do that?"

Egree shrugged. He clenched his fists and held them together. "Your heart is as big as this, Chief. It hangs in the middle of your chest, very slightly off center to the left. The hardest part would be sliding the weapon through the gristle between the ribs. An upward stroke through the diaphragm would be much simpler. You could hardly miss the heart once in fifty times. Usually under such circumstances the victim would remain ambulatory for from ten seconds to a full minute. He'd become comatose in a period of from thirty seconds to two and a half or three minutes. He'd be dead in from five minutes to forty minutes."

"Oh, this is so interesting," Larry said with with weary disgust. "Not more than five hundred people would like to kill him off. I think I am going to learn to miss this tiresome bastard. A heart attack would have been enough trouble. Thanks for being so thorough, Dr. Egree. Thanks a lot!"

"Happy to be of service," Egree said ironically. "Sam, when you go in there, palpitate that coronary artery. Pronounced arteriosclerosis, heavy deposits, constricted flow. He wouldn't have been with us much longer even without the—unfriendly gesture."

"He's the type," Sam said.

"So far," Larry Brint said, "are we the only ones who know it's murder?"

"Plus the emergency room nurse," Egree said. "I told her to keep it to herself. She will."

"If Division Street thinks it's a heart attack, we can get some information," Larry said. "If there's any rumor about it being a killing, we'll never find out who was with him."

And it worked as he predicted. I put Rossman and Raglin on it, and we began tapping all other sources. Kermer's manager had closed the doors of the Holiday Lounge, but the death was the big topic of conversation in all the other saloons and casinos. We soon learned a lot of people who hadn't been there were claiming they had. But we brought in a bartender who straightened it out, and it was the bartender who remembered that Kid Gilbert had been nearest to Jeff Kermer, and it had looked as if Kermer was trying to say something to the Kid.

I had him picked up and brought in, and thought it might work better if we used my office instead of an interrogation room. He walked in with Johnny Hooper, and I had Johnny close the door to the squad room.

The Kid's battered old face looked wary and curious. "What the hell, boys? What the hell?" he said in his worn whispery voice. "Sometimes I come to visit. I don't like this being brought in, you know?"

"You can't complain to Jeff about it. Not any more."

His eyes were quick and bright. "I can't think of anybody who can take over I wouldn't know pretty good."

"A heart attack is a terrible thing, isn't it?" I said.

He moistened his lips. "I never see one so close. I don't want to see no more of them, never."

"How close were you?"

"Too damn close. Like this. He was in the big bar, circulating the way he always does. You know, he gets a little bagged having a drink with this one and that one, and then he goes home. It's like his social hour. And that's when deals get made. Everybody knows it's a good time to hit him up for something. So he goes around the corner usually, into the next room there, when it's something private, a little kind of room where there's just a pay phone. He was coming from there when it hit him. I just happened to be crossing from the bar to one of the booths to talk to an old buddy when he comes walking toward me. His face was wet and shiny and sort of gray colored. He had both hands pulled tight against his chest. He was looking right at me and his jaw was going up and down like he was trying to say something, but it's noisy in there that time of night. His eyebrows were way up, making him look surprised, you know? I got to him as he started to go down, and I got just enough hold on him so I eased him down. I yelled and the place got quiet, and then some broads started screaming, and somebody was yelling to phone an ambulance. He was out cold a half a minute after I eased him down."

"Who was he talking to?" I asked. "Who did he have the private business with?"

"Oh, just some out-of-town broad. She's been around off and on the last couple weeks. Big blonde. Calls herself Nan something."

I looked at Johnny Hooper. We had the same idea at the same moment. He nodded and walked out. The Kid caught the exchange. "What's going on?"

"What kind of a deal do you think the woman was trying to make?"

"I don't get in on that end of the business."

"Would you make a guess?"

Kid Gilbert shrugged. "It would probably be some kind of woman thing. That's how she looked. Like she'd have five or six girls and got squoze out somewhere, maybe from the law or too big a cut working against her, and trying to make a deal to open up here, and she'd know she'd have to fix it with Jeffie because here you do it that way instead of greasing the law, and so it would be up to Jeffie to make the best deal he could, if he figured it wouldn't cut the take on the business he already has going for him."

Johnny Hooper came in with one of the pictures from Youngstown. "That's her?" he asked the Kid.

"Sure," he said. "The hair is different, and she's older than in the picture." He gave us his broken grin. "I answered fast, huh? So maybe I'm fingering her, and maybe I should have said I never seen her before, but Jeffie Kermer was nothing but nice to me ever since I know him, and now I got the idea it wasn't what it looked like."

"They caught it by accident at the hospital, Kid. She stuck a piece of steel into him, something thin and long, into his left side, toward the back, right up into the heart, something so small there was a good chance the wound would never be noticed."

He made his smashed hands into potato fists and looked a long way through my office wall. "I heard of it done in Boston with a piece of wire, once. Who'd she do it for?"

"Who do you think?"

"Everything else is quiet, so it would be McAran." He sighed. "And this would be just about the first chance she had, you know? The boys Jeffie brought in, they've been staying close. She had to see him three or four times before they'd pay no attention to her. She had that big straw pocketbook, big enough to hide it in. So maybe she could give him some figures to look at, showing what the take and percentages would be, and she moves a little behind him, sort of, and slips it in there fast. She came out a little behind him, smiling and talking, as if she hadn't noticed anything wrong with him. After everybody was around him, I didn't see her again. The way it is that time of night, if he yelled when she did it, nobody would have heard. You know, Lieutenant, that kind of a broad, she could do that to Jeffie, and it wouldn't be the first."

"Kid, we want her to think she got away with it. We want McAran to think she got away with it. The papers will cover it as a heart attack because they won't be told differently. If there is any leak, we'll know it came from you. And I think that with Jeff Kermer out of the way, we could make you very unhappy."

He spoke with a dignity which surprised me. "You don't have to say that to the Kid. You aren't going to make me any more unhappy than I am for Jeffie being dead. So I keep my mouth shut because you ask me to. I don't have to make myself big around this town by proving I know things other people don't. But I tell you one thing. I see that broad anywhere, and I am going to walk up to her smiling and hook her in the belly and cross the right, and you can have her from then on."

"All right, Kid. Do you know what kind of a car she was driving?"

"I never seen her outside the Holiday."

"How was she dressed?"

"Always pants and a sweater, high heels, fur cape, white gloves and a big purse, loud perfume, lots of paint, and a cigarette all the time in the corner of her mouth. No hat. What she drank—I heard her order—was vodka stingers, easy on the mint, with one rock. Deep voice for a woman. Built big but not fat, you know. As far as I could tell, she always come around alone, anxious to talk private to Jeffie. You want to kill a man like Jeffie, that's a good way. That's a real good way, goddam her." He stood up. "You don't need me any more? So I want to go by by myself. I'm going to miss him."

After he left, Johnny Hooper and I talked it over, thinking out loud.

We finally reached the conclusions which satisfied us to a certain extent. McAran had made the murder of Kermer part of the deal. Miller and the Frankel woman had joined McAran in the hills well before the jail break. And she, with the brass of the best grade of assassin, had kept coming into town until she had him set up just right, with, perhaps, a little parting message from McAran. Morgan Miller would be inclined to humor McAran in this matter because it would create internal confusions which would put a lot more strain on our resources of manpower and vehicles, and thus give their main project a better chance of succeeding. There would be a minimum of two cars, four men and one woman up in McAran's hide-out, but we could not overlook the possibility that Miller might have brought in some additional talent.

Johnny Hooper said, "Fenn, they've had a lot of time to plan something big, and they've had the money stashed to finance it. It could be a hell of a lot more ambitious than we figure. By now they'll be sold on their own luck. The only thing that's gone wrong for them has been Kelly getting hit. They may have the idea of cleaning out this whole town, of hitting us wherever the money is. You ask me, I'm damn glad Meg is going to be the bird dog. I just think it ought to be scheduled sooner than Sunday."

"You heard Major Rice. By Sunday we'll have it set up so nothing can go wrong. And all the week-end traffic of people coming back out of the hill country will cover us on moving into position. And on Sunday we can cover Meg with unmarked cars without making anybody suspicious. And we do have a hint on their timing, based on what McAran told the Perkins girl."

But we both knew, as did Larry Brint and Major Rice, that we weren't dealing with people whose mental processes we could predict. They had somehow reached into a maximum security prison and released their friends and helpers. None of them had anything to lose, and they were motivated by something beyond greed. They were riding

145

on the conviction of infallibility, ignoring the fact they could win in no final way, but were capable of attaining many more small bloody victories before the inevitable destruction.

xi

BY Saturday night, when I got home at nine o'clock, everything was properly set up for the next day. The weather forecast was good, and it promised to be one of those hot still days which would send the valley people up into the hills. Detective Chuck West's wife was going to stop by early Sunday morning and take our kids off our hands.

A joint operation was set up which we believed would cover every possibility. Sheriff Bub Fischer and his inept cronies had been quietly given leaves of absence, and one of the truly professional Sheriffs in the state, D. D. Wheeler, had been brought in from a neighboring county along with some of his top people. Major Rice had brought in a special cadre of troopers. Larry Brint had detailed our best men to it. The communications people had tied the three separate radio links into a single control system.

Not only had we brought in all the special equipment we thought we might need, but we also had a light plane standing by at the Brook City Airport equipped with a big photo reconn camera and Air Reserve technical personnel to operate it. And by a combination of good luck and savage threats, we had managed to keep the lid on any news leaks.

Without making any fuss about it, and by picking the right places for a continuing observation, we had every road out of the hills watched for the sudden appearance of the station wagon. Under D. D. Wheeler's direction, the hill area had been divided into six basic areas, so that once we knew which area we would be concerned with, we knew in advance the best way to move our people in, the best routes whereby we could escape observation, and the best places to use as observation points when we brought the patrol cars in to seal a much more restricted area.

I took one of the master maps with the overlay home with me and spread it out on the kitchen table and explained it in detail to Meg, using pennies and sugar cubes to show where the cars would be.

"You'll take off in our car at ten tomorrow morning, honey," I told her. "We'll have some unmarked cars up in there, and they'll look like people on picnics and Sunday rides. You don't have to know who they are. When you've gotten it pinned down, and you know just about where Dwight is, you come back out. Come out on 882 as far as that picnic place just this side of the bridge. I'll be parked there, ready to get the message back up to the unmarked cars."

"And what will they do?"

"They'll have their picnics at just the right places so nobody can leave whatever area you name without being noticed—if they leave by car. After dark we'll be set to move in close, and go the rest of the way at dawn."

"It's a big game, isn't it? A wonderful game of hunting. Guns and tear gas and even an airplane to take pictures."

"It isn't a game."

"Why do you have to make such a big thing out of it?"

"It's good police procedure, honey. It keeps people from getting hurt."

"Even Dwight?"

"Yes, dear.

I woke up on Sunday in the first gray light of dawn, not knowing what had awakened me. I was surprised to see that Meg was already up. I put on my robe and went looking for her. The kitchen light was on. There was a note to me on the kitchen table. Before I read it I ran out and saw that our car was gone. I hurried back in and read her note.

"Dearest Fenn, I couldn't sleep at all because I know that what I promised you is not right. I am afraid that you would have to kill him if it is done your way. Even if he is all alone, and knows nothing about the others you think are with him, it would fill him with a crazy, reckless anger to have people sneaking up on him before dawn. And I can't be sure that with so many people, someone might be too tense and shoot too quickly. For a lot of the years of my life I took care of him, and no matter what he is or what he has become, I would not want to live with knowing he died because I found out where he is and told people who think he is some sort of a monster. I am not especially brave, but I want to find him and go to him, so that if everything is all right with him, I can perhaps talk him into coming back out with me, so that nothing will have a chance to go wrong. I can't forget the look in Cathie's eyes when she told me she wishes him dead. Maybe he never did have enough of a chance with anything he ever wanted or tried to do, but I want to ask him about Cathie. I do not think he would ever hurt me, and if there are other people there, the ones from the prison, I don't think he would let them hurt me. I will try to come back out once I have talked to him, but I know there is the chance he or they won't let me leave. I won't tell him or anyone else what is being planned if they don't let me go, and once I have found out just about where to look for him, I will leave word with an old man named Jaimie Lincoln who lives on the Chickenhawk Road. If he's still living, he'll still be there, and if he isn't, I'll leave some sort of note for you. I am sorry if my doing it this way is going to spoil all the plans which have been made, and make people angry at you. But sometimes a person has to do things their own way. I will be careful, and you be too. I love you. Meg."

I raced to the phone. Raglin was on the desk. I told him to relay the word to Wheeler, Brint and Rice as fast as he could, and have somebody come pick me up right away, and have Mrs. West come get the kids.

By the time I got to headquarters D. D. Wheeler and Larry Brint were there, and Rice was on the way. They read the note simultaneously, Larry reading over Wheeler's shoulder.

Wheeler said in a tired, cold voice, "I knew something would go sour. I knew there'd be some damn fool complication. She got a hell of a start on us. But there's no need of letting her commit suicide. All we can do now is try our damnedest to pick her up before she disappears, and pray it takes her a long time to get a line on where they're hid out. Larry, let's get the description of her and the car to all points up there, and anybody you think might help. Damn fool woman! Hillyer, I wish you hadn't slept so heavy. Where's the map? Where's Chickenhawk, for God's sake? Get those unmarked cars bracketing that Chickenhawk Road, because from the note it sounds like that's the place she'll go last before she goes to see her brother."

"How about the airplane?" Larry asked.

"Hell, let's use that too." He turned to me. "Probably, if we miss her, that old man won't give a message to anybody but you, so soon as we get this organized, you and me are going in an unmarked car and find that old boy."

We left a half-hour later in a green sedan equipped with a short wave set. I drove. If Meg was picked up, they were going to alert us immediately.

The sun was up and beginning to be hot as I made the turn off Route 60 onto 882 and we started climbing. Wheeler didn't look like a Sheriff. He looked like those men who run carnival concessions, sallow, drab, cynical and tough, a sharp-eyed loner, with no fund of small talk.

The map indicated no good way to get to the obscure Chickenhawk Road. We had to go all the way to Laurel Valley, and then cut back on the old Laurel Valley to Ironville Road, potholed macadam, with blind unbanked corners, where the old hills closed in close around us.

"Rugged," D. D. Wheeler said.

"There's worse places. I used to drive back in here with Meg. There's some clay roads back in here that are passable only four or five months of the year." I remembered the secret valleys she had shown me, gloomy except at midday, the icy ponds, the black pine shadows, the jumbees of old gray boulders loking like the ruins of temples built before man walked the earth.

"Damn radio is bad," D. D. Wheeler said.

"The iron in these hills does it."

I drove as fast as I dared, yelping the tires, banging the shocks against the frame. He counted the dirt roads that branched off to the right, and we stopped at the fourth one. I saw a shack down on a creek bank, through the trees. I left Wheeler in the car and walked down to the shack, remembering everything Meg had told me about how best to approach her people. I made myself stroll. An enormously fat woman sat on a shallow open porch. A hound raised its head and made a low warning sound in its throat, audible above the spring clamor of the creek.

I stopped ten feet from the porch and said it was a fine

day. She nodded. The hound watched me. I said I was a stranger in these parts, and I was sorry to trouble her, but could she tell me if that dirt road there might lead to a place called Chickenhawk.

She hawked and spat and said, "It be."

"Does a man named Jaimie Lincoln live along that road?"

"I wouldn't be sayin'."

"I drove along that road a long time ago with my wife. I remember it was over ten miles to Chickenhawk and then about another twenty miles down out of the hills until we came out on the paved road from Slater to Amberton, east of the hills. I remember her pointing out where old Jaimie lived, but I can't remember where it was."

"She be knowing him?"

"From when she was a little girl, living over in Keepsafe."

"They be nobody to Keepsafe now, it being half-burnt out, and then the bridge gone and the road washed, all long ago. What was her name?"

"She's a McAran."

"They be a lot of them long long ago, sinners most all of them, but Jaimie's Ma was a third way cousin to some McArans, so she could be knowing him."

"I'd appreciate it if you'd tell me how to find Mr. Lincoln."

"What you be wanting of him?"

"A family matter. I can swear he'd like you to tell me."

She thought it over, spat again and said, "Go most of seven mile, you come to a hollow where the road winds north, and where it turns sharpest, is a path going south, where you walk in."

Wheeler was surprisingly patient with the time it had taken. The fresh spring grasses grew high in the middle of the dirt track to Chickenhawk, and he pointed to places where the grass was bruised and smeared with grease, and said, "Nice to know somebody used it since the Civil War."

Again I left him at the car, and I walked the path to Jaimie Lincoln's shack. When the path curved and I saw it in a small clearing, I stopped and called, "Mr. Lincoln! Mr. Lincoln!"

"Lord God!" a quavering voice said so close behind me I gave a great start of surprise. I whirled and looked at

151

an old, old man, as brittle, spare and dusty looking as a dried grasshopper. He stared at me with disgust. "You come through there like a bear wearing wooden shoes. She described you better looking than you be, but it must be you on account she said you got a long mournful face like a circuit preacher."

"She was here?"

He gave me a pitying look, stood an old Remington bolt action against a tree, shoved a shapeless old brown felt hat onto the back of his head and wiped his face with a faded bandanna. "Who the Lord Jesus am I talking of? Here well past an hour back, big handsome woman with tearful eyes, almost pretty as her ma, who died younger, and too rushed to set polite with an old man, but she says to tell you of a time a road was growed up with brush so she couldn't take you to see things she'd told you of."

"I see."

A cackle of frail laughter doubled him over. "Now look at you with a big secret like she thought she had, fooling an old man. Wanted to take you that old back way to Keepsafe, did she? Over the log road. She could have come to old Jaimie first, saving miles and questions. Old but I ain't deaf, and when I got twenty years of traffic roaring up and down in two weeks, I'm not just going to set here and wonder what the hell it is now am I? Just two miles more, and it goes off to the left, cleared careful so not to show much from the Chickenhawk Road, but cleared careless once you get back in. I circled over and clumb Fall Hill on a still night a time back and I see the auto lamps winding slow through all those woods, showing now and again like a fire beetle in the summer, the motor grinding slow until the sound was too far from my ears, and then coming out way over there just this side of Burden Mountain, onto the old-time road that was the way to get into Keepsafe afore the bridge was took out. Miss Meg looking for strangers, all she had to do was come right to Jaimie Lincoln, and I could even told her—which she didn't say no word to me about—one of them is maybe that mean son of a bitch half-brother of hers, the one stomped the face about clean off the middle Jorgen boy twelve, fourteen year ago, on account of a week ago yesterday I walked into Chickenhawk for salt and tobacco, and Bone Archer mentioned him, and his brother been over there to take a look in case it was the alcohol tax folks and said it was a McAran, of about the age to be the mean one come back from State Prison, camping in there with a bald city man and a big tit city woman. The way I see it—"

"Mr. Lincoln, I've got to go."

"Nobody has time to set polite, and there's no respect for age any more, and so many folks roaring up and down the Chickenhawk Road, I swear to God I'm moving clear over the other side of Fall Hill, this keeps up."

"Thanks a lot, Mr. Lincoln."

"Come back with Miss Meg when you can set, and if you want to just run through my dooryard, the two of you, like stung-up hounds, don't bother coming back."

I ran all the way back to the car. As I drove another two miles toward Chickenhawk, I told D. D. Wheeler what I'd learned from the old man. I watched the shoulder on the left and when I saw where cars had turned off I started to pull over. "Keep going!" Wheeler ordered.

"But I tell you she—"

"Keep moving! Can't you follow a direct order?"

I drove on. We went through the hamlet of Chickenhawk. Four miles beyond Chickenhawk, the road hairpinned down a steep slope, and when we were on the floor of a narrow valley, he had me pull over as far as I could and park.

"Brint kept telling me you're a smart officer."

"My wife is back there, Sheriff."

"Look at this map. Here's this cow path we're on. About here is where that logging road cuts off of it. Over here is where Keepsafe used to be, and it's high ground, and it's less than a mile from there to the top of Burden Mountain, which reads forty-four hundred feet high. There were some gaps where I got a look at it, and it looks pretty bare on top, like it was mostly rock. I looked over your list of the stuff McAran bought. There's binoculars on that list. That damn mountain looks down on every little road in the area."

I swallowed and said humbly, "Meg has told me about a trail to the top of the mountain. Look, we could go back on foot, maybe."

"Just the two of us? Real heroes? Sneak up on 'em and rescue the woman?"

"She's my wife!"

"She's a cop's wife, and you're a cop. Because she's been a damn fool is no reason for you to turn yourself into one, Hillyer. She found her brother and his friends over an hour ago. If she's alive right now, she'll probably be alive at dawn. If she's dead, they may stay there and they may try to move out, depending on how nervous it made them to have somebody dropping in. One thing sure, they won't let her go, because she saw too much in the first sixty seconds. I'll bet they knew a car was on its way in from the minute she turned in there. So get me some place where this damn radio will work, and we'll do all we can do with the idea they are looking down our throats every minute."

Three miles beyond the valley, when we came to a ridge that could not be seen from the crest of Burden Mountain, D. D. Wheeler had me stop. They couldn't hear distinctly enough in Brook City, so Wheeler used the State Police setup at the Slater Barracks as a relay.

He gave them the map co-ordinates for the aerial photography. He told them where to post four unmarked cars. He said we were coming in, the long way around, and to pull everything else out of the hills.

"She wouldn't be in this at all if I hadn't let Chief Brint talk me into it," I said.

"She wouldn't be in this at all if you hadn't taken up police work. She wouldn't be in it if the two of you had never met. None of us would be going to all this fuss if he hadn't hit the Hanaman girl too hard. If I had two heads I'd be living in a jug in a side show."

"All I meant was—"

"Shut up and let me do some thinking. We can't go in there the way I wanted to. We got to go in there like climbing a glass ladder barefooted."

"If they don't try to move out first."

"I don't think they will, somehow. Everything has been working for them. Your wife said in that note she won't tell them. And she sounds like a strong woman. She knows it's set up for dawn. Maybe she'll have a chance to move fast when we give those people the message. You see, Hillyer, people like Miller, Deitwaller and Kostinak have to get hit with a great big dose of helplessness. Right in that first tenth of a second is when you get your chance

154

to take them easy, when all of a sudden they feel as exposed as a bug in a bathtub, with nothing to hit back at. Every time a holed-up man kills a law man, it makes me feel sick at my stomach because it's never necessary. It comes about through a childish display of guts, or because somebody gets bored and careless. This thing is going to be run right."

And when we got back, they had a dirty surprise waiting for us. Rossman and Raglin had conducted the investigation, and Rossman repeated his verbal report for the information of D. D. Wheeler and myself.

"At ten this morning Mr. Theodore Perkins reported his daughter Catherine missing. He said her bed hadn't been slept in. He thought she was sleeping late because he thought she had probably gotten in late last night after he was asleep. Detective Raglin and I made the investigation. She had gone to the movies last night with a girl friend. We checked that out. They got on a bus downtown at about quarter of eleven. The Perkins girl got off the bus first. As the bus started up, the other girl saw the Perkins girl start to walk toward her home two blocks away, and saw a car which had evidently been following the bus pull up and stop, and saw the Perkins girl start over toward the car. She says it was a new-looking car, a sedan, possibly a Ford, gray or light blue, and then the bus was out of sight. Mr. Perkins said there was a phone call for his daughter at about nine o'clock, a call from a woman who did not give her name. He said he told her what movie the girl had gone to. We checked the houses in the vicinity of where the car had stopped. A man in the second house from the corner on the other side was letting his cat out at about five after eleven when he heard what he thought was a drunken argument. He heard a scream and a scuffling sound, and heard a man curse somebody. Then a car door was slammed and he saw the car drive away at a high rate of speed."

I explained the relationship between McAran and the Perkins girl to D. D. Wheeler. He cursed softly, steadily, thoroughly.

"Mr. Perkins said the woman on the phone sounded sort of tough," Rossman added.

"It doesn't make a hell of a lot of sense," Larry said.

"There's one way it makes sense," Johnny Hooper said

softly. "Suppose McAran told Miller he'd decided to send for the Perkins girl after the job was finished. If Miller didn't like the idea, and didn't trust the girl from what McAran told him about her, and couldn't talk McAran out of it, he could send McAran and the Frankel woman down into the town here to pick her up and take her back where Miller could check her out. Wasn't it a woman who got him messed up last time? And probably the Frankel woman has had some practice on picking a girl off the street like that."

"So we've got two of them up there," D. D. Wheeler said wonderingly.

"Why didn't they make it real easy for us?" Larry grumbled. "Why didn't they hole up in a kindergarten?"

"We've got work to do," Major Rice said firmly.

xii

MY wife didn't come down out of the hills and I knew she wouldn't. I knew when I read her note we wouldn't stop her, and she wouldn't come back out. I phoned Fran West and asked her to keep the kids another night. She sounded slightly teary, so I knew Chuck had told her about Meg.

All during the afternoon the news people kept moving in on us in ever increasing numbers. We no longer had anything to fear from newspaper coverage, but we knew that any leak over commercial radio might blow the whole thing. We had to settle for an off-the-record briefing, telling them that Meg's life might depend on silence.

When dusk came I could no longer sustain the sharp edge of my concern for Meg. I felt numbed and lost, as if I would never be able to feel anything very acutely again. I had the feeling that none of this was real.

After dusk the command staff moved five patrol cars into position, five two-man teams, and the unmarked cars were pulled down out of the hills. Two teams took their positions right at the mouth of the old logging road, after some difficulty in finding it. They reported back that the road had been recently cleared, that trees over ten feet tall which had grown up in the middle of the road had been hacked down and pulled out of the way. They examined the tracks with a hooded light and reported that it was so narrow Meg had obliterated previous tracks as she drove in, but it looked as if at least two other cars had used it recently, one of them leaving the distinctive tread marks of the new tires McAran had purchased.

They drove one car into the road, without lights, and parked it just short of the first sharp curve. They took up positions on both sides of the logging road and rigged a stationary flare which could be activated with a pull wire and made themselves comfortable for a long wait. The other cars were spotted to cover any alternate exits we might not know about, spotted on the roads those exits would have to feed into. We got the aerials at 8 P.M., fresh from processing. The superb lens and the very fine grain of the film provided incredibly clear enlargements of the whole Keepsafe area. Looking at them was like being suspended a hundred feet in the air over the little plateau where the hamlet had once been.

There had once been, as Meg had told me, a general store, a small church, a one-room schoolhouse and four homes in the village itself. The store, the church and one of the homes had been destroyed in the same fire. You couldn't tell what they had been. The rectangles marking the foundations were obscured by weeds and alders and berry bushes. Of the remaining houses, one had collapsed into an overgrown clutter of weathered boards. Another sagged on the edge of collapse. There were some rickety barns and sheds standing. But it looked abandoned for ten generations rather than only twenty years. It drowsed by a weedy road. Some big trees shaded the unused yards. There had been about a hundred acres of open fields around it. This land was thick with alder, scrub maple, young evergreen and berry patches. The plateau was tilted slightly to the south. To the north was the mass of Burden Mountain. At the south the land dropped steeply into a wooded valley. There was forest to the east and west of the cleared area. The photo technicians had pieced the enlargements together, so that the picture of the area was one huge photograph, six feet by four feet, but hinged by the tape on the back so that specific areas could be examined conveniently.

"Here's the fresh tire tracks coming out of these woods here at the west," Major Rice said. "They turn onto the road and come right up here. No mystery about what building they're using. These marks are where they've made paths through the tall grass, going over to this creek on the north. The cars are in this shed, from the way the tracks go. Here's footprints in the mud by the creek. Here's where they've fixed fires. No washing hanging out and no cans and bottles thrown around, and nobody outside, so they think they're being careful, but they might have just as well have written their names on the roof. This house is the center point of every pattern of tracks."

"Can we safely assume they're still holed up in that house?" Wheeler asked.

"Why would they move? I don't think the plane would spook them. If having the woman arrive gave them the jumps, they wouldn't set up a new place right in the same area. They might take off in the night for a new spot a dozen miles away. We're ready for that, if they go by car. But I say they'll stay put. They're confident. They wouldn't have picked up the Perkins girl if they weren't. Maybe having the Lieutenant's wife arrive this morning upset them a little, but McAran would know—and be able to convince the others—that she would be able to find them a lot easier than anybody else could. But let's not ignore the most important clue we have, gentlemen. They must be ready to make their move, otherwise they wouldn't risk detaining Mrs. Hillyer, or risk kidnapping the Perkins girl. Perhaps they even wanted the Perkins girl as a hostage in case something went wrong with the job they're planning. Now they have two."

After a few seconds of silence, Wheeler said, "Let's figure the positions for our three groups on the map. Three groups of ten."

"I want to be with the group you can spot closest to the house," I said.

As both Wheeler and Rick looked at me dubiously, Larry Brint said, "Fenn has earned that much, and it will be a good place for him to be. He'll do as he's told. And he has more reason than any of us to see it work out just right."

At midnight I avoided the night watch of reporters by going down the back stairs and out a side door onto the dark grounds behind City Hall. I walked through the deep shadows and sat on the base of the World War I monument. I lit a cigarette and looked toward the invisible hills, remembering how the top of Burden Mountain had looked in the midday sunlight.

I remembered Meg telling me, "There was a path up Burden Mountain, and I used to climb up there all by myself on clear summer days. There was always a smoky haze over Brook City. I knew it was the highest place in the world. Sometimes I could look down on the hawks flying. I used to pretend things, all those shiny and wonderful things, all the kings and castles little girls pretend. I kept a secret treasure back under the twisty old roots of a pine that grew out of the rocks. I kept it in a little square tin box—a Chinese coin with a hole in it, a real sea shell, a piece of red silk ribbon and a button with a green stone in it. I was certain the stone was an emerald. For a while I kept a note in there. I had printed it. All it said was 'I love you.' It wasn't written to anybody, and it wasn't supposed to be something written to me. It was just something to put in a treasure box. When I left, there wasn't time to get it. It's still there, I guess. Sometimes I remember it. Some day I'll go back and get it."

"Alone?" I had asked.

"You may come with me."

Suddenly a voice startled me. "Busy day, Fenn?"

I turned sharply and saw Stu Dockerty outlined against the lighted windows of the police wing. "No comment. Orders from on high. No comment about anything."

"I filed the last ounce of crud in person, and I was strolling back and saw your face when you lit the cigarette, Fenn." He sat beside me on the weathered black marble, and leaned back, as I was, against the chiseled names of the long dead. "As soon as they've aged a little, all wars are alike."

"What? Oh, I guess so."

"Romantic, gallant, kinda quaint."

"I suppose so."

"None of those guys had any personal problems you or I couldn't recognize in a minute, Fenn. The world changes, but everything stays just the same as it ever was."

"Tell me what my problem is, Doctor."

"Was I making it that obvious? I'm losing my touch. Your problem, my dear Lieutenant, is being afraid of warmth. I think you have some, but you've stowed it too deep. You refuse to trust emotions. You try to believe you can live in a rational world. You seem to think warmth is weakness, my friend. It makes you a bit of a prig. It starves your wife of her proper due, and it isolates you from your kids. And somehow I don't think it makes you any better in your job."

"Everybody seems to be judging me lately. You know, it might not do much good. I might have nobody left to apologize to."

"Pathos, eh? What froze you, Fenn? Your tragic youth?"

"There's nothing tragic about the way I grew up. It was a very ordinary situation. Very trite."

"No drama at all?"

"My father was a mill worker. You know that. My mother's people thought she'd married beneath her. But she was very happy. She laughed and sang all day long. She was a very emotional woman, Stu. She could cry at card tricks, like they say. She made everything seem—like wonderful games and adventures."

"Until?"

"Those things end."

"How did it end in your house?"

"I guess she sort of became the victim of one of her own games and adventures. Maybe things got a little dull for her. I don't know what happened. She didn't want to stay with us any more. She fell in love with a neighbor, a widower five years younger than she was. My father wouldn't agree to divorce. She stayed with us for a whole sorry year, and then went off with him to Cleveland. They both died in a fire. An apartment house fire. It killed a lot of other people too. I was fourteen when it happened. My brother was sixteen. He left a year later. Just took off. When I was seventeen my father had a stroke. There was a little money coming in. Insurance, compensation. I took care of him. Neighbors helped. He lived two more years. A woman in Oregon wrote about my brother. He died of flu in a lumber camp."

"Just an ordinary situation?" Dockerty said gently.

"Isn't it?"

"Meg knows all this, of course."

I do not talk to people about my life. Not to people like Dockerty. It isn't anybody's business. I don't need sympathy, praise, blame or participation. But it was a quiet night, warm in the valley, cool in the hills. And I had been numbed by what was happening to me. It did not seem so important *not* to talk.

"Amateur psychology," he said, "is an easy way for a man to feel superior to his friends. A million years ago, I suppose, some joker sat in his cave in the evening and told his friends why their luck in the hunt was so bad— a little carelessness about wind direction, and a badly balanced spear, and the wrong shape on the arrow heads."

"Go ahead with it, if you have to."

"Fenn, you had all that warmth and love, and you believed it was real. Then you decided it had all been faked, so you've never really trusted it—in yourself or anybody else, ever since."

"She left, didn't she?"

"Do you think about her much? Do you try to remember?"

"I remember how it was after she left."

"Remember the good part of it. She wasn't faking."

I didn't know what he was talking about. It had no application to me. It was meaningless talk. Meddling. Suddenly the tears were running out of my eyes, running down my face. I could not understand why it was happening. I felt a sob building up in my throat, threatening to burst out in a hard ugly sound, so I stood up quickly and coughed, and kept my face turned from the faint light. When I knew I could trust my voice I said, "I've got to go back in. We've got to brief the men we're taking up there."

"I'll be going along. Not all the way. Me and the big media boys, we'll watch you go in and wait for you to come out. They'll have the mountains wired for wide screen, and I'll keep out of their way, clutching my slate and nibbling my stylus. Be lucky, Fenn."

"That's about all I can ask for, isn't it?"

I was with Rice's group, attached but not in the chain of command. We sat near the black bulk of the truck parked next to the grassy ditch on the Chickenhawk Road. I sat a little apart from Rice's troopers, and we waited for the first light of Monday. They talked in low tones, cupped the glow of cigarettes in big hands.

A big man was saying, "This time of the night was when we'd be heading on back, so we'd come home just at first light. No eager patrols in our outfit, man. We didn't want to fuss with anybody, or go no further than we had to. We wanted to get out and get back alive. One time a gook patrol came within twenty feet of where—"

"Let's roll it," Major Rice said from the darkness.

I looked up, and I could just make out the treetops against the sky, even though it seemed as dark as ever. D. D. Wheeler took his people into the black mouth of the logging road first. Larry Brint had decided he couldn't

162

maintain the pace that would be required, so one of Wheeler's deputies took the second group. The troopers were the third and last group.

We had estimated the distance at four miles. There was a lot of blundering for the first mile, too much stumbling and falling, too much crashing into the brush where the road curved unexpectedly. The sound of vehicles would have carried too far in the night silence of the hills, and it would have been impossible to travel without lights. The stub of a hacked branch gouged my cheek painfully. Twice I stumbled and went down to one knee.

But after the first mile enough of a faint grayness came through the leaves to enable everyone to keep visual contact with the man ahead of him, and the going was easier.

Just before we came to the place where the logging road came out of the woods to join the old road to Keepsafe, we came upon my car. It is an odd and eerie thing to come across an object so familiar under such circumstances. Meg had driven it to this place in the brightness of the afternoon, and had been stopped by a long sapling trunk which had been wedged across the road from crotch to crotch at waist height.

We all edged by the car, stooped under the barricade and soon came to the edge of the woods, where Rice halted the group. Visibility was less than a hundred feet, looking out into the open. There was a perceptible pallor in the eastern sky. Scrub maple rose out of the ground mist in black silhouette, in a still and windless morning. The birds were making their first sounds. I heard the thin howl of a farm dog from beyond some other ridge. The four legged hunting things were going to ground, and the two legged hunting things had begun their work. Rice gave the first two groups their allotted five-minute lead. The hunt appeals to an area which lies below the heart of man. And man himself provides the most meaningful game. The flavor of the group was holiday, with a checking of weapons, hitch of belt, retying of shoes.

The first group had gone to the left, the second to the right.

"Okay," Rice said, and we headed out, crossing the old road, moving into the fields where fencing had rusted away, turning right a hundred feet beyond the road and moving

163

parallel to it, with about a ten-foot spacing. I was fourth in line, counting Rice.

It seemed to be growing light too quickly. Pallor in the east had a golden tinge. The trees were ceasing to be silhouettes as the leaves began to have definition. We went at a fast walk for a few hundred yards. The heavy dew in the tall grass soaked the legs of our trousers.

We swung away from the road, were slowed by hand signals, went at a crouch for a time, keeping out of sight of the house behind a half-acre tangle of raspberry thicket. From that point we crawled on our bellies through the wet grass, avoiding the nettles which had grown rankly in the old pasture, moving slowly, maintaining the interval. We stopped, and Rice came worming his way back. He changed the spacing slightly, and sent us, one at a time, at a right angle toward the house.

I moved cautiously, as ordered. Soon I could see the roof peak above the fringe of the tall grass directly in front of me. It was a dark gray triangle against the paler gray of the morning sky. I kept as flat as I could and moved forward. Off to my right, ten feet away, something bulked taller than the grass. I angled toward it, and found it was the wheel-less moldering carcass of an old farm wagon. It helped me orient myself more precisely. It had showed clearly on the aerial photographs, and was approximately eighty feet from the rear of the house, almost in line with the rear porch. Vines grew on it and the grass was rank around it. I moved to the far end of it and looked cautiously around it. I could see the house clearly through a curtain of grass, see the tumbled stoop, with the half-collapsed roof sagging over it, see the rear door, two ground floor windows and two upstairs windows.

I pulled back and looked toward the eastern sky at my left. It was streaked with lemon and rose and, above that colorful area, the sky was changing from gray to a pale clear blue. I closed my eyes and listened. I could hear the increasing clamor of the birds. I heard a thin remote droning and it took me a moment to identify it as the sound of a truck a long way away, going down a long grade in low gear. I could hear no other sound, but I knew there were men on either side of me, advancing to the closest protected positions they could find, using every advantage of terrain and cover. Wheeler's men would be in position on the east and south, covering the house, but not from the closeness we could achieve. The third group was on the south and west.

I rolled onto my side and hitched the holster around to where I could conveniently unbutton it and take out the hand gun I had chosen to bring along. It is not a duty gun. It is too bulky and unwieldy for such use. It is a thirty-eight caliber Colt revolver with an eight-inch barrel, heavy frame, custom grip to fit my oversized hand. As a confirmed gun nut I know it is a theatrical-looking weapon, but I have done so much competition shooting with it, I have replaced the barrel twice. It fits my hand. More than any other weapon I own, I have little sense of aiming it. The slug seems to go where I will it to go, with the little jolt of recoil coming as a surprise. I eased the hammer back to full cock. The acid sweet scent of gun oil mingled with the ripe smell of the spring grass. I moved back to where I could see the house. I hitched a little further and found I could see into the shed on the east side of the house. McAran's wagon was there, with its apparent load of lumber intact. It was headed out. Beside it, also headed out, was a gray Ford sedan, a new-looking car. As I was trying to make out the license on the Ford, I saw movement beyond the shed.

I moved slightly to cover it, and saw it was one of the troopers snaking his way through the grass. He disappeared beyond the edge of the shed and then I saw vague movement inside the semi-open shed, and knew he had gotten in with the cars. It made good sense. He could silently disable them and take his position there, ready to ambush anybody who tried to get to them.

The edge of the sun appeared, and all the gray went out of the morning. The long morning shadows appeared, and exposed places were touched with that silvery-white glare which announces a hot day. Down in the valley the light would be more golden, more diffused.

I had a strange vision of what would happen down in the valley. Fenn Hillyer and his wife were asleep down there, in the big double bed, with her arm across his waist. In a little while the neighborhood sounds would begin. She would get up and stand at the window and look at the morning. He would awaken when he heard the running of water in the bathroom. He would hear her get the children up for school, and hear her humming to herself in the kitchen.

That was reality. This dawn vigil was absurdity. My Meg could not be in that silent crumbling house, with men as dangerous as men can become.

Keepsafe drowsed as the sun climbed. The mist was burned away. Heat brought the insect songs. A hawk drifted, turning his head from side to side, his mind on a breakfast mouse.

The back door opened suddenly, noisily, and a man came out onto the back stoop. I recognized him from the mug shots we had studied. George Kostinak. He was a stocky blond man. He wore denim work pants. He was bare to the waist. His chest and shoulders were matted with pale hair. Where the skin was exposed, his meaty torso was sunburned a painful-looking red.

His vocalized an enormous yawn, scrubbed his head with his knuckles, then shuddered and hugged himself and squinted toward the morning sun. He jumped down over the broken steps, walked about six feet, then stood spraddled and urinated onto the baked poisoned dirt of the dooryard.

Just as he finished, a big, strong-bodied blonde woman came through the door he had left open. She wore a bulky sweater in a bright cheap shade of blue and tight lime-green slacks. Though her hair was tangled and her face, without make-up, had a doughy look, there was a vitality about her which made her curiously attractive. She had the purposeful, controlled arrogance of one of the big jungle cats. She exuded competence, recklessness and danger.

"I told you to go further from the house, George," she said. She held a toothbrush, toothpaste and a paper cup of water.

"You told me. Sure, Angie. You told me. But we aren't living here forever."

"Once a pig always a pig."

He laughed at her. "Who's calling who a pig, honey?"

She stepped down off the stoop. She looked at him in a deadly way. "You just took yourself off the list, friend."

"Now Angie," he said, with a wheedling note in his voice. "Now Angie, I was just kidding around. That's all it was."

"Two more broads around and all of a sudden I don't look so good?"

"I didn't mean anything like that."

"You got the happy idea you're going to get a chance at either one of them?"

"That's hard to say."

She stared at him with contempt. "George, you're a dreamer. How come it's always slobs like you think you're great lovers?"

"Aw, Angie, damn it, I was just—"

"Poor George. Poor ugly George." She turned away from him, spread toothpaste on her brush and began brushing her teeth vigorously. I felt a hard knotted something in my chest unwind slightly. Meg was alive. She was in that house, alive.

Kostinak moved closer to her. They spoke to each other in low tones. I could not hear what they were saying. Kostinak looked warily toward the house and took her by the arm and led her away from the house, directly toward me. I wished I could melt into the ground. They stopped not more than a dozen feet away from me.

"Morg is running it, isn't he?" Angela Frankel said. "You got complaints, you talk to Morg."

"All I'm saying, honey, and I'm saying it to you, not to Morg, everything was fine until Saturday night. Everything was fine until you and McAran brought that girl up here."

"You worry too much, George. You had the big argument about Kermer. That worked out, didn't it?"

"Okay. Yes, it worked out. And it was a promise Morg made to Dwight. But that was sort of part of it. But now we're getting too far away from how we had it all worked out. Frank Kelly is dead. And you were going to be the only woman here. Nobody figured on three. And we're moving faster than we figured. You and Herm and Morg, my God, you act as if everything is just fine, but I got the feeling everything is going to hell."

"Maybe you're too nervous for this kind of work."

"Doesn't it bother you at all, a cop's wife showing up?"

"Nothing bothers me, George."

"If she found us so easy—"

"We'll be gone before anybody else does. Long gone."

"Sure, Angie, but gone where? There's going to be too

much heat. I don't see why you and Morg don't understand that. Too many people know too damn much about it. They can tie you into it after they talk to the women."

To my relief they had turned so they were facing the house.

"Do you think Morg is losing his touch?" she asked with a strange note of insistence in her voice. "Do you think he's going to leave a lot of loose ends?"

"What do you mean?"

"I could tell you some things you don't know, Georgie. They might make you feel better."

"What things?"

"McAran was wrong about the Perkins girl."

"He sure as hell was!"

"Morg has changed his mind about McAran, George."

"But—we need him. The way it's laid out, we need him."

"But how long do we need him?"

"Oh."

"You were going to find out later on, after we split the take at the motel. That's where they'll find McAran, like he died in his sleep, with the station wagon parked outside the door. So there'll be no nonsense about sending any postcard to the husband of that Meg, about where to find his tied-up wife."

"Do it to McAran like you done it to Kermer?"

Her voice deepened. "With the little meat skewer, Georgie. That Kermer gave one little yip when it slid into him, and turned on me with the color going out of his face, and I said, 'McAran says hello,' and he turned like he was tired out, and went walking out into the bar. It was very nice, George."

"You give me the creeps, Angie."

"He was number three for me. One was quicker and one was slower, but whether it's quick or slow, it gives you the feeling you're taking somebody else's turn away from them, and it will take that much longer before anybody can take your turn away. Like if you could do it enough times, you'd live forever."

"Just thinking about a knife makes me feel funny."

"Not a knife, lover. Just a little skewer."

"I seen it. To me it's a knife."

"Morg promised me another thing, Georgie. When we're in the cars, all ready to go, I'm going to be missing my purse and run back in, alone. And it's going to be so quick, Dwight won't suspect a thing. Zip, zip, and I won't even stay to watch their faces change, and Morg will be gunning the motor in case either of them squeal a little. So see how nice and neat it's going to be? See why you're worrying too much? It could be a year before anybody finds the broads. Maybe it'll be noon tomorrow before anybody finds McAran, and by then we'll all be on our own, except Morg and me, back in Youngstown like nothing happened."

"Herm know all this?"

"Not yet, lover."

"I've never got messed up in *anything* like this."

"What have you got to lose?"

"That's what Morg keeps saying."

"When he tells you how we're doing it, be surprised."

"Sure."

"Feel better?"

"I don't know yet. Maybe I'm not going to feel better until I get far enough away from you, you can't try that damn thing on me too."

She laughed. "Don't give me any ideas, Georgie. Don't tempt me."

"You got yourself hooked on it. Maybe it won't work so good with McAran. Maybe he'll last long enough to get his hands on you, Angie."

"That's why you and Herm and Morg are going to be here—to grab his hands, dearie."

They moved slowly back toward the house. There was a sudden sound of tinny music from inside the house. Kostinak said, "Morg's trying to catch the seven o'clock news."

Morgan Miller came out onto the shallow stoop carrying the transistor radio. He turned the volume down. He wore khakis and a hunting jacket. A brown felt hat covered his baldness.

"One of you could have started the coffee," he said accusingly.

"I was just going to," the Frankel woman said, "soon as I go see a man."

"So go unfasten Sister and take her with you," Miller ordered.

"I'll make another trip. How's the debutante?"

"Didn't you look at her when you got up?" Miller asked.

"I took a look at her," Angela admitted rather sullenly.

"So what did you think?"

"I don't think she looks so good. I think she looks like hell. I think it was a waste of time wiring her ankles to that pipe. She breathes funny. Maybe you figured clubbing her across the back of the head would improve her health?"

"Don't get smart with me, Angie. If she got through the door and we lost her in the dark, you would have got the clubbing for giving her the chance."

"She moved awful fast," Angela said. "She was quiet all the way from town. But if you hit her too hard, it doesn't make too much difference does it?"

"Except I was going to have her ride in the front of the wagon with you if she worked out."

"But she didn't work out like McAran thought."

"Is that my fault?" Miller demanded angrily.

The Frankel woman shrugged. "I'll make a second trip with Sis."

Kostinak stepped up onto the stoop. The woman turned and came toward me. None of them could guess how many people had overheard them, nor could they know the enormous tension of this moment. If the Frankel woman spotted one of us while the two men were watching, it was all going to turn sour in a single moment. I reached back stealthily, hooked a finger into the thong of a spring-handled sap and eased it out of my hip pocket. She changed direction slightly, angling away from me. The two men went back into the house, the faint music fading as Miller carried the radio inside.

After she had passed by me, I turned and watched her. I saw the flexing of the heavy green-clad hips as she walked along the narrow path they had made through the grass. She had gone between me and the man on my right. We were playing it by ear, waiting and hoping for the chance to take Meg away from them before they discovered the elaborate trap.

As the Frankel woman walked further out into the field, she passed beyond my range of vision. I was so flat against the ground the nearby grass obscured her. The last I had seen of her was the blonde hair. I suspected she would return by the same path. If our luck was good, she would return and then come back in a little while to take Meg out into the field. Then the whole thing would be easy.

I guessed that close to three minutes elapsed before I saw the blonde hair again. She would pass within eight feet of me. I told myself it was most unlikely she would see me, because if she turned toward me at just the right place, she would be looking into the sun.

She walked slowly, frowning. She stopped when she was closest to me, and I thought my heart would stop with her. She put a cigarette in her mouth. A slight breeze had sprung up. I wonder how many times the unthinking winds change the life of every man. The breeze was from the east, and so she turned her back towards me, lit the cigarette with a match and tossed the match aside. But as she did so, she suddenly became so motionless that the hand which had released the match remained out at that odd angle. She thrust her head forward, staring into the tall grass on the other side of the recent path. I saw her body stiffen, and knew we could not risk a cry of alarm or sudden flight.

I plunged up toward her, careless of the sound I made. She heard me, and started to spin around, and began to make a hoarse sound of alarm, but I snapped the six-ounce lead ball, wrapped in black leather, against the solid mastoid bone behind her right ear, striking through the cushion of her harsh hair, so that the impact had a squashing-pumpkin sound. Still turning, she fell heavily, face down, and the beginning harshness of her cry turned into an audible sigh as the mechanism of her throat went limp. I crouched, grasped her wrists and yanked her back behind the shelter of the farm wagon, sprawled full length, then crawled quickly to retrieve the gun I had laid aside, crawled over her inert legs.

When Rice put his hand on my shoulder, I nearly leapt out of my skin.

He put his mouth close to my ear. "She saw Ritchie's legs. Nice going. Keep your eye on the door."

He pulled her further back. I could hear isolated phrases in the morning newscast. Miller had turned up the volume. When I glanced back at Rice, I saw him lashing her wrists together with a short length of line. When I risked another look, he had levered her onto her back. He was barefoot, and he was solemnly packing his socks into her slack

171

mouth. He tied the wadding in place with another length of line around the nape of her neck and through her jaws. He tied her ankles, wedged her, face down, as close to the side of the cart as he could get her, and put his shoes back on.

He came close to me again. "This will do it. Stay sharp, fella. Chunk her another time if she fusses. I'm going to go pull the boys on the left in a little closer." I nodded. He wriggled off into the grass, keeping the wagon between him and the door.

The voice had ended. I heard music. It stopped in the middle of a bar. Morgan Miller came out onto the stoop. He stood tall and looked out across the field. I suddenly realized why he seemed familiar to me. He was being Humphrey Bogart every moment, in every move. Nature imitating art. In that moment of empathy I knew what that man thought of himself. It made him no less dangerous, but it made him seem smaller, more manageable, slightly pathetic. His breed was obsolete. He had been gunned down a generation ago, way back when Federal agents were called G-men. The world had left him no runningboard to ride on. Television had parodied him so many times, he had become a comedy figure. But a clown who doesn't know he's a clown can kill you without a smile.

"Angel?" he yelled. "Angel!"

Kostinak appeared in the doorway, spooning something out of a can. He stared out at the field. "There's fifty bushes she could be behind, Morg."

"What the hell is keeping her?"

"Maybe she went all the way to the creek to wash up."

"She have a towel?"

"I didn't notice. You know how she is. You chew her for something, she just does it again. You give her that chewing about the coffee, so she takes her time."

"Maybe." Miller stood, his chin high, looking across the field. He began to seem increasingly wary and apprehensive. "George, go get those guys out of the sack."

"Hell, they got blind last night, Morg. They'll need all the sleep—"

"Get them up! Now!"

"What the hell is the matter with you?"

"I don't know. I don't know what the trouble is. But I want them up. I want everybody up, fast."

172

"Sure. Okay. Right away." George went into the house.

Morgan Miller jumped down and took three steps into the dooryard, spun around and went back inside. He reappeared moments later with a military carbine in his hands. He checked the clip and the action.

Deitwaller came through the doorway, buttoning his shirt, and stood beside Miller. "What the hell is up?"

"I don't know. Angie went out into the field and didn't come back."

Deitwaller yawned. "So she'll be back. Don't get in a sweat. Damn, I feel terrible." He was a cadaverous man, tall, with a sunken chest, bad posture, a skeletal face, a crust of dirty black whiskers.

"It's too goddam quiet around here, Herm."

"For God's sake, Morg, it's *always* quiet around here. Haven't you noticed? It's so quiet I can't sleep unless I get stoned."

"It's a different kind of quiet," he said. *"Angie."* He cocked his head and listened. "No answer."

"She didn't like Sis showing up, so maybe she walked out."

"Not Angie. Not her."

I knew exactly what I wanted, and I knew I wouldn't wait for any kind of approval. I wanted Kostinak to come out onto that narrow sagging porch, and then I was going to take the one closest to the door first, and the other two in the same breath.

"Coffee!" Kostinak yelled. I recognized his voice.

Deitwaller shrugged and went inside. McAran come out. He filled the doorway. He made the others look shrunken. He had on jeans and a plaid wool shirt, unbuttoned to the waist.

"George says you got the jumps, Morg."

"Angel disappeared."

"She's just trying to upset you. Shouldn't somebody be getting up onto that mountain? It's George's day."

"Shut up. I'm running this."

"Everybody knows you're running it, Morg. Especially I now you're running it. Ever since I tried to tell you it was kay to send Meg right on back out I've known you were unning it. But whether you're running it right is something lse again. It would have been okay to let her go and—"

173

"There's no heat yet. There was nothing about her on the news."

"Can I at least untie her, now that she can't sneak off in the dark? She wants to come outside and—"

"Nobody moves an inch away from this house, you, Herm, Meg, nobody. Not until I say it's okay. Get your guns."

"Hell, you *are* jumpy! Can I untie her?"

"Yes, but she doesn't leave the house."

"Okay, okay, okay."

A few minutes after McAran had gone inside, Miller wheeled suddenly and went in. I could hear their voices, but I couldn't distinguish the words.

Perhaps three minutes later, I heard a shattering of glass and a splintering of wood. It sounded to me as though it came from the other side of the house. I waited for a sound of shots, but none came. I found out later that the noise had been caused by Morgan Miller as he kicked a window out, a dormer window in the small attic, opening out onto the west slant of the roof. He climbed out, clambered up the slope of asphalt shingles, and stood cautiously erect, astride the rooftree. I caught a glimpse of movement and looked up with great care and saw him walk to the north peak of the roof and stand, looking out across the pastureland. It seemed to me he would be able to look down and see over the wagon, see the bright blue of the Frankel woman's sweater. He turned slowly and carefully and walked out of sight. I let my breath out.

He walked to the other end of the rooftree, I learned, and looked carefully around. Two of Wheeler's men were behind the stone foundation of the church. One was crouched close against the wall. The other was prone. Miller spotted his legs. He swung the carbine to his shoulder, aimed with more care than any of us would have expected, and smashed a knee to junk and ruin. The instant he released the shot, Miller was running recklessly down the slant of the roof toward the dormer window. The injured deputy gave a high whistling scream of shock and pain. Several men took snap shots at the moving target, but Miller made it back into the attic.

"Hold your fire!" a huge voice ordered. I knew that voice. It was the emotionless voice of D. D. Wheeler, vastly amplified by the battery-operated bull horn his people had packed in. "Hold your fire!" The voice echoed and rumbled off the hills.

"Morgan Miller! Morgan Miller! Answer me."

"Bastards!" Miller yelled from inside the house. Compared to the bull horn, his voice sounded thin and hysterical. "Dirty cop bastards!" He yelled curses and obscenities until his fury was spent and his voice had begun to grow hoarse.

"Miller, you're surrounded by State, County and City Police. Every possible exit from that house is covered. You're not going to get another shot at anybody. We got all the tools we need to pry you out, you and Kostinak and McAran and Deitwaller. So do it the hard way or do it the easy way, it comes out the same any way you play it. We got all summer at full pay. By tonight, if that's the way you want to play, we'll have generators trucked in here, and light you up like an operating room. So come on out now. You'll live longer."

There was no excitement in that voice. It was cold, final, almost bored.

There was a long silence from the house.

"Talk it over and walk out with your hands tall," the big voice ordered.

When the echoes ceased, McAran yelled, "Fenn? You out there, Fenn?"

I had no authority to answer him. The Frankel woman suddenly lurched over onto her back. She stared steadily at me, with leopard-cage eyes, with a hatred nothing could diminish.

"Hillyer, report here," the big horn brayed.

I called to Ritchie. He crawled over in a hurry and I left him there to watch the woman. I went back through the grass, circled east, and stood up when I was behind the half collapsed house, the place preselected as a command post. Brint, Rice and Wheeler were behind a four-foot field-stone wall. Rice sat solidly on his heels, nibbling a grass stem. Brint sat on a derelict kitchen chair, a broken leg braced on a flat stone. He looked tired. Wheeler sat on a pile of rocks with the horn between his knees. He could watch the house through a cleft in the wall.

Larry looked at me and said, "It isn't the way we hoped, boy."

"It looked better for a little while," I said. I moved over

to Wheeler in a crouch, went down onto one knee, looked at him inquisitively.

"I want you here to listen to any deals," Wheeler said. He raised the horn to his lips. "Hillyer is right here."

"I want to hear his voice."

Wheeler handed me the horn. "Press the trigger. Speak in a normal tone."

"I'm here, Dwight."

"You know we got your wife in here, buddy boy."

I hesitated, offered the horn to Wheeler. "Go ahead," he said.

"We know she's in there. She's your sister, Dwight," I called.

"My loving sister? Sure enough? Listen to her."

There was a woman's yell of pain which turned my heart over like a heavy stone. And then she yelled thinly, "Come kill all these filthy——" The sound was abruptly stopped, as though somebody had clapped a hand over her mouth, or hit her again.

"A strong woman," Rice said gently.

"Fenn!" McAran yelled. "She's our green stamps. She's what we trade with. But she's not all we've got in here."

Wheeler took the horn. "One thing you've got is no surprises for us. We know you've got the Perkins girl in there, and how you picked her up and why. We know you killed Kermer, and how you got through the roadblock, and we know one of you strangled Kelly, and why. We know your time has run out."

"Five minutes!" Miller yelled. "Five minutes you've got to clear the way for us. In five minutes either you tell us it's clear, or we throw an ear off this cop's wife out into the yard. One minute later we throw out the other ear. And then we start on the fingers. And if you throw any tear gas in here, or try anything cute, I swear I'll slit the throat of both of them. We got nothing to lose by it. Nothing at all."

I put my face in my hands and bit down hard on my lip.

"So what if we play it your way?" Wheeler asked.

"We'll come out with the woman. We'll leave the girl here. She's sick. When we're in the clear, we'll let the woman go."

"We'll need more than five minutes to alert our roadblocks to let you through, Miller," Wheeler called.

"How much time?"

"How about twelve minutes? It's now twelve minutes to eight."

There was a silence while they apparently held a conference. "When we come out," Miller yelled in his increasingly hoarse voice, "we'll have a gun against the woman's spine. We'll go in the wagon, and we want that Plymouth shoved out of the way, and the log out of the way."

"We've got no radio setup, Miller. I'm going to have to send a man down there on foot to the first block we've got set up, right where that Plymouth is parked."

"So sent him! Get it all set. Let us know."

Wheeler put the horn down and sighed and turned to one of his men and said, "Get Danielson here on the double." The man hurried away. Wheeler took out a handkerchief and mopped his face. "We can't let them move out. I guess you know that well enough, Hillyer. They should know it too. Those people never do. We'll have to play along, hope for the chance."

"But how will you—"

"Easy, son," Larry said. "Ride with it."

Danielson appeared, slightly winded. He was a smallish, tidy, sandy man with huge hands and wrists. He held, with an obvious tenderness, an old '03 Springfield with a bulky Zeiss scope mounted on it.

"You heard it all, Willy?" Wheeler asked.

"Yes sir, I did, Sheriff."

"You'll get one damn chance when they come out with the woman. You set for it?"

Danielson frowned in a troubled way. "Honest to God, I don't know. I was careful, but maybe I thumped it enough coming through the woods, that first mile or so, to be off. I got to have a chance to test fire one time anyhow, Sheriff. She could be off too much."

"You fire it, they aren't going to like that," Wheeler said.

"Unless," Larry said, "they knew it for a signal."

Wheeler snapped his fingers and picked the horn up. "Miller, I'm sending a man on down to lift that roadblock, and he's going to signal back the all clear with two spaced shots. We'll give the same answer to show we heard it, so don't get nervous."

"Just you don't send them shots this way," Miller yelled.

Wheeler borrowed one of Rice's troopers and sent him off on the run, circling wide but in plain sight of the house, with orders to go to the entrance to the logging road and fire the two shots.

"What'll the distance be, Sheriff?" Danielson asked.

D. D. Wheeler scowled. "Shortest way to the cars is out the back door, so we'll gamble on that. Agree, Larry? Paul?" Rice and Larry Brint nodded. "So they'll have to go through that narrow place into the shed single file. Take a look through here, Willy. See the place?"

"I can go around the other side of this here barn for a good angle, Sheriff. Hundred feet. No fuss, if this damn girl is dead on." He looked around. "That shed back there is close enough." He went into the prone position, bracing his left arm in the leather sling, aiming through the scope at the tilted side of the shed. "Couple little knot holes show up good."

"Take two slow ones after we hear that trooper sound off, Willy."

"Sure, Sheriff."

I moved closer to Danielson. "What power is that?"

"Six."

"A lot to hand hold."

"From prone it's like in concrete. I'm steady. I got hand loads in here, with the lead checked on a jeweler scale and the powder right to the grain."

I wanted to talk. I wanted to keep saying things so I wouldn't have to think. But I had no more words.

Suddenly we heard the first shot, a distant *thwack* which seemed to initiate echoes louder than the first sound. As the echoes began to die we heard the second one. "Okay, Willy," Sheriff Wheeler said softly.

I saw him take the breath and let some of it out. The big hand squeezed tenderly. The crack of the rifle merged with the smack of lead against dry wood. He shifted slightly, fired again. He turned and grinned at Wheeler. "Dead on, sir. Punched both them little knots clean on through, about the size of dimes."

"Go for the gun, Willy."

Danielson looked disappointed. "I was figuring a spine shot would—"

"And you'd drop him every time. We know that, Willy, but one time out of ten maybe his finger gives a little twitch, and we can't take that chance."

"It could ricochet into her, Sheriff."

178

"I like that chance better. She can be hurt but not dead."

"He was on the roof with a carbine. What if that's what he's got on her?"

Wheeler thought for a moment. "Then you take the base of the skull, Willy, and you damn well place it right, and you blow those nerves to hell before any message gets down to that trigger finger."

"He'll never hear my girl speak to him."

"What's the big fat delay out there?" Miller yelled. "You working up to something cute?"

Wheeler lifted the horn. "We want your promise to release Mrs. Hillyer unharmed, Miller, or there's no point in our co-operating with you."

"When we're in the clear, we'll let her go."

"Right out a car door at seventy miles an hour," Rice murmured.

"All you men hear this!" the amplified voice brayed. "Those men are coming out with the woman. We're letting them through. It's eight o'clock, Miller. You're free to leave any time. But you'll be picked up, sooner or later."

Danielson had drifted away. I moved quickly, hoping to get back to the good place by the ruined wagon before they came out. I heard Larry call me, but I kept moving.

I reached my previous spot. I could see a little way into the kitchen. The Frankel woman was still there, glaring at me. I saw movement inside the kitchen. And then they forced Meg through the door into the sunlight. Her coppery hair was tousled. There was a purple bruise on her left cheek. Her face was flushed, set, and angry. They came out behind her, closely grouped, the four of them, their heads moving back and forth almost in unison as they looked vainly for any sign of life. To my relief, Miller was off a little to one side, the carbine in both hands, aimed almost straight up. Deitwaller was the man directly behind her, lean, hunched, his chin almost on her shoulder. McAran was behind Deitwaller.

I saw that Deitwaller had hold of her wrist.

"And nothing cute from you either, Miz Meg," Miller said. "Herm can snap your wrist and it won't change a thing."

"I'm scared to death," she snapped.

They moved down into the yard in the same tight formation. Somebody accidentally kicked Angie's toothbrush off the edge of the stoop into the dirt. Kostinak carried a big blue forty-five caliber automatic pistol, and moved it aimlessly back and forth, so that I felt as if I looked straight into the barrel each time it swept by. McAran carried a short-barreled revolver. It looked like a standard police weapon. He held it aimed at the sky, his right elbow sharply bent. His face was quite blank. He kept licking his lips and seemed to be trying to walk on tiptoe.

Miller paused and yelled, "We're taking the station wagon. We got to have time to unload some stuff off it. Okay?"

"Okay," the big voice said.

"Nobody is going to get careless," McAran yelled, but I heard a slight tremor in his voice.

Wheeler did not answer. They had moved far enough to my left so that I could see the gun in Deitwaller's lean gray hand. It was another automatic, smaller than Kostinak's. He held it firmly against the base of her spine. Her favorite blouse was rumpled, and her paler blue skirt looked soiled

As they neared the shed they began to move a little fast-er, too fast, I was certain, for Willy Danielson to put that single slug where he wanted it. But as they reached the narrow entrance, Kostinak had moved up parallel to Meg, and they paused in momentary confusion. Kostinak stepped into the shed. I was holding my breath. Suddenly there was the flat familiar bark of the Springfield, and a ricochet song. Herman Deitwaller went into a crazy, stomping dance, turning around and around, whinnying thinly, holding the unbearable agony of his right hand tightly against his belly. The trooper in the shed came quickly around the back end of the station wagon and blew Kostinak's head into a sickening shapeless paste. Meg was suddenly running directly away from the house and shed, running out toward the tall grass, lifting her knees into the big strides, her hair flying. She could not know it, but she ran directly toward the guns of the men who could have cut the others down immediately. I saw Miller wheel and swing the carbine toward her. I was standing without any memory of getting to my feet. The heavy revolver bucked three times in my hand, taking him squarely in the chest each time, so that it rammed him back against the shed, his arms swinging up, throwing the carbine into the air. He rebounded from the shed, took a single drunken step and sprawled forward, hitting on his shoulder, tumbling over onto his back. Deitwaller fumbled for the carbine with his left hand, his face squinched with pain, but the trooper who had been in the shed had stepped over what had been Kostinak, and moved swiftly, and clubbed Deitwaller across the back of the neck, stepping on the carbine as he did so.

I knew somebody was running, running back toward me. I wanted to look at him. I knew it was McAran. But I couldn't take my eyes from my wife. She seemed to be running with an unbearable slowness. I glanced at McAran just as he took the quick shot at her, and out of the corner of my eye I saw the long and horrid limpness of the way she fell, and as I swung the muzzle of the revolver toward McAran, something hit me high on the left shoulder, a quick, sharp, stinging blow as though I had been hit by a tack hammer. It turned me off balance, and seemed to daze me for a moment, and he went by me, fifteen feet away, running hard, weaving in an illusive way. People were yelling my name. It made no sense. I found out later they wanted me to drop so they could knock him down. But I went running after him. They were still yelling at me. I was still in the way. I ran in a straight line. He weaved and dodged. We made about the same speed. A few were at a good angle to try for him. They missed.

He ran beyond the house, and he swerved and headed for a barn. The big door had been off the rails for a long time. It lay rotting on the ground. He ran into the gloom, and I ran after him without breaking my stride. There were holes in the floor. There was a ghost smell of hay, of animals. He he ran by empty stalls, through patches of light from the holes in the roof, he tripped, caught his balance, turned, came up hard against the far wall, faced me as I, too, came to a stop fifteen feet from him, both breathing hard, both aiming hand guns at each other as in some ridiculous western stand-off.

"Had to get cute," he gasped.

"I'm going to kill you. I have to tell you first, so you'll know." I heard voices outside, heard footsteps inside the barn, coming toward us.

He looked beyond me. Suddenly I saw that familiar rocky grin. He flipped his gun aside. It thumped and skidded across the old worn planking. He put up his hands. "What could I do? Those guys moved in on me. They took over. They borrowed my car. What could I do? I guess you'll try me for something, but I don't know as it'll be something real important."

"You shot her."

"A lot of people were shooting, Fenn. A lot of people. Why should I shoot my loving sister? Anyhow, even if you thought so, you wouldn't shoot me. You're a cop, fella. I got my hands up. You follow the rules. Take me in."

The footsteps had stopped not far behind me. I looked at McAran, my brother-in-law. I knew he read it on my face. His mouth and eyes went wide.

"No!" he said. "Hey! Fenn!"

The gun nudged back against the heel of my hand and the barrel kicked up as it always does. The hole appeared in his right cheek, close to the nostril. He took a step back. His eyes were out of focus. He sat down with a surprising care, with but the smallest of thumps, made a shallow coughing sound, bowed his head down toward his knees, then spilled over easily onto his left side, flattening against the floor, making a last sound that was like somebody trying not to cough in church.

"Get back!" Larry Brint yelled. "Get back, all of you!" I turned. I saw them in the wide doorway, in silhouette against the daylight. They moved out of the way, and the doorway was empty. I don't know how he had moved so fast, or who he had bluffed out of his way.

He trudged forward, holding the Magnum he treasures. "Too bad you missed him that time, boy," he said. He put the revolver McAran had dropped back in the slack hand, aimed it toward the wall, fired it twice. He straightened up, put his heel against the body and shoved it over onto its back.

"Then he missed you."

He took aim. The Magnum made it's heavy-throated, authoritative bark, and he put one slug into the facial hole where mine had entered. He put a second into the belly. Each one bounced the body off the floor an inch or so, and raised small clouds of ancient dust.

"But then I got him, Lieutenant," he said. He came toward me and looked at me in a puzzled way. He reached toward my shoulder and pulled his hand back and nodded. "He hit you one time. That's good." He gave me a slightly vacant smile, and then he made a giggling sound, totally out of character for him.

"He had his hands up, Larry, and I—"

182

"No, he didn't. He didn't give up. I killed him. She wouldn't want to know you killed him, boy, no matter how it was done. She raised him. She'd think about that. It's better she'd know I did it."

"But he shot her, Larry."

"If she's dead too, son, then it doesn't matter, does it? But we don't know that for sure."

"But you saw me do it. He'd thrown his gun away—"

"Shut up, Lieutenant. You beat me by a tenth of a second."

They came in and they looked silently at the dead animal on the floor, a splendid animal, muscled like the dreams of boyhood. I noticed the revolver in my hand when I turned away. I lowered the hammer, holstered it, clicked the flap down, hitched it back out of the way and walked slowly to the big doorway and blinked out at the sun. There was traffic on the road. Keepsafe was busier than it had been in years, perhaps busier than it had ever been before.

I walked slowly across the field toward the dooryard of the house. I had never felt so tired. I saw Rice with his walkie-talkie trooper—the communications link he'd told Miller he didn't have—and I knew he'd cleared the logging road and called the standby ambulance in. I saw it on the road, following a state car, heading for the house, and I lengthened my stride.

She was where she had fallen, nested in the grass, a blanket over her. Her face was slack and bloodless, and her lips looked blue. I knelt beside her. Somebody behind me said, "It's a head wound. She's still breathing."

There was an ugly tear in her right cheek, bleeding slowly. I stood up as they moved her with professional care. A young man in a white jacket appeared in front of me and said, accusingly, "You're hurt."

I looked stupidly at my left shoulder, at the oily gleam of the soaked fabric. "Yes," I said. "Yes, I guess so."

D.D. Wheeler's face appeared. It materialized the way faces do when you are very sick or very drunk. He looked angry. "Exposed yourself! You and the damn fool with the smashed knee. I didn't want anybody hurt in this thing!"

Somebody turned me away from him and guided me, holding my right arm, leading me toward a car. I wanted to stretch out somewhere and go to sleep. I wanted to make a nest in the spring grass, and sleep the summer through. I wanted to be so sound asleep, so deeply asleep, there would be no dreams at all.

The car they put me in could not move out until the ambulance was out of the way. So I saw the professional gentleness with which they eased the two women into the ambulance. I saw Cathie Perkins rolling her head from side to side, her eyes wide and blank. But Meg was without motion.

Cathie survived a severe concussion, so severe her memory was impaired for a long time. But in time she recovered, and married a man in his middle years and bore his children.

We followed the ambulance as it moved so slowly and cautiously through the forest shadows of the old logging road, and then down out of the morning hills, down into the city. We followed the high constant scream of the sirens, and it seemed to me that every face was turned toward us and every face wore the same expression.

xiii

IT was a small wound. It had taken a tiny bite out of the top of the collar bone and been deflected up at a small angle, and ripped out through the muscle. It was not enough to cause shock, yet by the time they brought me in, I was gray, trembling, sweating profusely, icy cold and unable to think clearly.

The damn fools would not tell me whether she had died yet. They kept giving me their medical smiles and saying she was fine. They had dressed the wound. They were giving me plasma for shock. I lost patience with them. I pulled the needle out of my arm and got off the table and started away to find her, but as I reached the door the room lurched, tilted and blurred, and I felt the cold tile floor smack my cheek just as the world faded from gray to black.

I awakened into a drugged nighttime, into an underwater feeling, where each thought was a massive labor to create, and once it had been made tangible, drifted like a heavy log in a slow current, nudged its way past me and was gone.

"You hear me, Fenn? You hear me okay?"

I raised fifty-pound eyelids and looked at the moon face of Dr. Sam Hessian. "Help me get up, Sam," I mumbled.

"You lie still. You're giving these good people too much trouble around here. Can you understand what I'm saying?"

"Help me up."

He reached and pressed one finger against the back of my head, high on the left side. "The slug went into her right here."

"Watching her," I said laboriously. "Frozen. Damn fool thing. Could have taken him—taken him easy."

"Shut up! It went in here. Made a little radial fracture like a BB will do to a window." The finger began to move up and over the crown of my head. "Traveled under the scalp, boy." He traced the line down across the right side of my forehead, down the right temple, close to the eye. "All the way along this line." His finger touched my cheekbone.

"Hit the bone here and was deflected out through her cheek Can you hear me? She's resting. Pulse, respiration, every thing checking out fine."

I held my eyes open with a monstrous effort, staring a him. "Lying," I said.

"It's the truth! I swear it by—by my county pay check.

I was holding onto the bottom rung of a ladder suspende in space. It was very tiring. I closed my eyes and let go.

Angela Frankel and Herman Deitwaller were as sure-fir candidates for murder in the first as you could ever hop to find, and after a courtroom circus which made and un made some minor political reputations, and after the usua ritualistic legal delays, they were sent on their delayed wa to join McAran, Kostinak and Morgan Miller. But before was over for them, Deitwaller disclosed their plan of opera tion. In appropriate coveralls, he was the one who had bee assigned to check over the presses in the basement of th Hanaman Building, and leave the timed explosive char Miller had brought to their rendezvous, the heavy and leth tool box found in the hiding place inside the apparent loa of lumber on the station wagon, found resting on the broa dark staining where Kelly had bled. The proximity of th Hanaman Building to the Merchants Bank and Trust Con pany guaranteed a maximum confusion at the bank and the street, enough to make Brint believe the bank job mig have worked.

No one directly involved in that final violence on th summery Monday morning in that abandoned hamlet in t hills can properly describe the concentrated attentions of t national news media. It did not last long. The world mov and news fades as quickly as the retinal image of a fla bulb. But Johnny Hooper has observed that while it w going on, it was like being trapped in a burning firewor factory along with ten thousand starving ducks, after havi been rolled through an acre of poison ivy. As Albert E stein once observed, the ideal news photographer shou come from a very large family where the battle for nou ishment and attention precluded any possibility of learni taste, sensitivity or manners. The gatherers of our news sho so many simultaneous questions, they never hear the a swers. So the odd role Meg played in the whole affair v lost, because it was too intricate to be told loudly, and in

bsence of any other plausible explanation, they inferred she
had been kidnapped and that made it easier for both of us.
The national coverage made much more of the ingenuity of
the hiding place in the station wagon than of the emotional
involvements.

With our national compulsion to find Huck Finns in every
walk of life, Willy Danielson emerged as a national hero,
grinning into a hundred lenses, showing up on television
programs carrying "my girl" in his big hands, quickly learning to give the right Aw shucks quality to the scripts they
made him memorize, and doing nothing to contradict the
stirring legend that when the men in command had decided
the only thing they could do was let the criminals leave
with the girl, Willy had begged for the chance to show his
skill, had shot the gun out of Deitwaller's hand, had killed
Lostinak and Miller micro-seconds later, and would have
nailed the remaining two if the girl hadn't fled directly toward him. His cold, jolly, sniper's smile enchanted millions,
and when a heroic script was written for him, he turned his
leave of absence into a permanent resignation, quietly di-
vorced his wife, and moved into the congested nasal passage
world of serial television, where the scripters taught him to
put the "o" in option at fourteen hundred yards—offhand.

An agile promoter put the appropriate parcels of land
together, improved the logging road, set up a ticket booth,
a parking area, a refreshment stand, hired a cast, dressed
them appropriately, and re-enacted his version of the seige
and slaughter six times a day all summer long, and quit right
after Labor Day with a substantial profit. Five shots had been
fired in that barn to which McAran had run. In the new
production, enough blanks were fired to make it sound like
a infantry fire fight.

Three sturdy and lovely young hill girls played the parts
of Angela, Meg and Cathie. They screamed enthusiastically,
and the scantiness of their clothing was enhanced by strategic
rips in the fabric.

For me there were two endings, or two beginnings.

Meg recovered more slowly than the doctors anticipated.
There was a listlessness about her. Several times I tried to
tell her that the whole thing had been my fault, that she
wouldn't have been in danger if I'd refused to ask her to
lead us to McAran, but she wasn't interested in whose fault

it was. She had bad dreams, many of them based on that moment when Cathie had tried to run and Miller had struck her down. Meg tired easily. She seemed remotely affection ate, but more out of a sense of duty than desire. Outward ly, except for the star-shaped scar on her cheek, she was unmarked.

One day in late September I suggested we leave the kids with somebody and drive up to Keepsafe the next day, if i was nice. "If you'd like to," she said indifferently. I don' know why I wanted to take her up there. I knew it migh hurt her. I think I wanted to shock her back to life.

So we went up. The paint of the abandoned concession stand was fading, the green wood warping. We parked th car on an empty street paved with bottle tops and filter tips She got out of the car and looked at the deserted place The summer throngs had shuffled the grass flat and carve countless messages in the weathered wood.

She pointed to the foundation where a house had been "That was where we lived." She turned and stared at th house where she and Cathie had been held captive. "Tha was the Belloc house. I cried when they moved to Ironvill So did Mary Ann. She was my best friend, the only gi my age I knew."

She walked toward the house and I followed her, slowl She leaned against a gate post and stared at the front doo

"I didn't know him at all," she said wonderingly. As I wa about to speak I suddenly realized she was talking abo Dwight. I remained silent. Sam Hessian had told me it wou be a good thing for her when she could bring herself t talk about him.

"He was just like the rest of them. I'd come looking f him, to help him. I'd had trouble finding out where he mig be. They yanked me inside and they were all yelling at m The woman hit me. I turned toward him, starting to c because I was confused, and he hit me in front of ther And I told myself it was what prison had done to him, b I knew it was a lie. I knew nothing had ever changed hi He had always been just the same, and I had always be able to pretend he was somebody else, because I needed th somebody else—who didn't exist. That's when the somebo else died, the day before he did. The person Larry kille I'd known him only one day, so I couldn't mourn him. Ma Ann and I played in that attic. We cut the ladies out of

188

ld Sears Roebuck and pasted them on a cardboard and
ad big tea parties. Dwight went up there once and tore all
eir heads off, all their pretty heads clean off."

I came up behind her and put my hand on her waist. She
oved away in instinctive, hurtful rejection. She looked be-
ond the house.

"I'd like to go up the mountain, Fenn."

"Do you feel well enough?"

"The path isn't too steep. We don't have to climb fast."

The trail was obscure. Squirrels cursed us, and jays sounded
e alarm. There was no view until we reached the top. Most
f the top was a huge gray rounded stone, like the back of
me incredible lizard. From there we had the illusion of
oking straight down into the village. Our car was a beetle
the dust, shiny in the sunlight.

"It's cooler up here," I said.

"Always."

She walked to the other side of the summit, to a place
here the stone had fallen away so as to form sitting places.
e sat and looked toward Brook City. I sat next to her
a lower place, half-facing her. I looked at her calm profile.

"I used to know that all the glamor of the world was down
ere, Fenn. I would grow up and go down there and be a
eat lady. I would give my own tea parties."

"Please, darling," I said, and my voice was husky.

She looked down at me with a puzzled expression. "All
tle girls have those thoughts and dreams. I wanted to be the
center of something. I wanted to be terribly *needed*. So
cre would be a lot of things I could do. But my children
ed me. I can be sure of that, at least. I thought Dwight did,
t I was wrong. So, I'm not complaining, dear. I can make
"

She smiled. Something which had been trapped and tied
thin me moved then with a terrible, gasping strength, and
oke free, flooding, spilling, choking me. I ground my
e against her skirt, and heard my voice saying, "Help me.
lp me. Please help me."

When I could look at her, my tears blurred the look of a
rtled wonderment on her face. She said, "But—you don't
lly *need* anyone. You're so—complete, dear. I'm glad you
love me in your own way, but you've never wanted me
—give more than a little. It's always made you uncom-

fortable—even a little thing like me telling you I love you
I'm used to—making do with what I have."

One word hit me harder than all the others. "Complete!"
I said. "Without you—I'm nothing. All the world has been
turning to ice. You're the only warmth. Nothing else is
worth a damn. I just can't—can't—"

And then her arms and her warmth were around me. I
talked for a very long time. Some of it, I guess was in
coherent. In the most special sense, I had never talked to
my wife before. In another sense, I had never talked to
another person—I had never let anyone see inside me. I
had never known how many defensive layers there were un
til I stripped them all down, one after another. It was
brutal therapy, emotionally exhausting.

When it was over, we knew each other. I saw all the
love revealed in her eyes, and in the shape of her mouth
a luminous confrontation, so that I could not get enough of
looking at her. There are no cold men or cold women. There
are only people so lonely, so frightened, they hide all which
can be hurt.

When it was done, we were like lovers soon after the
have first met. There was a feeling of celebration and antic
pation. She reached under the twisted roots of an ancien
pine which grew out of the rocks, and found the treasure
of her childhood. The box was intact, but rusted shut. I
pried it open.

I held my hand out and she gave me the treasures, one b
one. A spotted sea shell. An oriental coin. A tarnished but
ton with a green glass jewel. Some fragments of red ribbon
A disintegrating bit of notebook paper, with a small girl
printing in ink which had faded so I could just manag
to read it.

She looked at me with a considerable pride.

"See?" she said. "I love you. It was for you all alon
waiting right here for you. And for all the rest of our live
you are going to have to remember this date, and alway
give me something, because maybe this is the day we met

The other part of it came a week later, in Larry Brin
office.

"I can't see it, Fenn," he said, shaking his head in
troubled way. "The place is beginning to come back to lif
Two plants re-opening, and they'll be breaking ground f
the brand-new one next month. And Davie Morissa is wea

190

ing Kermer's shoes, and it's going to work out just about right for everybody, so by the time you're set to take over this desk, you ought to be in a position to do more with it than I've ever been able to do."

"I'm sorry, Larry."

"The way everything turned out, you're completely acceptable to the Hanaman group, Skip Johnson, everybody. You can't give up this kind of a deal, boy."

"I have to."

"You're giving up your security."

"That money that was impounded, the money found in the locked glove compartment of McAran's car is finally being released to Meg. Kowalski had to put up a hell of a fight to get it. The net she'll get will be about two thousand."

"Enough to retire on, obviously."

"Enough so we can go away and look around for a place where we'll feel like settling down."

"I have to say you don't look worried. Fenn, tell me. I know you're sort of an idealist-type fella. Is it because you're fed up with the kind of compromises and deals we have to make here in Brook City to give the people as much law as we can afford?"

I shrugged. "That's bothered me. I guess it always will. I'll find it wherever I go. There'll be more of it some places and less of it at other places. I'm able to live in a world I can't change."

"Is it because you told her it was you killed McAran?"

"I told her that. We both think we understand it. We can live with it. It isn't the easiest thing in the world to live with, but we can manage. It wouldn't drive us away from here. I told her a lot of things, Larry."

"Then *why* the *hell* do you think you have to leave?"

"I don't think it will sound like much of a reason to you."

"Try me."

"I'm turning into another kind of person, Larry. It isn't easy. It's making me happier than I've been. I'm learning—emotional honesty. But all the old grooves and habits are there. They slow me down. It's worth it to both of us to have every aspect of our life as new to us as—as this is. Maybe I won't be as good a cop as before. Meg seems to think I'll be a better one. But we have to find out somewhere. Can you accept that?"

"I have to, I guess." He sighed. "I'll write the references you want."

"One month from now okay?"

"It will be okay, Fenn. The city fathers will return to you exactly fifty per cent of what you've put in the pension fund, out of the kindness of their hearts, so you better apply soon. They move slow in the Treasurer's office."

Halfway to the door I stopped, turned and looked at that worn, schoolmaster's face. "Thanks, Larry."

"For what?"

"For a lot of things, but right now, thanks for not putting it on a personal basis, for not asking me as a personal favor to you to stay on."

"I thought of it. What would you have said?"

"Do you think I ought to tell you?"

"Probably not, Fenn. Probably not. One answer would tempt me, and the other answer wouldn't make either of us feel any better."

Dockerty caught up with me as I was going down the wide stairway. He looked like a man on his way to an embassy reception. "What are you smirking about, old boy?" he asked me. "That's a lecher's look if I ever saw one. You must have something tasty lined up. It isn't like you, you know."

"Very tasty," I said.

"And with no prejudice against a policeman?"

"A little maybe. But I can talk her out of it. I'm on my way to phone her."

"Who is this idiot creature you're seducing, Lieutenant?"

"My wife."

After ten seconds of silence he sighed and said, "I'll make no comment about her taste, old friend. But yours is beyond reproach."